Dead Ringer

The Stairway Press Edition

Allen Wyler

Dead Ringer—*The Stairway Press Edition*

Other books by Allen Wyler (fiction)

Deadly Errors
Dead Head
Dead End Deal
Dead Wrong
Changes
Cutter's Trial
Deadly Odds
Deadly Odds 2.0
Deadly Odds 3.0
Deadly Odds 4.0
Deadly Odds 5.0
Deadly Odds 6.0

Other books by Allen Wyler (nonfiction)

The Surgical Management of Epilepsy

Dead Ringer 6.0 ©2024 Allen Wyler, All Rights Reserved

Print ISBN 978-1-960405-24-1
ebook ISBN 978-1-960405-25-8

Visit Allen online at www.allenwyler.com

Cover design by Guy D. Corp
www.grafixCORP.com

STAIRWAY≡PRESS
STAIRWAY PRESS—APACHE JUNCTION

www.stairwaypress.com
1000 West Apache Trail, Suite 126
Apache Junction, AZ 85120 USA

Chapter 1—Hong Kong

A DARK, ILL-FORMED premonition punched Lucas McRae in the gut so hard it stole his breath. He froze, aware of something drastically wrong involving someone close to him.

Laure? Josh? Were they safe?

A second later it vanished, leaving only a lingering vague sense of foreboding.

He'd heard stories like this—a mother suddenly awakened, knowing her son was just killed by an insurgent's RPG half a world away. He rejected these tales as nothing more than folklore. Mental telepathy—or whatever you wanted to call it—was scientifically impossible.

But, Jesus, this thing, this awful feeling in his gut...

"Doctor McRae, over here."

Lucas looked toward the voice. To his right, over the roof of a taxi and beyond the hotel loading zone, Jimmy Wong waved from the rolled-down window of a red compact. A Toyota of Nissan, but a model that isn't available in the States. Thankful for the distraction, Lucas trotted over to the car. But the free-floating, ill defined dread returned, burrowing in his gut.

He slid into the passenger seat, his skin already sticky from the thick tropical humidity and sinus-clogging smog. He buckled in and shut the door.

Wong Yiw-Wah, or Jimmy to Westerners, extended a hand.

"Welcome to Hong Kong."

The president of the Hong Kong Neurosurgical Society had a friendly, oval face of indeterminable age. Wong's temples had turned gray, like Lucas's.

Lucas shook hands and said, "Thank you. It's an honor to be here."

Wong merged into morning rush hour traffic and accelerated.

"Sorry our group cannot afford The Peninsula. Your hotel accommodations are adequate?"

He spoke with a slight British accent. Lucas figured he'd probably been schooled in England.

"Yes, very nice. Thank you."

The Harbor View International Hotel was an okay, no frills, three-star place to sleep at night and shave in the morning. With spending the day at the meeting, a fancier place would've been a waste of money. It could be quieter, though. A rattling elevator door across from his room woke him repeatedly throughout the night.

"And your flight over?"

"Perfect."

That was one of those white lies you tell a host.

"Sorry I was unable to meet you at the airport, but the operating theater became frightfully backed up and my case dragged on and on. Certainly, I don't have to tell *you* how those things go." Wong glanced over his shoulder, preparing to change lanes. "The car picked you up without a problem, I am told. True?"

"It did. Thanks."

Lucas had rolled in about eight last evening. He was dog tired, coated with a layer of stale sweat, and had eyelids that felt lined with sand. He didn't bother with dinner, just showered and then poured a minibar scotch to use as an Ambien chaser before hitting the sheets. The combination worked like a sledgehammer to his brain, putting him out within minutes. Otherwise, with the change in time zones, he would have been wide awake until just before time to get up again. Business trips. He hated the fatigue jet lag caused. Especially when you were expected to socialize at cocktail parties and dinners.

"Very good, then." Jimmy cleared his throat. "I hope you are up to demonstrating your skills today. Your audience will be keen to see you work."

Lucas nodded, but his mind returned to the god-awful premonition from moments ago.

What was that all about?

He tried to distract himself by watching the city's buildings fly by as Jimmy Wong sped down West Kowloon Highway. Hong Kong: a vertical city of breath-stealing Western architecture built to ancient *feng shui* standards. But hard as he tried, he couldn't shake it. Something bad had happened.

What?

This wasn't stage fright. Demonstrating tricky surgeries had become second nature to Lucas and was a well-earned by-product of an international reputation. Years ago, he experienced little shivers of anxiety at the start of a talk or a demonstration, but not anymore. Besides, this feeling was entirely different. It had nothing to do with the immediate future. Rather, he knew—just knew—something bad happened within the past twenty-four hours.

Again, he tried to ignore it and concentrate on today's tasks.

He had made a career choice years ago. Rather than being good at general neurosurgery, he became outstanding at a few extremely tricky surgeries. His expertise became a double-edged sword; he derived comfort from knowing his chances of screwing up were low because he had mastered the difficult techniques. The price, of course, was monotony from doing the same cases over and over. Not only that, but the subsequent notoriety forced him to become even more specialized. Initially, he took satisfaction in being referred problems no one else would touch. But he quickly learned the downside: fear. The high-risk cases were also the ones to very quickly and unexpectedly blow up in your face, leaving the malpractice lawyers licking their chops.

Today would be easy because he would be using a cadaver instead of a live person.

So why did he feel like something terrible had happened?

Well, there was Laura. As it turned out, this trip couldn't have come at a worse time in their failing marriage and decision to talk to their separate attorneys. But this was not something he could have foreseen when invited to be the guest lecturer ten months ago. Truthfully, it was nice to escape the tension for a few days.

The harder he tried to identify the cause of the foreboding, the more it danced away, like a familiar word on the tip of his tongue. Maybe it was just his imagination. He hoped so.

For a distraction, he asked Wong, "Your case yesterday, what was it?"

Chapter 2—Queen Victoria Hospital, Hong Kong

AFTER THEY CHANGED into green scrubs, Wong led Lucas down the hall to the lounge of a classroom—a cozy room of blond wood paneling, industrial beige carpet and two leather couches. Eleven scrub-clad surgeons milled around chatting animatedly, most of them holding white Styrofoam cups of steaming tea.

The drab sameness of hospitals struck Lucas.

This could be anyplace in the world—Cincinnati or Calcutta—and he wouldn't be able to tell the difference. Well, except for the Chinese characters on the plaques covering a trophy wall.

Wong introduced Lucas to each surgeon, one of whom an older man with the face of a bulldog—he'd already met. The guy had accompanied Wong to Seattle to watch Lucas in action. Two weeks afterward Lucas received an invitation to be the society's guest lecturer. Thankfully, Lucas remembered the man's name before embarrassing himself. Strange how the mind worked. As a premed student he memorized the periodic table, but at parties he forgot a person's name within seconds of being introduced.

For the next ten minutes Lucas made sure to spend a few

moments chitchatting with each participant, all of whom were trained with English as their second language. Then Wong ushered everyone into the classroom, a large utilitarian corner room smelling of overheated electronics and formaldehyde.

The space had been laid out to optimize this type of demonstration and benefitted from natural light from two walls of windows. At the front was a table on a six-inch riser. The remainder of the room was filled with tables, each with two chairs on opposite sides. Suspended from the ceiling above each table were parabolic surgical lamps and two Sony HDTVs. Except for the televisions, this could've been one of his old classrooms in med school.

Wong led Lucas to the demonstration table where a blue surgical towel covered a cantaloupe-sized mound on a stainless-steel tray. This, Lucas assumed, was the cadaver head he'd be using. Three boom-mounted HD cameras were aimed at the tray, one on each side with the third directly overhead. Similar cameras were set to monitor four other tables. Wong explained that the cameras would record the demonstration while providing the audience different close-up views of the dissection. Wong then asked Lucas to sign a recording release.

Lucas dropped into the chair and inspected the tray of surgical instruments. Central supply apparently provided the one he'd requested. Like all surgeons, he had preferences. And like all surgeons, this bordered on superstition—especially when working under the microscope.

After verifying each camera was sharply focused and recording, Wong nodded for Lucas to begin.

Standing behind the table, Lucas addressed the group.

"The first demonstration will be the anterior approach to the clivus." A tricky way to reach the base of the brain is by cutting through the back of the mouth. "I assume you've all read the articles I emailed Doctor Wong?"

They nodded in unison.

"Any questions before I start?"

They glanced at each other, but no one spoke. Lucas picked up a Sharpie in one hand and a corner of the towel with the other.

"As with any craniotomy, it's extremely important to plan your incision correctly."

As he withdrew the towel, Lucas said, "We start the incision here," and looked down at the head. He froze. For three long seconds he was unable to tear his gaze from the gray, bloodless skin. Then he spun away, spewing vomit on the wall and the floor.

Lucas crouched on his haunches with the room swirling around him. He fought to keep the stench of his own vomit from triggering another retch. He wanted to move away from the mess he'd made but wasn't sure he could stand without passing out.

He felt a firm hand on his shoulder, heard Wong asking, "What's wrong? Dr. McRae, are you all right?"

Aw, shit...

Another gut spasm hit. He dropped his butt onto the floor, put his head between his knees, and thought, *Glad I'm in scrubs instead of my suit.* In the next instant he realized how inane that last thought was.

"Are you okay?"

Lucas raised a hand, silently asking to stay like this for another few seconds. He sucked a deep breath. The room began to settle down. Something was sticking to his lower lip. He brushed at it with the back of his hand, glanced down, and saw his hand covered with partially digested food chunks. The sight triggered another spasm.

Thank God for gloves.

He felt stable enough to finally stand and pushed up without looking at the head. Then he was on his feet again, the room back to normal. Carefully, he stripped one glove into the other, forming a ball of latex that he dropped into a nearby wastebasket. After another breath, he stepped away from the pool of vomit.

The room was stone silent now, every eye on him.

Wong said, "Lucas, speak to me. What's the matter? Perhaps you should lie down. You're white as a sheet."

He realized Wong was holding his left arm, steadying him. For some reason Lucas noticed another man, the only other Caucasian in the room, standing in the doorway, watching.

Where'd he come from?

On shaky legs, hands flat against the black soapstone counter, Lucas sucked down two more deep breaths to clear the stench from his airway.

"Sorry," he muttered and started to look down at the decapitated head, but stopped.

Not yet.

"Are you all right? Can you continue?"

"One more second." Lucas raised a hand and glanced at the exit. "Where's the nearest men's room?"

And then he couldn't keep the realization at bay any longer. It was Andy. His friend Andy, whose head he was just looking at.

"If you don't mind, I will accompany you."

Wong led him through the lounge, down a hall to a door with a frosted glass window.

The lavatory was small with barely enough room for both men. White tile walls, a stall, a urinal, a sink. Bending over the sink, Lucas splashed cold water over his face and lips. With cupped hands, he rinsed his mouth several times to wash away the foul gastric taste and clear the smell from his nose, but there was little he could do to get rid of the burning at the back of his throat.

Straightening up, he checked his face in the mirror, found it clean but more haggard than when shaving earlier. As a matter of fact, he looked like shit warmed over.

"What happened? Are you ill?"

Lucas propped his butt against the sink, said "Oh, man," and patted his face again with a paper towel.

He felt calmer now.

How could his eyes play such a trick?

He'd seen Andy just days ago.

"Should you lie down? Shall I take you to the Casualty Department?"

"No, that's not necessary. It's that…" Lucas nodded toward the other room. He couldn't say the word *head*. "I thought I knew the person. But it can't be."

What a huge understatement. He and Andy were best friends—that is, if you could manage to be best friends with someone your spouse hated.

Wong stared.

"The specimen? You know him?"

The specimen. Jesus!

It dawned on him. That was what he'd always thought of it: the specimen. Never someone's head. But it was. And the one in the other room couldn't possibly be Andy's.

Then again…

"Surely you must be mistaken," Wong said incredulously.

"I know. I know. It's just he looks so much like him."

He shook his head at the thought. Only days ago, they'd been at Safeco Field drinking beer, watching the Yankees cream the Mariners, Andy cracking him up with sarcastic wiseass comments that Laura considered juvenile.

He felt more stable but still shaky. Hopefully, he'll be able to think more clearly.

"Tell you what, I can do the demonstration…I just can't do it on that particular specimen. Can you have someone exchange it for me, please?"

Wong said, "Absolutely. Give me a minute."

As Wong left the small lavatory, Lucas removed his cell phone from his pocket and checked. He had a signal, so dialed. Andy's phone rang through to voice mail.

What time was it in Seattle? Evening, maybe?

Andy could be out.

"Andy, Lucas. Call me on my cell as soon as you get this."

He rinsed his face again. While he was drying, the door opened, and Wong spoke.

"Let's get you a fresh pair of scrubs before you go back in.

As Wong herded everybody back to their seats, Lucas slipped on a new pair of gloves. Someone had replaced the surgical towel over the specimen he would use and had cleaned up the mess around the table.

The other surgeons sat at their tables, watching curiously, probably wondering what was wrong. Wong didn't explain.

Then slowly, carefully, Lucas pulled back the saline-soaked towel and this time saw the face of a woman, her hair clipped off but with black roots, relatively young.

Lucas asked Wong, "These specimens, are they fresh or preserved?"

"They're fresh. No formalin."

Formalin, a saturated solution of formaldehyde, water, and another agent, usually methanol that is perfused through the body to replace blood. The preservative alone can distort tissues. Slightly. But there wasn't a factor here, and with the blood drained out the color was so...dead.

Lucas sucked a deep breath, looked at his audience and said, "As I started to say..."

Chapter 3—Ditto's Funeral Home, (DFH)

WENDY REALIZED SHE'D been too engrossed in planning the interview to notice the woman approach. Now the matronly receptionist stood directly in front of her, lips pressed into a forced smile, hands clasped primly at the waist. A dead ringer for Mrs. Thatcher, her sixth-grade teacher, the one the boys swore had a corncob up her ass.

"Mr. Ditto will see you now."

"Thank you."

Wendy stood, smoothed her navy slacks, picked up her empty can of Diet Coke. She glanced around for a wastebasket. Seeing none, she held on to the can and followed the woman down a beige hall to a solid wood door. No sign or room number. The receptionist knocked softly before opening it and motioning for Wendy to enter. The woman kept a death grip on the doorknob as Wendy passed.

What immediately struck Wendy was the size of the office. On second thought, it wasn't the size—ten-by-fifteen feet at best—but the unobstructed view over Lake Union to Capitol Hill and downtown Seattle from a wall of floor-to-ceiling windows behind the desk. Tastefully decorated. Expensive. The showstopper was an ultramodern desk made from brushed metal. Aluminum, maybe. German design, she figured. No other designers could come up with something so industrially utilitarian yet so esthetically sensible. An Italian would've incorporated more flair, probably from some black lacquer and a rare, obscure burled African wood. To her, the room's only flaws were the framed posters, one of a thin-faced dude wearing a sports jersey and two Detroit Tigers posters.

Why put sports posters in a room with such a lovely desk?

A man glanced up from behind the desk with a look of surprise, as if he hadn't heard the knock or been informed. It caused her suspicion meter to set off a silent ping.

Where he stood was an imposing figure—six feet four, two hundred-twenty pounds, early fifties, jet-black hair gelled straight back with a moustache/goatee combo expertly dyed to match. She suspected the dye job because any man his age should have at least some gray.

She immediately felt something off-putting about him. Couldn't say exactly why, but she would figure it out later.

"Robert Ditto?"

"I am." He came around the desk offering his hand. He wore tan slacks and an expensive-looking black polo shirt. Cashmere maybe. Made her feel inadequate in the navy pantsuit she'd been so delighted to discover at the Nordstrom Rack sale last year.

She shook his hand, saying, "Detective Sergeant Wendy Elliott, Seattle Police," as if the receptionist hadn't already clued him in.

Then she offered identification.

He waved it off.

"No need. I'll take your word for it."

He gestured for her to sit in one of two contemporary black leather chairs facing the desk.

"Nice office." Wendy glanced around for a wastebasket to dump the empty Diet Coke can. Seeing none, she held it up.

"There a wastebasket I can throw this?"

"Trash? Oh no." Ditto hurried back to her, a pained expression on his face, and extended his hand. "Here. Let me have it."

She gave it to him.

He stepped over to a wet bar.

"Forgive me for preaching, but do you realize how much landfill is required just to handle recyclable waste like this? Waste that otherwise could be used again and again? It's huge."

"No."

Wendy felt her face warm with a mixture of embarrassment and belittlement.

Should've just left the fucking thing in the car and let it go flat.

But no, she just had to finish it because the only thing worse than warm Diet Coke is flat Diet Coke. Now Ditto was at a wet bar sink rinsing it out. The entire dynamic of this interview had suddenly gone sideways.

She watched him turn the can over, drain the water, shake out the last drops before putting it in a blue plastic recycle bin under the counter as if this were some sort of religious ceremony.

"There."

He faced her again, drying his hands on a bar towel.

"Who's that?" Wendy asked, pointing at one of the posters.

Not because she gave a rat's ass, but because she wanted to put some mental distance between the empty can fiasco and the point of this interview.

Am I being over-analytical again?

It was a trait Travis always accused her of.

"Mr. Hockey." Ditto smiled with unabashed reverence and awe. "Gordie Howe's his real name. Probably the best damn hockey player to ever hit the ice. Played for the Red Wings." He stared at the poster, momentarily transfixed. "Know much about hockey, Detective?"

Perfect. He seemed relaxed talking about something he obviously knew a lot about.

"Nothing."

She settled into one of the chairs. To her, any activity that involved freezing your ass off seemed ridiculous.

Ditto folded himself into the desk chair and faced her.

"You know what a hat trick is?"

"Tell me," Wendy said as if she meant it. She crossed her legs and relaxed, getting more into character.

He grinned.

"In sports, a hat trick is doing something successfully in three consecutive tries. Three home runs in three times at bat. Three touchdown passes in a row. That sort of thing. In hockey, a Gordie Howe hat trick is to score a goal, do an assist, and get involved in a fight during a single game. That's how good he was."

Sounded like testosterone bullshit, but there he was, talking.

"You from Detroit?"

Ditto nodded.

"Born and raised in Hamtramck. A suburb of the Motor City. Everyone calls it a suburb, but I call it an armpit 'cause of all the garlic-stinking Polacks."

She realized he'd said this in all seriousness and felt herself squirm.

"Now what can I do for you?" Ditto asked, straightening his posture, getting down to business.

"Does your company own a black Suburban?"

Wendy knew damned well it did. DMV showed it registered to Ditto's Funeral Home Inc.

Ditto's smile vanished; his posture straightened more.

"Ah yes, we do. Why?"

"We're investigating a missing person report. A routine inquiry."

Lupita Ruiz's disappearance, however, was anything but routine for her. They were close friends, especially after Lupita rescued her from what could've been a very ugly rape. On the other hand, Redwing, her commanding officer, couldn't care less about Ruiz or the other missing working girls she'd been investigating since her transfer from the Vice to Missing Persons.

Ditto said nothing, just sat watching her, expecting her to explain further. She held his gaze for a moment and noticed Ditto looked more nervous with each second of dead air. Interesting.

She waited a few more beats before asking, "I assume it's a company vehicle and not your personal car?"

Ditto seemed to consider his answer.

"Yes, that's correct."

"So that means you have a list of people who use it?"

He shifted in the chair, gaze drifting towards the ceiling.

Wendy swore she could hear his mental gears grinding.

"Any one of my employees can use it."

"Have a sign-out sheet, some kind of record of it?"

"We do, but why do you want to know?"

She debated how much to tell him. Ditto seemed very tense. She couldn't tell if it was irritation or something more sinister, which made her even more interested in the interview.

"Fair enough. Let me be more specific. Do you know who was driving the vehicle on the tenth?"

Ditto pursed his lips and seemed to think about it.

"The tenth of this month?"

"Yes."

With a frown he turned to his computer monitor, nudged the keyboard closer, and started typing.

"It wasn't used that evening." He shook his head for emphasis. "At all."

Her pulse quickened. Her lie meter pinged. From the back of her mind came a whispering suspicion that this might finally be the break she'd been looking for.

"Let me make sure I have this straight. You're saying no one drove it the night of the tenth?"

"Right. No one drove it that night."

Ditto's forehead glistened with sweat in spite of the AC cooling the room.

She decided to give him one more chance to pull himself out

of the hole he'd dug.

"You're absolutely certain about that?"

Ditto shot her an icy stare.

"What did I just tell you? Are you accusing me of something, Detective?"

Wendy looked him directly in the eye as she asked, "Is it possible there are times when an employee might use the vehicle without you knowing?"

He seemed to relax a bit.

He nodded.

"It's possible, I guess. After all, someone's on call round the clock, so, yes, since you put it that way, it's entirely possible."

"And they could have done so without it appearing on that log you're looking at?"

Ditto said, "What I'm saying is, there's no record of a pickup that night. None at all."

Rather than press the question, Wendy decided to change tactics.

"You have staff here twenty-four hours a day?"

"No. Yes. I mean *I* live here. And, uh, so does another employee." Ditto looked down at his desk for a moment, then added, "Let me clarify. I have an apartment in the building. Another employee rents space on the second floor. We don't, uh, live together."

Curious. Wendy wondered if the employee was male or female. Not that it made a difference, but still…

Ditto licked his lips again.

"See, my business requires someone to be available 24-7. What I mean is, if we get an after-hours call—that's nine to five—the van might be used, depending on the call, but that's precisely why I'd have a record if it had. See what I'm saying?"

Not really.

What she did see was Ditto verbally backtracking, and this made her more intrigued.

"So what you're saying is, it's unlikely the vehicle would be off the premises if it wasn't used specifically for business purposes and therefore would have shown up on your log?"

Ditto shook his head and looked down at the edge of the desk he gripped. He relaxed his hands, met her gaze.

"Help me out here. What does my van have to do with a missing person? That's what you said this was all about, didn't you?"

Wendy said, "The missing person's a prostitute. She was last seen in an area that is under video surveillance. A camera happened to record a Suburban there at approximately the same time she went missing."

Well, sort of. Close enough to the truth to sound convincing.

Signs posted on utility poles along that particular stretch of Aurora Avenue—a high drug and prostitution area—warned of video surveillance. What actually happened was a patrol officer noticed a black Suburban illegally parked in an alley. The officer ran a routine license check, which meant the location and the time were officially recorded. When Wendy ran across it, she included it as part of her weekly investigative report about a string of missing women she'd been working up.

Ditto gave a nervous laugh.

"Excuse me, but all this concern about a hooker?"

"Yes."

Would he be as dismissive when she shoved the search warrant up his ass?

She reached down to grab her purse.

He seemed to realize a change in the interview mood and sobered immediately.

"Hey, the city's full of Suburbans. There're probably hundreds on the streets around here. Why come to me?"

Wendy chose to give him something to sweat about.

"Your license plate was a partial match to the one seen."

"I see." Ditto drummed a pen on the desk, saying nothing. Then he carefully returned the keyboard to its original spot and cleared his throat.

"So, we finished?"

Smiling, Wendy stood and smoothed her pants.

"One more thing. What exactly is that vehicle used for?"

He stood too and seemed befuddled by the question.

"Like I said, for business. Why?"

"This is a funeral home, right? I thought morticians used a hearse."

His eyebrows rose in surprise.

"True, we are a mortuary, that's how I started this business. But I've long since expanded."

When running the license plate, she had wondered about the name *Medical Research Center of Seattle* the car was registered to, thinking it sounded a little strange.

"What kind of research does a mortuary do?"

Ditto cleared his throat.

"We're the biggest supplier of anatomical parts on the West Coast."

"Say what?"

"You know. Body parts for surgical demonstrations."

Wendy clutched her purse, a little freaked.

"No, I don't know. Mind explaining that?"

"See, you got new technologies and devices emerging all the time. A new type of hip replacement, a new way to take out a slipped disk. Surgeons got to learn how to do it, so they take a course. In the course you got to use something, right? And it's got to come from someplace. That's what we do. We provide the material."

This said with a look of pride.

Her stomach knotted. "Just so I understand, what you're saying is, you supply dead bodies?"

"Yes, yes, of course. But not necessarily whole bodies. Maybe an arm or a leg or whatever part they need."

Suddenly the room felt ice-cold. Wendy felt as though she had to get away, get some air before she fainted.

Ditto's phone rang.

18

Chapter 4

THE PHONE CALL gave Ditto a thank-you-Jesus excuse to cut the conversation short. Maybe buy him time while he got his goddamned thoughts together.

"Excuse me. I need to answer this."

He wanted the bitch out of the office so he could figure a few things out and, if need be, do some fucking damage control.

He picked up the phone.

"Robert Ditto here."

"Got us a potential problem, my man," Gerhard said. "You free to talk?"

Leo Gerhard was in Hong Kong running some sort of teaching session for a bunch of Chink brain cutters. Supposed to be routine with no glitches anticipated. But the edge to Gerhard's voice tripped a tingle in Ditto. Problems occasionally developed during acquisition trips but never during routine demonstrations.

Fuck.

Great timing.

"Someone's in the office at the moment," Ditto said. He stifled the urge to look up to see how much Detective what's-her-name was tracking. He knew she was listening to every word, probably evaluating his every move. Hell, he'd be doing the same if the tables were reversed. He also knew he wasn't completely hiding his nervousness. She'd be an idiot not to pick up on it. Never had been good at lying, which was why he never played poker anymore. And he *was* worried. Fucking Suburban... But, he reminded himself, he didn't even know if it was connected to anything. Not yet at least.

"It's important," Gerhard said with obvious concern.

"What's the problem?" Fucking Chinks were always a pain in the ass. Problem was, their money was as good as anyone else's. And in this competitive business, you never wanted to lose even one account. "Can't it wait?"

"No."

One word. That's all Gerhard had to say for Ditto to understand this *was* important.

Well, shit, only one thing to do.

Ditto said into the phone, "Hold on a sec." Then turned to the detective. "Sorry, this is an extremely important call, and I need to take it in private. You can find your way out, can't you?"

She pulled out a business card and tapped it on his desk.

"Here's my contact information. Ask around. Check specifically if your vehicle was used the night in question. Maybe it was, and you just don't know about it. Let me know for sure what you find out, one way or the other. Okay?"

"Yeah, yeah." Ditto moved to the door as a way of herding her out. "I'm on it the moment I'm off this call." He opened the door for her and then, with the calm undertaker's smile learned at his father's knee, said, "It's been a pleasure, Detective."

Ditto closed the door behind her, waited a second before cracking it to peek out, just to make goddamn sure the bitch wasn't trying to listen. Good, she was almost to the reception area now, walking with the purpose of someone very impressed with herself, maybe because of being a detective and all. Had to admit, though, nice ass.

Then he was at the windows again, the phone to his ear.

"Sorry. That took longer than I thought. Tell me what's up."

"The surgeon, the one doing the demonstration? Fucker claims to know the donor."

Ditto replayed that comment in his mind twice.

"Wait a second. I'm not sure I follow. You're in Hong Kong, right?"

"Right."

"Say again. What's the problem?"

"Let me back up. I'm at the Honk Kong Neurosurgical Society or whatever, right?"

Ditto dropped into his desk chair, pulled over the keyboard. "Yeah?"

"The thing is, the cutter doing the demonstration isn't from here. He's American and—get this—he's from Seattle. Can you believe that shit?"

Ditto's gut tightened.

"Go on."

"Thing is, the course organizer, Dr. Wong, says this Seattle doc says he knows the guy whose head it is."

Ditto sat back in the chair.

Was that possible?

Yeah, possible. Just not highly fucking probable. But Murphy's Law said that it could happen in spite of their policy of shipping specimens to places as far away as possible from where they'd been procured.

He'd heard a story once from a professor at a medical school. A kid's mother died while the kid was in premed, and her wishes were to have her body donated to the medical school. Problem was, nobody gave the anatomy department a heads-up that the donor's son was an incoming freshman. Murphy's Law pretty much predicted what would happen. And sure enough, it did. First day of gross anatomy, the kid's mom was on a dissecting table ready to be taken apart.of his hand

Ditto asked, "What's his name?"

"Who? The doctor or the donor?"

Idiot.

"The doctor."

"Lucas McRae. Know him?"

He thought about all the courses that had been held in the classrooms downstairs and came up with a blank. He'd remember the name Lucas because of the John Sandford character. Loved that dude.

"No, doesn't ring a bell."

Gerhard didn't say anything.

Ditto asked, "The specimen, what's the identifier?"

"Got it right here. Figured you might want to know."

"Hold on a sec." Ditto set the phone on the desk and pulled up the Hong Kong order on the computer. There it was: an order for four heads. No specified sex or decade of age, which made it easier to fill. The problem was some guy named Wong had specifically requested fresh material, meaning the heads couldn't be preserved with formaldehyde. A request occurring more frequently these days because some asshole claimed non-preserved material more closely resembled the texture of living tissue. Well, duh. Fresh was fresh; that's why they called it fresh. It pissed Ditto off.

Didn't those prima donnas realize how much hassle that caused him?

Orders for formalin-fixed material were easily filled from inventory. But fresh material? Unless you were lucky, the specimens were never in stock the day the order came due. Mostly because inventory was difficult to maintain. Just like steaks from the butcher shop, the tissue begins to spoil and break down if stored too long. So, if he didn't have the items in inventory, he had to buy them from a competitor. Which he hated because those heartless bastards knew that he was up against the wall and charged him up the ass. And they loved to see him squirm.

But this Hong Kong order...*fuck*. Each specimen number had an asterisk beside it. That was Ditto's code to designate it had been "procured." He swallowed and double-checked.

Heart racing, he picked up the phone.

"Still there?"

Gerhard's words had the watery, echoic quality of a low-grade satellite connection.

"Something wrong?"

Then a thought hit: what were the chances of this conversation being monitored? After all, with that detective being here…or was he being overly paranoid?

"Hold a second longer."

Ditto slicked back his hair and took two deep breaths, then stared at his favorite Tigers poster, the 1968 original he'd framed for its inspirational value. On the last day of the 1967 season the club had been eliminated. But the next year they returned with a vengeance, rebounding from a 3 to 1 deficit to beat the favored Cardinals in game seven of the World Series. *That* was the kind of strength he needed now.

He heard Gerhard's voice on the phone.

"Bobby?"

"I said, hold on a second."

Wiping sweat from his eyes, he tried to think, tried to take a step back to look at things objectively. Point number one: the detective was looking for the hooker, not her john. Point number two: even if some surgeon recognized the face in Hong Kong, what he was going to do about it?

Not a goddamned thing.

The hooker no longer existed, having been completely harvested within hours of procurement. Her ligaments were used for replacement parts in knee surgery and her skin for bandaging burn patients. Bones cut up for jaw reconstructions or spine fusions. Hair sent to wig makers. They would've used her corneas, but her head was worth a lot more intact if left in its primo condition. Same with her john.

He felt deep pride in his ethics for dealing with such tough choices. Choices that weren't always easy. What benefited society more? One set of corneas for only one person or a head used for teaching twelve surgeons?

In this case the answer was obvious, but there were other times when it wasn't. He always erred on the side of the majority because that made the most sense. Choosing the course that benefited the most people was always the right thing to do. Doing the right thing was something else Dad had taught him.

"Waste not, want not," was one of the rules of life Dad drummed into him.

In their family no bottles were ever thrown in the trash; they were recycled. No faucet dripped very long before being fixed. Lights were turned off when leaving a room. Some people called such frugality a depression-era ethic, as if once the Great Depression ended people were free to waste things. They weren't. He fucking despised waste.

Ditto clicked on that record.

"The person in question was Andy Baer." He remembered seeing the john's real name from the contents of his wallet before turning it into ashes along with his clothes. "Never leave evidence" was another cardinal rule Ditto unwaveringly observed. "This the same guy your doc thinks it is?"

"Don't know, didn't ask. You want me to find out?"

"If the opportunity arises. If not, let it pass. No sense drawing attention to ourselves."

Call finished, Ditto drummed his thumbs on the desk and mulled over what had just happened.

It was bad, these two things coming—bam, bam—right in a row. A sign.

He believed in signs. Not like some of those over-the-top whackos who saw signs in everything. But now and then something appeared you'd be a fool to ignore because it could end up being a sure path to destruction. That detective and the doctor both somehow connected with the two specimens was a very creepy sign.

But what was the honest-to-God risk here?

The two bodies had been completely harvested and the

24

remains cremated. So, there was nothing left to incriminate him.

Except for the heads.

And the moment Gerhard came back with the heads, they'd go into Old Smokey and the ashes disposed of.

There was nothing to worry about.

Well, except for that detective.

She still gave him pause.

Damned Suburban.

Chapter 5

DITTO SWIVELED HIS chair around to face the window. As he stared outside, he contemplated the potential pitfalls. The customary records for the two bodies? No problem there; there was none. The tissue would be disposed of. Leaving what? He and Leo Gerhard were the only ones who knew the truth. And Gerhard? A rock solid, stand-up guy he'd trust to never admit to anything.

He remembered how they met in the army—both eighteen, new to Fort Lewis, Gerhard assigned to the bunk above his. They were sitting on Ditto's bunk polishing their boots.

Gerhard casts him a glance and asks, "Why'd you sign up?"

Ditto laughs, spits on the boot toe, working it in with a circular motion.

"Look at it this way: I'm from fucking Hamtramck, Michigan. Ever been there?"

A broad smile flashes across Gerhard's face.

"Hell, man, I'm from Detroit."

Ditto stops working.

"No shit? You ain't black and don't look like one of those fucking Polacks. Who the hell else lives in that godforsaken town?"

"*Germans,*" *he says proudly, flashing a Heil Hitler salute.*

"*My man!*"

They high-fived.

Gerhard asks, "*How did you end up here in the mortician corps?*"

With a grunt Ditto sets the boot down, picks up the other one.

"*Wasn't my choice. I signed up to be a Delta. But you know how that goes. They agree to fucking anything, but then once you enlist, they fuck you over. So the fucking CO sees that my dad runs a mortuary. They figure I don't have a problem being around stiffs, so here I am. Fucking can't seem to get away from it. You?*"

Gerhard gets a faraway look in his eyes.

"*I dunno. Always sorta liked dead people. Sure as shit more interesting than live ones. Least most of 'em, anyway. Delta, huh? You really wanted to go through all that shit?*"

"*Actually, what I wanted was to play pro hockey, be a Red Wing, another Gordie Howe. But, you know, those fuckers are crazy. Have no regard for their own bodies.*"

"*And Delta ain't crazy?*"

"*Yeah, but they're the best. So what's your story?*"

Gerhard shrugs, then spits on the boot in his hand.

"*I was forced to join. Sorta.*"

"*Sorta? The fuck does that mean?*"

Gerhard sets down the boot, leans forward, elbows on knees, staring at the floor.

"*I used to hang at a boys' club a lot on account of my folks are always gone. Dad shucks steel. That is when he ain't blotto and can get work. Mom works. So...*" *He shrugs.* "*Anyways, this fucking counselor, fucking fag, tried to get friendly. Know what I'm saying?*"

Bobby nods.

"*Fucking queers. Hate 'em.*"

"*One day I had enough. I got this ice pick and stuck him in his belly to send a message. Wasn't trying to kill him or nothing. Let him know he couldn't punk me. Fucker damn near dies, ends up paralyzed. Me, I end up in juvie. Judge gives me the choice of doing hard time or signing up. What kinda choice is that? But now that I'm here, I kind of like it.*"

Ditto thinks about that a moment.

"Paralyzed? You stuck him in the gut? How the hell does that work?"

"Judge asked the same thing, and a quack told him I hit some blood vessel. Shit, I don't know exactly, but that's what they said."

Ditto says, "Hey, we got forty-eight hours coming up Saturday. What do you say we go get some pussy together? You know, double team some bitch?"

Gerhard shoots him a look of gratitude.

"Hell yeah. There's this place, been there a couple times."

That Saturday afternoon Gerhard takes him to a shotgun cottage. Flat roof, clapboards flaking faded green paint, striped awning on the window. Gerhard knocks.

A woman answers, barefoot, in a royal blue satin robe, hair slightly mussed.

Gerhard leans on the jamb.

"We looking for some pussy."

She spits on the concrete at his feet.

"Get on your way. Thought I told you, don't want your type round here no more."

Slack-jawed, Bobby watches Gerhard bust open the door, grab her by the neck, and squeeze, glowering in rage as her face flushes from red to purple, gagging the whole while. Finally she stops moving and Ditto realized she is dead. Never says a word. Not one fucking word. Just drops her in a pile on the throw rug.

Then they're out the back door, running down a dark alley, Ditto wondering what the hell he's gotten himself into.

No one ever questioned them. But Ditto knew this would always give him leverage over Gerhard.

Three and a half years later Ditto's army stint is winding down, and he's making plans for after discharge. He and Gerhard were playing chess in the enlisted men's quarters.

It was Ditto's turn to move, when he asks Gerhard, "Hey, why not come to work for me?"

Gerhard glances up from the board.

"Work? This is the fucking army, man. This is work."

"I mean after we're discharged."

With a derisive grunt, Gerhard shakes his head.

"Ain't leaving. I re-upped."

Ditto can see the Army life working for Gerhard. Structured, no decisions to make, put in your twenty years and walk away with a pension. Not great money, but enough to live on. If you wanted to live in a single wide out in Buttfuck, Nowhere. Made him a little sad because he'd grown close to Gerhard, and discovered they shared a lot of the same ideas.

Ditto says, "Well, I've had enough of this shit. Just remember, you got a job if you change your mind."

Gerhard sits back, pushes his metal frame glasses up his nose, crooked.

"You serious? What kinda business?"

"Only kind I know how to do. Funeral home."

"Who you gonna work for, your dad?"

"Nah, fuck Hamtramck. Too many blacks and Polacks. I'm thinking Seattle. And I'm not working for nobody ever again. I'll start my own."

Gerhard nods, looks back at the chess game.

But Bobby is really getting into it now, excited over his new idea, wanting to run it by someone even if that person had an IQ on par with a snail.

"Thing is, everyone wants to save money, right?"

Gerhard glances up again, as if irritated for being distracted from the game.

"I guess."

"Yeah, they do. Everybody loves a discount. Think about all those coupons people clip out of the newspaper. Shit, even Rockefeller would probably want to save a buck if he could."

"So?"

"I start a discount funeral home, run specials on budget cremations. Something everyone, even a field worker, can afford. Call it Ditto's Budget Funeral Service. Advertise on AM radio, on those stations that play geezer music. Cater to your potential customers. It'll work. I know it will."

Dead Ringer

Gerhard points to the chessboard.
"Gonna fucking move or what?"

Two years later, Ditto, his business up and running, read an article in the *Seattle Times* about a morgue worker in Los Angeles busted for selling body parts on the black market.

How stupid not to have seen it. A cremated body represented huge profits that were quite literally going up in smoke. So he did a little research into the cadaver business and discovered just how much could be made from a fully harvested, disassembled body. Not only that, but there were demands for body parts for surgical demonstrations and medical schools.

He added two optional programs to his menu of traditional funeral service: the medical research program and the body recycling program. The research program pitch went like this: the mortuary would cremate your loved one free of charge if the body was first donated to science. Meaning it could be used for teaching purposes. Once the teaching was completed, all the parts would be collected and cremated, and the ashes returned to the family.

The recycling program had a different spin. Body parts would be donated to recipients. The brochures stressed the heartrending need for corneas, skin, and bone, playing up how much this helped the grateful recipients' quality of life.

The problem was that although the discount funeral part of the program caught on with people who couldn't afford a traditional mortuary, to Ditto's dismay, the option of donating bodies or body parts for medical research didn't fly. People just couldn't seem to get their heads around chopping up Mom or Dad for the advancement of science. Ditto took this as a prime example of people's callous disrespect for fellow human beings.

Then it dawned on him: why not take the parts anyway? So many people were opting for cremation there was plenty of opportunity.

Fuck it. No one was looking.

And here was the beautiful thing: he could steal what he

wanted—a little skin here, a few ligaments there—and who would be the wiser? Especially since cremated remains always seemed to weigh more than people expected considering the size of the box. Who would know if Grandma's ashes were intact? And from that day on, they never were.

If you thought about it, each body had two legs, two arms, a head, and a torso. Each piece is profitable. But if you sold off all the parts, where did you get ashes for the family? Easy. Once in a while, he took care of the bodies of the homeless. His civic duty, as he saw it. Those ashes that nobody wanted, he could "bank" until he needed them. Plus, who the hell could tell if they got all their loved one's ashes? Holding back a little here and there, he could build up quite the savings account. Then, when a primo body came in, all the parts could be sold off and the family given banked ashes. And when things got tough and the bank low, there were always dogs and cats to cremate.

Ditto and Gerhard stayed in contact, and two tours of duty later Gerhard mustered out and came to work at the funeral home. One evening they were sitting in Ditto's living room drinking beer and listening to Bob Seger complain about working men's problems and bullshitting just like old times when Ditto asked.

"You like this job?"

Gerhard shrugged.

"Guess so."

"You like the money?"

Gerhard grinned.

"Sure."

He salted away every cent. Only God knew what he was saving for. Ditto sure didn't. No kids, no wife. But he knew Gerhard had grown up dirt-poor and probably had a fear of ever living like that again.

Ditto said, "I'm paying you fifty grand a year, right?"

Plus benefits.

Gerhard walked to the kitchen with the empties.

"Ready for another?"

On call that night, Ditto thought better of it.

"Nah, but go ahead."

He heard the clatter of cans drop in the recycle bin.

Gerhard returned, levering the tab open with a *pffsshh*.

"Yeah, I guess fifty grand. Why?"

"How'd you like to make more?"

Gerhard grinned again.

"Could always use a bit more. What're we talking about?"

"What if I kicked it up to seventy-five grand?"

Gerhard's face sobered. He just stood there like he wasn't going to allow himself to get sucked into being the butt of a joke.

Ditto said, "I'm serious."

Gerhard took a long pull of a Labatt's.

"Then hell, yeah. What you expect me to say?"

"See, here's the thing. You know how we're always short on bodies? Well, I've been thinking about a way to deal with that."

"Yeah?"

"We don't wait for them; we just take them. People no one will miss. You know, homeless, hookers, addicts. Who gives a shit about 'em? Follow?"

Gerhard took a pull and made a question into a statement.

"Kill them, huh."

This convinced Ditto that Gerhard's only issue was the money.

"Thats right. That's what I'm thinking."

Now it was out in the open, but if there was one person on this earth he could trust with a proposition like this, it was Gerhard.

Gerhard nodded slowly, thinking it over.

"But there's a problem."

Uh-oh.

"Yeah?"

"Seventy-five's a little on the low side for that kinda work."

Ditto breathed a sigh of relief.

"What's a more realistic figure?"

"Ninety, thereabouts."

Ditto had already done the math. Even at ninety it was a steal. He held out his hand.

"Deal," he said.

Chapter 6—Hutong Restaurant, Hong Kong

A WAITER WEARING white gloves and a tux held out a round black lacquer tray to Lucas with a traditional martini glass perfectly centered.

"Your drink, sir."

A spiraled lemon rind floated in Bombay Sapphire, one end hooked over the rim, looking like it was right out of an *Architectural Digest* advertisement.

"Thank you."

Lucas sampled the drink. Perfect. Exactly what he needed. Especially after today.

Man, what a bitch it'd been.

Once he'd recovered from the initial shock of seeing a man who looked like his friend, he'd gone on to do the demonstration, but only after Wong exchanged that head with another one, which turned out to be a female with her hair clipped off too. From the natural color of the roots and the lack of lines around the eyes and mouth, he guessed her to be mid-twenties.

Which was also depressing.

How could a woman so young be dead?

It caused him to worry again about his son Josh.

Was he okay?

He was supposed to be chatting up the other surgeons but couldn't bring himself to do it. They seemed to sense this and left him alone, standing in small clusters, chatting and munching serious-looking hors d'oeuvres served by an attractive Chinese woman in an embroidered red silk dress with a mandarin collar and provocative slit up the side to show a little leg. With her killer smile and long legs, she wove effortlessly through the group.

With the start of the morning session delayed an hour, they'd finished later than scheduled, so Wong had shepherded the group here directly from the hospital, giving Lucas just one chance to call home with his cell phone, only to get no answer. How frustrating. He checked his watch and calculated how much longer until the party might be over so he could go back to his room. Hopefully, dinner would be mercifully short.

He took another sip of the martini and attempted to distract himself by looking more closely at the restaurant. Impressive. The society had reserved a separate dining area of the Hutong, a restaurant renowned for its bird's-eye view of Hong Kong from the twenty-eighth floor of One Peking in Tsim Sha Tsui. Nice place. And in a better frame of mind, he'd certainly would've enjoyed the guest of honor role. But not after this morning.

Drink in hand, he stepped to the floor-to-ceiling windows to peer down on Hong Kong Island and Victoria Harbour where two Star Ferries passed each other in opposite directions. He checked his watch again, trying to convert Seattle time, vaguely aware of a fifteen-hour time difference.

A familiar voice asked, "You feel better now?" Wong stood next to him, teacup in one hand, saucer in the other.

Lucas said, "Let me ask you. How did you obtain the heads?"

"We ordered them from a supplier. M-E-R-C-S." He said each letter individually. "With all the demonstrations you do, I'm sure you must have heard of them. Perhaps you have even been an instructor for one of their in-house courses?

"No, never heard of them." But it made sense to obtain anatomical parts this way. The specimens were always there for him at the demonstrations, and he'd never given it much thought. Besides, his primary focus was on the dissection, not how the parts were supplies. But now... Suddenly his mind flooded with questions. "So how does it work? You just call up and say I want four heads for such and such a date, and they show up?"

"Essentially, but the process is not as capricious as that. First, you must be able to document a legitimate need. In this case, we were required to verify our status as a valid medical organization made up of licensed physicians."

This was another point he hadn't considered. "When did they arrive?"

"Yesterday. In fact, the courier is over there." Wong nodded to his left.

"Courier?"

"Yes, of course."

Lucas looked in the direction Wong indicated and saw the Westerner from earlier. He'd forgotten all about the paunchy bald guy with thick glasses. Now, seeing him again, Lucas remembered him hanging around the periphery of the class, never quite interacting yet never leaving. Like muted patterned wallpaper: there but never noticed. He wore a cheap brown business suit, and the front of his white dress shirt hung sloppily over his belt. His tie was pulled loose, and his top button was undone. A squat glass of amber liquid—scotch or bourbon maybe—was held in his right hand, his little finger extended in a delicate manner. An odd affectation, Lucas thought.

"He *brought* I them? I mean, personally?" He just took it for granted the material would show up, maybe using DHL, FedEx, or a similar overnight service. Maybe all you had to do was fill out an order form on the Internet, and at the scheduled time the material appeared. But now that he thought about thtat, it seemed incredibly idiotic for various resons. The biggest being that packages were sometimes lost or delayed. There had to be better delivery assurance than an Internet tracking number.

Wong appeared puzzled by the question. "I'm not sure I understand what you are asking."

"You say he brought them. How?"

"In his luggage."

Jesus. He imagined arriving in a hotel room and unpacking—shirts here, pants there, and arms in the fridge.

"May I introduce you?"

Lucas was already heading toward the man, intent on asking whose head they'd used today.

Wong caught up with him in time to say, "Mr. Gerhard, allow me to introduce our honored guest, Dr. Lucas McRae."

With a salesman's smile, Gerhard offered a beefy hand. "Glad to meet you, Doc. Watched you a bit today. I'm no surgeon, but it sure seemed to me you got yourself a great pair of hands."

Lucas's guard immediately went up. No one gives you that kind of verbal blow job without an ulterior motive.

They shook hands. But Gerhard didn't let go. Instead, he pulled Lucas's hand closer. "May I inspect it?"

"What?"

"Your hand." Gerhard carefully turned Lucas's hand over, gently thumbing the palm. "Just as I expected, no calluses. Certainly not the hand of a journeyman." He inspected the back of the hand, fondling a finger in the process. "So long and delicate. I've never felt a neurosurgeon's hand before. It's exactly what I imagined."

Regaining his composure, Lucas jerked free of Gerhard's grip. He stifled the urge to wipe his palm with a napkin. He couldn't keep the thought out of his mind: *I've been slimed.*

"I'm curious. How do you obtain your, ah, material?"

Gerhard rocked back onto both heels. "Donations."

"Donations?"

"Sure. You know. People donate their bodies to science. For medical research."

Maybe some donate for that cause, but not Andy Baer. Especially for a cause as open-ended as "medical research." That could mean a thousand things, and Andy was very specific and precise. Was? Jesus, he was already thinking in the past tense.

"Dr. Wong said you brought them with you," Lucas said. "Is that right?"

"Yes."

"So how does that work?" Lucas asked.

"Not sure what you're getting at."

Gerhard's adenoidal and whiney voice and roly-poly sloppy demeanor was the opposite of what Lucas expected.

Then again, what did he expect?

He never thought about couriering body parts before.

"I'm asking how you physically transport them."

"In a Halliburton."

"An aluminum suitcase?" This immediately triggered more questions.

Gerhard gave him a look.

Lucas asked, "You brought four heads, right?"

"What's your point?"

"I'm interested. Mind explaining how that works? I mean, you show up at the airport with four heads in a suitcase. Is it some kind of specially made suitcase? I mean, the dimensions of a head are pretty specific, and I assume you'd want to keep them—or any body parts—pretty well cushioned. And what about the authorities? Every piece of luggage is x-rayed or inspected." He imagined a TSA agent's reaction to several human skulls suddenly popping up on the screen "Doesn't that raise a few eyebrows?"

Gerhard laughed dismissively.

To Lucas, the laugh sounded hollow and strained, and the smile that went with it seemed forced. As Gerhard sipped his drink, Lucas suspected the man was sizing him up, like the kid on the playground who's deciding whether or not to throw a punch.

But Lucas was still working up to the main point of the questioning. "Well?"

"For us, it's a bit different than when you pass through security. First of all, before we ever begin a transport we got to meet several requirements."

"Like?"

Gerhard's smile tightened.

"Like I said earlier, you got a point to this line of questioning? This don't seem to me like your typical cocktail conversation."

"It's a little bizarre, walking through an airport with human heads in a suitcase, isn't it? I'm curious how it works is all."

Gerhard studied his drink a moment, rattling the ice cubes. He drained his glass in one long gulp. "Understand something. The business is regulated. We got ourselves a series of hoops to jump through including the CDC. What's more, the Department of Commerce requires us to carry a certificate at all times. So, before we ever set foot inside an airport, there's a ton of paper we got to fill out. We got to notify the airline and the TSA. And for international trips like this here, we got to clear it through customs days ahead of time. Once we got all that done"—he shrugged—"we're free to go. That answer your question?"

Lucas asked, "Why not just FedEx them?"

Gerhard snorted. "I'm surprised you even ask that."

"Well, I'm asking."

For a moment Gerhard's eyes flashed anger but quickly changed into a dead-eyed poker mask. He coughed into a fist and cleared his throat.

"You got all sorts of reasons. We got to bring every little chunk of body part back home so it can be buried or cremated just as if it were whole again. That's the agreement we make with the families. See, they don't mind their loved ones being used for research, just as long as we bring back the body. Just like in the army, we don't leave no one behind. Satisfied?"

"Okay, I understand the process better. Thanks. Bear with me for one more question. You maybe use a head here and a leg somewhere else. How do you keep track of everything?"

Gerhard seemed befuddled by the question.

"Keep track? Simple. I return with everything I take."

"No. What I mean is, you came here with four heads, right? What's to say you don't go back with an arm and a leg instead? Who keeps track?"

"The fuck you talking about? If I come with four heads, I go back with four heads."

"No offense. I don't mean you personally. I'm talking hypothetical here. What I'm asking is, does anyone actually check what you take in and out of the airports?"

"The FBI checks to make sure every scrap of tissue that goes out comes back. End of discussion."

Yeah, right. As if the FBI has the manpower to do that.

He didn't believe that for one second. Still, he hadn't asked the most important question.

"Then I guess DFH Inc. keeps good records?"

"Yeah, yeah, precise records. This conversation is over."

"Just this one more thing. What's the name of the man whose head I saw this morning?"

Raw anger flashed through Gerhard's eyes.

"Why?"

"I think I know him."

"Oh, bullshit. You know as well as I do that a detached head don't look the same as when it's attached. No way to tell who it was."

"No, I know him." Still, doubts lingered in Lucas.

What are the odds of it really being Andy? Damned small.

Gerhard's eyes narrowed to slits; his hands balled into tight fists.

"Back off, doc. I'm not giving you any names."

"Why not?"

Gerhard glanced around, balling and unballing his fists.

"You give out medical records to anyone who asks for 'em?"

"The person I'm talking about is dead, for Christ's sake. His death certificate is a matter of public record. I'm asking his name, not the *cause* of death."

Asshole.

He glanced at Wong for support, but he didn't say a word.

Gerhard started to turn away, stopped, smiled. "Tell me the name of the guy you *think* it *might* be, and I'll tell you if you're right."

"Andy Baer."

"Nope, not him."

"You're lying."

Gerhard nodded to Lucas, then to Wong.

"Been a pleasure, gentlemen."

He walked away.

Chapter 7—West Seattle Precinct, Seattle Police Department

LIEUTENANT RANDY REDWING was talking to Wendy.

"What exactly are you saying? That this Ditto character is responsible for your missing working girl?"

Tilting his chair back, left foot on a partially open desk drawer, Redwing clasped his hands behind his head. His face stayed expressionless, making it maddeningly difficult to read. Wendy hated that.

Redwing, a Native American from Fargo, grew up in South Dakota. Wendy knew this because of the *Fargo* movie poster and a high school banner proudly displayed on his office wall. His bronze skin, dark brown eyes, craggy features, and high cheekbones reminded her of some famous plains chief you might see in a painting from the Wild West. All he needed to complete the picture was one of those headpieces made of eagle feathers or whatever they were. He meticulously kept his coarse salt-and-pepper hair in a severe military brush cut, which went along with his scrupulously honed reputation for being a real hard ass as the commander of the Missing Persons Unit. He was especially tough on the minorities in the department.

Before working Missing Persons, Wendy served a stint in Vice as a decoy, hanging out in a high prostitution area wearing a miniskirt, flashing her legs and luring guys into negotiating a price as the two male team members monitored the discussion from a car on the next block. She thought about the first time she'd met Ruiz.

Wendy stands under the blue neon sign of the adult video store—a cinderblock rectangle off Aurora Avenue that sells porn and sexy toys—waiting for a potential john to proposition her. It's chilly for hot pants and a halter, so she wears her lightweight pink parka to keep warm enough as she paces the Aurora side of the building.

She sees another woman come around the corner of the store from the parking lot and head toward her. She tenses, not knowing what to expect. The woman comes right up to her. She's Hispanic, attractive, still young—probably in her twenties—but "the life" is etched in her face, and it makes Wendy sad.

"You police, right?" the girl says, more as a statement than question.

Wendy's caught off guard and doesn't answer.

"Yeah, you police. You ain't got real street moves. Look, we need to talk. I got a room there," with a nod at the two-story run-down motel the next block north on Aurora.

Wendy doesn't move. She's not about to go into an unknown room with a hooker.

"About what?"

"A deal." Lupita glances down the street. "But we can't stay here."

"No way."

Lupita shakes her head, looks directly at where the hidden microphone is taped to Wendy's chest just below her breasts.

"Nah. This gotta be strictly between us."

Just before Wendy enters the motel room she says to the microphone. "I'm entering room 104, request you move up."

She figures, screw it, her cover's blown, so why not at least have her backup in the parking lot in case they're needed? Her transmitter isn't powerful enough to reach the car from inside the room, especially with the door closed.

Inside, standing next to the queen-size bed, the girl says, "Name's Lupita. Yours?"

She'll be damned if she's going to divulge personal information.

"Cop."

"Then make one up, I don't care. Me? Street name's Charmane."

To Wendy the statement seems honest and open, and she likes that.

"What you want to talk about?"

"What if I could give you information on the crew bringing in them Asian girls?"

"What kind of information?"

For a year now Vice has been investigating the illegal importation of young women from Asia for use as "sex slaves." Some girls were found in a shipping container at one of the piers. But little headway had been made in the case. Any good information would be welcomed.

"Like where they keep them. Once you guys know that you can work it back, find out who's behind it."

"And what do you get out of it?"

Wendy expects a dollar amount.

"Here's the deal. Got me some friends, their hearings are coming up in a few days. They need to get cut some slack."

There it was.

"What friends?"

"Some girls I know. Friends. I'm taking care of one of their daughters until...shit, I can't see her doing time, not with her daughter out on the street...and I can't keep on taking care of her. Got my own problems."

Wendy puts her hand on Lupita's shoulder.

"I don't know if I have the juice to do a deal, and I sure as hell don't know anything about your friends. Give me their names, let me look into it, and we meet tomorrow. How's that sound?"

Next day in a small café off Aurora, Wendy tells Lupita, "That's the best I can do. We cool?"

Lupita nods.

"Thank you."

Those two words carried genuine gratitude.

"But there's a catch."

Lupita looks up.

"There always is. What?"

"This won't be our last conversation." She pauses to let that sink in. "You will, of course, be compensated."

"Such as?"

Wendy is amazed at herself, negotiating this deal, her commander letting her work her first confidential informant.

"You know how it works. The price of the product is only worth its value. Depends."

Lupita sips her coffee, glances out the window.

"I take that as agreement." But it worries Wendy, the responsibility this suddenly places on her shoulders. It feels heavy. She's now responsible for this woman she has somehow connected with. If she fucks up, Lupita will be the one to pay... "Excuse me for asking, but why are you doing this for these girls?"

Lupita seems surprised by the question.

"They're friends."

"What I mean is, this can get dicey. You sure you're up for it?"

"Hey, just 'cause I'm in the life, doesn't mean I like it. Some of these players are mean motherfucks. If I help a few friends while taking some of these fuckers down, I'll be happy. None of us chose to do this. But it's what we do."

Wendy realized Redwing was staring at her, waiting for an answer.

"Her street name was Charmane, and yes, I do think Dittos is involved. Somehow."

She realized she was frowning, which would piss him off. Not a smart thing to do when requesting his help. Especially since he was always sucking up to the brass, bragging about how happy the members of his team were.

"You think he's a killer?" Redwing said with a trace of annoyance.

"I'm not saying he's involved directly. What I'm saying is that particular Suburban is registered to DFH Inc. It was documented to be in the immediate area about the time she went missing. And a couple of my girls noticed it cruising her territory earlier that afternoon."

Charmane's territory. As if Lupita were a company sales rep or something. An adult bookstore and a couple cheap motels occupied the block she worked, so it wasn't like *Mister Rogers' Neighborhood*.

"That's pretty slim evidence to go on," Redwing said.

"Maybe, but Ditto started acting guilty as sin as soon as I started asking questions."

Redwing picked at a wart on the back of his index finger.

"In what way?"

"In every way. You name it." She threw her arms up. "Eye aversion, hemming and hawing. Exactly what you'd expect from someone who's got something to hide."

"We both know you don't have enough here," he said, shaking his head. "You need way more than a gut feeling to get a court order. As long as he claims the vehicle wasn't out of the barn that night, there's not a damn thing we can do about it. You want to have it looked over, hand me something solid. I refuse to deal with bullshit supposition."

Frustrated, Wendy pressed her temples and wondered if this discussion would trigger another migraine.

"You telling me an officer running the license plate is nothing more than bullshit supposition?"

"No, that's factual. What I'm saying is your impression that Ditto is lying is nothing more than an impression. Impressions aren't solid, and they sure as hell aren't evidence. There is nothing to say his vehicle had a damn thing to do with that girl's disappearance. Or have I missed something? Something you didn't tell me?"

"I'm telling you," she said, emphasizing every word. "I know when someone's lying. He was flat-out lying through his teeth.

Allen Wyler

There has to be a reason. And I want to know what it is."

Redwing bit his fingertip and spit a speck of skin at the wastebasket. "Give me a break. The man could have ten thousand reasons he doesn't want you knowing what he was doing at the time, none of which are likely to be remotely connected with the missing girl."

"Like?"

"Aw, hell, use your imagination. How about he's a married man and sees a hooker who works that block? Give me a minute, and I'll come up with at least another ten bulletproof reasons."

Wendy leaned over, hands flat on the desk, and locked eyes with his.

"The man is lying. The vehicle was there. That right there makes me interested." She didn't bring up her suspicions about the other missing girls and Ditto's business. "What's not to see?"

Redwing wasn't buying it, so she added, "Fine. If you say he's not involved, what about the possibility someone used the van without him knowing? First he tells me that's possible and when I pressed him, he tells me there was absolutely no pick up that night."

"Well, then?"

What did it take to convince him? And, why wasn't he listening to her? She wanted to scream.

"He's *lying*. He doesn't know for sure whether the vehicle was used or not. He based his answer on a sign-out sheet."

"You know that for a fact?"

"Yes. He looked it up on his computer. Haven't you been listening to my report?"

"I have. But have you been listening to *me*? You don't have enough for probable cause. Besides, why are you burning so much time on this particular case? If you don't have enough work to do, let me know. We have a backlog as long as your legs."

Wendy shot him a warning look. She didn't get this far in the department to put up with asshole comments about her looks. Not even from her boss, a man who wasn't exactly known for his

47

sensitivity to women.

She knew he was right about the evidence, but she also knew in her gut Ditto had lied. The Suburban *had* been in the area that night. There had to be a connection. But any connection between Ditto and Ruiz's disappearance was up for grabs. What he didn't understand was that the girls looked out for each other. They noticed things that seemed unusual. Three of them had spotted the vehicle that night and told her about it. Sure, their sixth sense wariness wasn't something that would stand up in court. But Wendy believed them.

Sometimes the law sucked.

And there was the bigger issue. About a year ago she noticed girls missing. Not that it was unusual. Working girls disappeared all the time, especially with it being a high-risk trade. Some simply left town. Others got busted. Others dropped out for a myriad of reasons. But she knew of three who vanished without any reason. Since then, she'd been keeping track.

Who knew how many had vanished before then?

"What up girl?" Wendy calls out as she approaches a tall black woman in the parking lot of a convenience store.

"Nothing. That's the problem. Business been down."

Wendy pulls a pack of Kools out of her purse, offers her one.

"You seen Tanisha round?"

The girl takes a cigarette.

"Not really." She scans the lot. "Got a light too?"

Her small purse is so thin it can barely hold the condoms.

Wendy holds her Bic flame up to it.

"When the last time you seen her?"

The girl shrugs, checks out the occupants of a car pulling up to the front of the store.

"Three weeks ago, maybe. Why you so interested in Tanisha?"

"Ain't seen her neither," Wendy says. "Gives me worry."

"True that."

That conversation took place six months ago. She suspected another Green River Killer might be working the area. She'd started nosing around, asking questions. Some of the other girls had noticed the same thing, but no one kept track or wanted to discuss it. But they silently shared the same fear of a serial killer. Every one of them knew the stories of the sickos who preyed on prostitutes. It heightened the girls' vigilance and their communication network. Several started passing on information to Wendy. So, yes, it wasn't her only case. But no one, including Redwing, seemed to give a shit about Ruiz.

She resented having to explain this.

"Because I care about her."

"Just as long as it doesn't interfere with your job. Don't forget you got other cases to work."

She was being dismissed.

"Not a problem. But sir?"

He looked up from his desk, eyebrows raised, like it was a big surprise she was still there.

"Yes?"

She intended to keep an eye out for any of the other street girls she knew.

"Make sure I continue to get a copy of *every* missing persons report that comes through."

Chapter 8—Harbor View International, Hong Kong

UNLIKE SOME OF the party hearty Japanese and Korean neurosurgeons Lucas had met over the years, these guys weren't into slamming down whiskey until the wee hours of the morning, so when dinner wound down the group disbanded. Fine with him. The sooner he could get back to his room and try to reach Andy again, the better.

Wong dropped him off at the hotel with a handshake and a thank-you for being their guest speaker and doing the demonstration and wished him a safe flight home.

His room was typical for that level of hotel, a long and narrow space divided into closet, bathroom, and bedroom. Two single beds separated by a console built into a common headboard and a desk with a wall mirror that doubled as a dressing table. Two tall windowpanes angled outward to form a bay window, providing an almost 180-degree view of the harbor.

But Lucas wasn't interested in the view. Instead, he sat in the chair by the window and dialed Andy's cell phone. It rang ten times before flipping to voice mail. Same with the condo and office numbers.

Maybe he just didn't hear it ring.

Lucas stripped off his coat and tie, dumped his wallet and room key on the console, splashed cold water on his face, and came out of the bathroom toweling off. He looked at the clock again. Only four minutes had passed. Back in Seattle, Andy would be leaving his downtown condo for the short walk to the brokerage where he worked. It was possible he didn't hear his cell ring because of the traffic noise.

He balled up the towel and threw it on the other bed before dropping into the chair by the window.

Damn it, Andy. Where the hell are you?

Andy...gregarious, fun loving, always cracking him up with stupid puns. He drank a little too much at times, but hey, who didn't? It wasn't as if it got out of hand. No, it wasn't the drinking that caused Andy problems.

After graduating Stanford, Andy became a trainee at Merrill Lynch. He sailed through apprenticeship and became an account executive. Lucas signed on as his first client, even though Lucas was scrimping to get through medical school and didn't have a cent to invest. Andy conned him into starting an IRA, pitching the idea of socking away a fixed amount into a mutual fund every month even if it was only a couple dollars. Dollar cost averaging, Andy called it. And guess what? It worked. Over the years Lucas contributed more as his income grew, never losing sight of the original discipline. That account was now a sizable nest egg. When Andy moved to a small firm, Lucas moved his accounts with him.

Money had always been the major difference between them. Andy's family was well off. Lucas's parents made enough to get by, but certainly not enough for the Sun Valley ski vacations and trips to Maui Andy enjoyed. To his credit, Andy never developed that entitlement attitude some other rich kids had. Personal wealth came so naturally to Andy that Lucas wondered if it was a genetic trait. It would've been easy for Lucas to envy Andy's wealth but didn't. Instead, he let Andy teach him as much as possible about managing money.

"You need to give back," Andy tells him. They sit in Andy's office reviewing Lucas's taxes.

"What do you mean?"

"You're making some money now. Don't save every penny. Take some and give it to organizations you believe in, like the ASPCA. I know you like that one. You'll help them and, in the process, feel good about it."

Lucas checked the clock again. Okay, good. By now Andy should be in his office. He dialed the office number.

"This is the office of Andy Baer. I'm either out of..."

Aw, shit.

"Andy, pick up, goddamn it!"

Maybe he's sick.

He dialed Andy's condo, listened to dead air as the connection worked halfway around the globe, heard the phone ring ten times before, "You've reached Andy Baer..."

Come on, man, where are you?

When the greeting finished, Lucas said, "Hey, Andy, pick up. It's Lucas."

He waited, heard a beep and the recording click off, then sat in the hum of the air conditioner while staring out across the harbor at the Space Museum and Star Ferry Pier. His gut was killing him with worry.

He rummaged through the tiny refrigerator and found a scotch, chugged half. He wanted to stand and sit at the same time, just do anything to make this feeling go away. He inhaled a deep breath and glanced around the room. At the blank television, the worn bedspreads, the beige phone, his open suitcase with the change of clothes set out for the morning. The impersonal hotel room left him feeling alone and isolated and slightly afraid.

He downed the other half of the bottle and decided if there was a flight out within the next couple of hours, he'd take it instead of waiting another sixteen or whatever hours. Hurry and he could be at the airport in, say, an hour. He could sleep on the flight. If he could sleep at all.

On the desk was a leather folder with a list of numbers. He found United's and dialed. It rang until finally went into a recorded message telling him to hold for the next available agent.

This time of night it probably meant a long wait.

Finally, a voice came on the line with, "May I help you?"

Lucas learned the only other flight to the West Coast was through LA but with a long layover, so by the time he arrived in Seattle it'd save him only thirty minutes. He decided to stay put.

Shit.

He turned to the window, massaging his temples. How realistic could it be that it was Andy's head? Maybe he was wrong. Maybe his jet lag and the fact the head was bloodless distorted his judgement.

Where are you Andy? Of all the times to not answer the phone…

He should try to sleep.

Yeah, as if that's possible.

He showered, changed into scrubs, then tried to watch TV. He couldn't concentrate. He grabbed the remaining scotch from the fridge before dialing Andy's office number again. And got the same voice mail. *Shit.*

He dialed his home number.

"Hi, Laura, it's me."

Laura's voice carried the temporary rasp of sleep.

"Lucas?"

He pictured her on her stomach, stretched across his side of the king-size bed for the phone.

"Sorry, I thought you'd be up by now."

"I should be. I turned off the alarm about three this morning when I couldn't sleep."

"Look, could you please do me a favor?"

"What?"

"I'm worried about Andy. I tried his condo, office, and cell but there's no answer. Could you track him down, please? I'll call you first thing in the morning." Which, for her, would be afternoon.

"You know how I feel about him."

Despise was the best word to describe her feelings.

"This is important. Can you just put that aside for a moment and do this one simple favor for me?"

"Why's this so important?"

He explained.

When he finished, she said, "Out of the billions of people in the world, you see Andy's head in Hong Kong? That's ridiculous."

That was exactly what he wanted to believe but couldn't.

Laura's disdain for Andy had become another reason for the estrangement in their marriage. Ironically, if it hadn't been for Andy, they never would've married.

A group of first year medical students meet every Friday after classes at The Blue Moon, a university district tavern. Maybe not exactly the same guys each week, but enough regulars to make it like family. Beer and pizza, argue politics, bitch about professors, that sort of thing. Tonight he, Andy, and four other guys sit in a booth. Lucas watches four co-eds slide into the next booth. Especially one. Oh yes! He can't stop staring at her. And twice she catches him, the hint of a smile at the corner of her mouth.

After maybe ten minutes of this Andy says, "Hey, McRae, what the hell you looking at?" and turns to look in that direction.

Lucas whispers only loud enough for Andy to hear.

"No. Don't look."

So, all the guys are looking at him now. And of course, Andy smiles and slowly turns to check out the girl, making a big deal of it. Lucas is dying, his face on fire.

After a moment Andy says to Lucas, "Go on, ask her out."

Yeah, sure. Maybe Andy can do something like that. But walking up to a girl he's never seen before and asking her name? Christ! Especially now with everyone aware of what's going on. He slouches further in the booth. Either the girls at the other table haven't noticed or have more refined social skills than these turkeys because they continue to ignore his booth. But he thinks he hears one or two giggles.

Half an hour later the girls stand to collect coats and purses.

Theo says to the group, "Hey McRae, she's getting ready to go. Last chance to meet the love of your life."

Think I didn't notice? Disappointment hits. He'll probably never see her again. His only chance to meet her is slip-sliding away. But he's frozen in place.

So, of course, Andy has to turn and look again. Shit!

She starts for the door.

Andy says, "Excuse me," pushing Angelovic out of the booth so he can slide.

Aw, Jesus...

Two excruciating minutes later Andy is back, slaps a piece of paper on the table in front of Lucas. "Name's Laura. Call her."

Lucas gripped the phone harder. "I don't want to get into another argument about Andy. Could you please just do it for me?"

"*You're* the one who's arguing," she said.

He massaged his forehead and tried to think of a way to cajole her into calling him but couldn't. She wasn't going to call. Period.

The reason Laura despised Andy? Because he was a womanizer. That, and the fact that she and Trish, Andy's ex-wife, were good friends.

Regardless, he and Andy had been friends since grade school, and right now he was worried about him.

"Please just do it for me?"

"Oh, all right."

From her tone he knew she wouldn't do it. And if he asked her tomorrow, she'd claim he never answered his phone or give some other excuse.

But what could he say?

"Thanks. I'll check with you in the morning."

"Good-bye." She hung up without waiting for his good-bye.

Lucas returned to the window to stare out at the harbor.

"You did what?" Lucas asks, shocked.
Andy is obviously embarrassed.
"I gave Trish a case of clap."
"Aw, Jesus, Andy..."
"I know, I know...it's just...it wasn't a hooker, this time."
"That makes it okay?"

The infection caused enough fallopian tube scarring to make Trish infertile. This, in turn, sparked bitter emotions between the couple. Laura instantly sided with Trish and condemned Lucas for not cutting off his friendship with his lifelong buddy. Both Trish and Laura developed an openly hostile attitude that seemed to generalize to all men. Lucas tried to reason with her, but it only mired him deeper into quicksand.

The next huge test of the Baer marriage came three years later when Daivd, their son, turned fourteen. Andy took him on a skiing vacation in the Bugaboos for some adrenaline pumping downhill. David lost control on a steep slope and ended up sailing over a cliff, while Andy could do nothing but watch in dumb horror. By the time rescuers reached the broken body, David was cold and dead.

Trish and Laura never forgave Andy. Trish filed for divorce two months later.

Staring out the window, he sipped scotch and wondered how his own marriage had become so entangled in a thickening bramble of constant little irritations for the past two years. This phone call, for example. What was the Chinese saying? Death from a thousand little cuts?

The really frustrating thing was being totally powerless to change the downward spiral. His personality—typical of a surgeon—was to diagnose the problem and fix it. Simple. This approach didn't work for his marriage because Laura refused to talk about their problems or see a marriage counselor. To make matters worse, he believed, was her agitated depression. Angry explosions over seemingly nothing, leaving him mystified.

"Laura, maybe you're depressed. Maybe a small dose of an antidepressant might help."

"Oh, now I have mental illness? Perhaps you should look at yourself, Lucas. Have you ever thought of that? Who's going to argue with the neurosurgeon?"

"Is this what you want? To always be on edge around each other?"

"What do you mean, 'around each other'? You're always at the hospital, always have more important things to do. Maybe you should've shared some of the responsibility of raising Josh?"

So, where did that leave them?

On the slippery slope toward divorce. And he hated that. He wished he could find a way to change things back to the way they'd been five, ten years ago as a happy couple. He thought of the shared joy of buying their first house and the work spent together making it *their* house: Painting walls, cleaning out the basement, reworking the garden, buying their first furniture as a couple. The Christmas trees that they had decorated. That joy seemed so distant now.

He thought of Josh. Of how proud he made him. With their marriage disintegrating, his most important goal in life was to see Josh launched into adulthood as a well-adjusted, healthy young man.

The last drops of scotch went down as he watched another Star Ferry cross the harbor, the sight deepening his sense of isolation. If only he could put his arms around Josh and hold him close and know that wasn't Andy's head…

He dumped the bottle in the trash with the other and climbed into bed knowing sleep wouldn't come without an Ambien. Even then, maybe not. Didn't matter because tomorrow he'd catnap on the long flight home.

Soon as he landed in Seattle, he'd find Andy.

Chapter 9—DFH Inc. Seattle, Washington

PERCHED ON A kitchen stool in his penthouse great room, Ditto savored his second cup of Starbucks Kenya roast when the phone chimed with the distinctive ring for his private line rather than the DFH after-hours line.

He set down the *Seattle Times* sports section and glanced at the glowing digits of the clock in the microwave. Damned early for a personal call. Then he remembered turning off the cell phone—the phone most of his friends called him on—and plugging it into the charger. The battery really needed to be replaced, but it pained him to think of it being dumped into a landfill. Good thing about RadioShack, they recycled batteries. Or so they said.

The phone rang again. Most likely either Gerhard again or the on-call person. Sometimes they called for advice.

This was a perfect example of how this job was killing him, what with the constant grind of always having to backstop employees. It had even become an issue with his girlfriend. He couldn't get Cathy to understand there was no way to predict when Joe Blow might shuffle off to the great unknown and he'd be called to pick up the body. She thought he should delegate more responsibility to Gerhard so they could get away for a few days.

Gerhard was competent but didn't have the flair for customer service Ditto had. Then again, the two state universities, UW and WSU med schools, were DFH's only regional competition for body donation, so that wasn't really a big issue. Made him laugh because neither institution accepted bodies outside their local area unless the family agreed to pay the transportation costs. Was that idiotic or what? If all he had to worry about was the discount cremation part of the business, it'd be okay for Gerhard to manage for a few days on his own. But the body parts business required constant diligence. For obvious reasons, he'd never explained any of these details to Cathy, so he couldn't expect her to understand.

The front door opens and a woman—a real looker—stands in the doorway.

"Oh, you're here already."

For a moment he's struck dumb by her beauty.

Then he recovers with, "I'm sorry for your loss."

"Thank you, but I'm just a friend. The family's in the living room. This way."

Gerhard follows her, pushing the collapsible stretcher covered with a purple blanket into the next room. The couch has been made into a bed, medications and tissues on the nearby coffee table. A woman is on the couch with the unmistakable pale of death. Three other people are in the room.

Minutes later, after the body has been loaded into the hearse, Ditto stands at the door with the woman. He hands her his card.

"Here. If there's any time in the future I may be of service, just call."

She exchanges the card with a slip of paper.

"Thank you, Mr. Ditto."

On the way back to the hearse, he unfolds the note. The name Cathy and a phone number are printed in neat block letters.

He laughed at the memory of meeting Cathy while at work in the funeral home—which preempted any need for the awkward, eventual question, "What do you do for a living?" With other women, when that topic inevitably came up, his answer was an immediate turn off. Not so with Cathy.

They sit in a booth in an Indian restaurant on their first date, eating tandoori chicken, naan, salad, and drinking a bottle of wine.

Cathy asks, "How'd you get started in the mortuary business?"

"Simple. When I was a kid, I worked for my dad. So when I joined the Army, they made me a mortician. I got out and wasn't quite sure what I wanted to do, so went to work for one." With a shrug, "Here I am."

She hangs on every word.

"No, I mean, how did you get the idea for the budget business. That's really very canny."

He smiles at the memory. "I went to Wal-Mart one day. As I got out of the car—it was raining hard as hell—I looked up, saw the sign, thought of their slogan, Live Better, Save Money. The rest just followed."

"And the body parts business?" she asks.

"I figured it shouldn't have to cost a family an arm and a leg to pay for a cremation."

They both laugh, but she has no way of knowing that's his and Gerhard's private joke.

She seems to enjoy hearing about his business…so Ditto piles it on.

"Med schools use bodies mostly to teach normal anatomy, so they're very picky about what they accept."

She flashes him a get-serious look.

"I'm serious. Check out the UW's website. It's all there. We won't take your body if you have diseases like hepatitis, HIV, or obesity. Damn ridiculous, if you ask me. Obesity? Hell, bring it on! A fatty has more skin than a skinny macrobiotic. And there was nothing wrong with a fatty's ligaments, bones, or hair either. Why waste any of it? What we do is recycling at its best.

By the time he and Cathy finished the wine he was explaining how conscientious recycling was a mind-set he valued so much he'd made it the cornerstone of DFH's corporate culture. Throughout the building he'd placed color-coded bins for paper, plastic, glass, metal. He believed every attempt to recycle, no matter how seemingly insignificant, helped Mother Earth survive the heavy footprints of our wasteful society. She nodded agreement, then blew his brains out with a smile. Damn! A looker and a believer.

He still couldn't believe his luck.

He answered the phone, not bothering to check caller ID.

"Ditto here."

"It's Gerhard. Okay to discuss business?"

"Yeah. I'm alone. Shoot."

Gerhard's voice sounded strained.

"The news I got isn't what you're gonna want to hear. Apparently, McRae does know him."

Fuck.

High as the odds were against this happening, apparently it had. Ditto started pacing.

Last night Ditto had spent hours tossing and turning, staring at the shadowy ceiling, considering the consequences of this possibility. If it had happened at any other time, he'd shrug it off, and say "So what?" What was McRae going to do about it? Long as that specimen got back here and into the oven, McRae wouldn't have diddly squat to back up his claim. It'd be his word against our DFH Inc. records. But there was that fucking detective too. That changed the equation. Despite what the records showed, it really had been Baer in the back of vehicle. Who knew what might be found if the cops went over the Suburban looking for evidence.

"This McRae, what's your take on him?"

"You asking if he's going to be a problem? Fuck, yes. He threatened as much."

"He can threaten all he wants. We just need to make sure no

one believes him. Get the specimens back here tomorrow."

"Got it. Thought you'd want to know is all."

"I do. Thanks for the heads up. But what *you* need to know is a detective dropped by asking about the Suburban. Apparently, someone noticed the other night when you made a pickup."

"Shit."

"Yeah, shit is right. But nothing's going to come of it if we take care of things correctly."

"You can count on me."

"I do. And thanks. Have a safe trip."

Ditto clicked off and replaced the phone in its charger. He returned to the counter to finish his coffee. But now it seemed too strong and bitter, and the mug felt heavy in his hand. Should've gotten rid of the damned mug at the same time he got the divorce from Linda Lee. That unfaithful bitch. Jesus, what a clusterfuck this thing was turning into. First the detective, then the doctor...

He took a deep breath and started to go through it again.

So, a Seattle doctor in Hong Kong claimed to know the person whose head was used for the dissection. Big deal. That could be handled by simply claiming a case of mistaken identity. After all, DFH had clean papers on the donor.

Who the hell was going to prove it differently?

No one.

But then there was the Suburban. Even if someone saw it near a motel the hooker used, so what? He was no lawyer, but common sense said if that was all the detective knew, he was okay.

Still...

Ditto took another sip of coffee, decided it hadn't improved with age, and went back to the newspaper.

As long as nothing unexpected happened, he'd be all right.

Chapter 10—Health Sciences, University of Washington

WENDY DOUBLE-CHECKED the number to the right of the doorjamb against the one she'd scribbled on a Post-it. A door identical to every other door along both sides of a long echoing hall painted institutional beige. No nameplate, just the alphanumeric TT425 engraved in an eye-level plastic plaque. She knocked.

"You may enter."

You may enter?

She opened the heavy door.

"Professor Boynton?"

"That's right." He flashed a charming smile of perfect teeth.

He was the polar opposite of what she'd imagined after hearing his voice on the phone. Or maybe she'd been influenced by the title Professor, Department of Biological Structure. She'd envisioned a bald seventy-year-old with Dumbo ears hunched over an old desk filled with high stacks of papers. Yoda in a white lab coat. Instead, this dude was tall, buff, tan, early forties and wore a Tommy Bahama shirt. Certainly not even close to any professors she'd seen at junior college.

They shook hands, and he pointed to the guest chair and said, "Please."

The room felt more like a walk-in closet than a professor's office. Barely enough space for the vintage oak desk, matching guest chair, and floor-to-ceiling bookshelves. A solitary window allowed a restricted view of Northeast Pacific Street. That is, if you could see through the thick layer of grime coating the glass. A seventeen-inch laptop on the desk. The faint smell of incense caught her attention.

He took his chair and leaned back, arms folded across his chest.

"Now what exactly may I do for you?"

During the call, she'd mentioned needing some general information about the medical school's Willed Body Program but hadn't delved into particulars. She certainly hadn't wanted to get into any sensitive questions without a face-to-face conversation.

"First, thank you for taking the time to see me, Professor."

He flashed another smile.

"Call me Bill. Professor sounds too formal."

"Okay, Bill. You're in charge of the Willed Body Program here at the university?"

When she'd Googled *willed body program,* it popped up with the UW Department of Biological Structure. Boynton's name was on the site.

"Yes."

"The information on your website answered a lot of questions, but I still have several more I need answers to."

"Ask away."

"It states bodies are used for medical research. What exactly does that mean?"

He pushed the laptop aside, knitted his fingers together, and leaned on the desk, eyeing her in a way that made her want to pinch her blouse collar closed.

"Means a lot of things, but probably the most common use is education. Teaching students." He seemed to savor those words. "I guess in the strictest sense student teaching is not truly research, but in the more global sense it is. I like to believe that training new professionals is the only way to assure a supply of future researchers. Don't you agree?"

Wendy believed the question was rhetorical, so she didn't answer.

Without giving her time to answer, Boynton continued.

"There are always questions about the biological structure of the human body that aren't fully answered. So, I guess you'd say much of the material is used for rather straightforward pedantic research."

She had no idea what that meant but nodded.

"I see."

He seemed to be done and waiting for a new question, so she jumped to the real reason for the visit.

"Are you familiar with a local facility called DFH Inc.?"

His expression changed to disgust.

"Ditto's endeavor?"

My, my, what an intriguing reaction.

"What can you tell me about it?"

Boynton studied her a moment.

"What exactly do you want to know?"

"Let's start with the business. Can you explain it to me?"

He pinched his lower lip.

"So, really, you came to ask about Ditto's business and not about our Willed Body Program; am I correct?"

"Yes, you are."

"And I assume you've spoken with Bobby-Bobby?"

"Who?"

Boynton snickered.

"That's what we call him behind his back. Bobby-Bobby. You know, Bobby *Ditto?*"

"Oh. Got it." Wendy cleared her throat to refocus him. "Yes, I talked with him. But there are still a few things I don't understand, things I was hoping someone outside of DFH could explain."

"This part of an investigation?"

He sounded curiously hopeful.

"Why would you ask that?"

Boynton flashed a knowing grin.

"Because I've always suspected something amiss over there."

Interesting.

She reached into her purse and triggered a recorder.

"Do you mind if I record this?"

He shook his head.

"Is that a no?"

"It is if you want me to be truthful."

Wendy held up a small notebook.

"Then do you mind if I take notes?"

He pointed at the notebook.

"Would that be discoverable?"

"Yeah, probably. Depending on what happens."

"Then I mind that also."

"Any particular reason?"

"Because I get the impression you're investigating Ditto. Knowing him, it means sooner or later he'll end up in court. And that means anything I put on the record today will end up there too. That happens, he'll know exactly where it came from even if I'm not named as the source. That dude's one vindictive hombre. What I'm saying is, if he were to win in court, he'd come after me with a vengeance. That's not exactly a career builder now, is it?"

Another rhetorical question.

"Well, if what you say is true, that he ends up in court, what makes you think he'll get off?"

Boynton laughed.

"Because he's far from stupid. In fact, he's one of the cleverest hombres I know. Never went higher than high school, but he has a business sense that's uncanny. He's also an expert at reading people. He plans well and executes effectively. Whatever you have going on, be careful. That's all I can say."

Wendy dropped the notebook into her purse, sat back, crossed her legs.

"You were saying, about his business?"

He glanced at the ceiling, rubbed the back of his neck.

"You have any idea what the market is for bodies?"

"You mean, like for kidney transplants?"

"That too, but no, not living organs like kidneys and hearts. I was referring to intact cadavers and cadaver parts. Organ donations are regulated by DSHS, but the cadaver business isn't."

"Interesting."

Earlier Wendy had looked up a couple of cases—one at UCLA Medical Center, another in Virginia—where body parts had been sold illegally by employees in the morgue. But the news service articles didn't provide the information she needed. She planned to dig up more when she had the time.

"In this state at least *body* donation is wide open, and it's a huge market." Leaning back in his chair, Boynton tapped his pursed lips with steepled fingertips. "Here's how it works. Say you're one of the big medical instrument companies, and you develop a whiz-bang new artificial knee. How do you train surgeons on how to implant the appliance correctly?"

"You tell me."

"The company conducts training seminars. You might hold a few at the big national meetings, but you also set up a series of workshops in major cities around the country. However you choose to do it, you'll need a constant supply of actual knees. And they have to come from somewhere. That's where DFH steps in. They're a major supplier. Not only that, but their fancy building over by Lake Union…you ever been inside?"

"Yes, but only the lobby and Ditto's office."

"Well, it has some of the most elegant teaching facilities I've ever seen. HDTVs, webcasting pods, wood-paneled lecture halls…I'm telling you, this building"—he held out his arms—"sucks in comparison."

From the little she'd seen, it sucked regardless. The West Precinct was the Taj Mahal in comparison.

"The demand for cadavers isn't just for medical education, either. There's other needs you might not think about. Forensic studies, as an example. There's a guy in Tennessee who's made a name for himself by studying the life cycle of maggots in decomposing bodies. He's the world expert on the subject. He had fields of corpses and adds new corpses to them all the time. Can you imagine a field of rotting bodies? I'm sure you must have heard of him."

Wendy nodded, but in truth this was the first mention she'd heard of him and what she envisioned made her nauseous.

"Then you have accident reenactments. Although there are companies that make gelatin body simulations for those, the biomechanics are never as accurate as a human corpse, so the demand remains high," Boynton said with a shrug.

He's really getting into it. Probably one of the few times he's lectured to someone actually interested.

"These are all legitimate uses that make us as people better off." He paused. "But back to your point. Have any idea how much Ditto is paid for a whole body? Especially one in pristine condition?"

She assumed from the way he asked that it would be high.

"Tell me."

"Get this." Boynton leaned closer as if disclosing confidential information.

"How does three hundred thousand dollars grab you?"

He sat back and crossed his arms with a smug expression.

"That's three *hundred* thousand?"

He smiled.

"Staggering, isn't it?"

She whistled.

"Man!"

His smile widened as he laid down his trump card.

"But *selling* bodies is illegal."

"Then I don't—"

Boynton raised a hand, cutting her off.

"Here's how it works. Say your father has a massive heart attack and dies, and you don't have the money for a casket, much less a funeral. You're torn. You want to do something nice for dear old Dad, but you simply don't have the money. And God knows, you have to do something with the body. Can't very well just toss him in the Dumpster late at night. What do you do?"

"You call DFH Inc."

He flashed a thumbs-up.

"You bet you do. And what's not to like? Ditto's crew promptly arrives, whishs away the body. If you opt for his medical research program," making quotes with his fingers, "there is no charge. It's free. He cremates the body and gives you the ashes or disposes of them for you if you prefer. But wait," he said with a dramatic flourish, mimicking a TV ad, "there's more. If you want, they'll even give your loved one a nice memorial service in their own chapel free of charge. It's a huge win for everyone involved. Not only does Dad get a funeral, but he's contributed to the advancement of science. Whether you're down on your luck or rolling in the dough, you don't have to end up paying several thousand bucks to have Dad cremated or buried with a ceremony. You got to love it. And people do."

"So how—"

Up went his hand again.

"How can Ditto get three hundred thousand grand for Dad and stay legal? Easy. He charges the customers—medical schools or medical device companies, for example—huge storage, transportation, and" again miming quotation marks, "handling fees. That part *is* legal."

"Meaning there's an illegal part?"

Boynton nodded slowly.

"Didn't hear it here, but yet, I'm convinced of it."

Wendy stole a glance at her recorder. The red record light was glowing, so she was catching every word.

"Go on."

"What I'm telling you is only what I suspect. I don't have proof. We clear on this?"

"Yes."

"Okay, then. First, there's a huge black market for body parts. There's also a huge demand. So, say you're Ditto and you pick up a fresh body, one that's still warm and in perfect condition. If you know what you're doing and work quickly, you can salvage everything—corneas, skin, heart valves, ligaments. I could give you a complete laundry list, but I think you get the idea. He doesn't deal in kidneys or other living internal organs for transplant—because that gets a completely different level of state scrutiny—but still, there's enough tissue to make a jaw-dropping amount of money from dealing in cadaver parts. And it seems like such easy money that every year you read about some dumbshit morgue worker arrested for helping himself to parts of the deceased."

She thought back to the few cases she reviewed.

"Donating your body isn't for everyone, and I'm here to tell you it doesn't happen every day. For a variety of reasons. Most of all, not everyone knows it's an option. And if you do know, you might not like the idea of being dissected in a classroom full of curious med students. Maybe you're worried about being naked in front of an audience. For others, just the thought is intrinsically repugnant. Maybe some have religious law or belief against it. The point is—and this is a biggie—the number of annual donations doesn't come close to meeting the demand. Yet somehow every year Ditto's business grows. How does he do it? I can't understand where he gets all his material—it must be a huge supply. Something's not right."

She wanted to know exactly where he was going with this.

"Can you be more specific?"

"All I know is how many bodies come to us annually. It's not close enough to meet our needs. So, I can't for the life of me see how it can approach what Ditto's numbers are. Granted, he aggressively advertises his discount funeral part of the business and that helps. But think about it. There shouldn't be any material left over from that. At least not if he really is cremating the entire bodies. So where do all the body parts come from to supply the cadaver parts business?"

"What exactly are you saying?"

"Did I say something?"

"No, but you sure implied something."

He wagged an admonishing finger.

"I told you I'm not going on the record with this."

"Look, if you have any proof of anything, say it. Now's the time."

"No, I don't. I already told you that."

"Then give me a hypothetical. What do you *suspect* is going on?"

Boynton seemed to choose his next words carefully.

"Ditto runs three businesses. The one everyone knows about is his budget funeral service. No problem there. The second is his medical research program where bodies are used for various teaching programs. Supposedly, after the body or limbs are used, all the parts are returned and cremated together, and the ashes disposed of according to the family's wishes. The third business is supplying cadaver parts—bone fragments, ligament, whatever— for use in surgery. I simply don't see how he gets enough material to keep that third part of the business so robust."

When he paused, Wendy said, "Go on, tell me what you think is happening."

"Obviously, he needs bodies to meet demand. How does he do it? First, there's the possibility of getting unclaimed or unidentified bodies from the medical examiner. But they don't give away freebies. Besides, by the time the ME finishes with a body, it's usually too decomposed to be good for anything. There's only one other way I know to acquire a freshly dead person."

"What's that?"

"Like I said when we started, Ditto's a vindictive guy. I don't want him coming after me."

"Okay, but it's just us here. What are you saying?"

"Think about it," Boynton said. "You need a fresh body. Where you going to go?"

She waited for him to make another comment, but he just shook his head.

She asked, "Anything else to add?"

"You free for dinner?"

Chapter 11

USING A CAMPUS map from the main hospital information desk, Wendy threaded her way back to the parking lot thinking about Boynton's unexpected dinner invitation. She'd been caught off guard and hoped she hadn't been too rude when she turned him down.

The parking lot was on the south side of Husky Stadium with full sunlight frying her motor pool Caprice. She opened the front door and stood there waiting for heat to waft out before climbing in. No matter how hot Seattle became, it paled to the car-searing summers she's endured growing up east of the mountains in Moses Lake, Washington.

People always said, "Yeah, sure, but that's a *dry* heat."

As if that made a difference. Dry, wet, whatever, to her it was frigging miserable.

Her dad had been an air traffic controller for the air force, stationed at Larson Air Force Base outside Moses Lake. The base became decommissioned just about the same time his tour of duty ended. With 4,700 acres and a 13,500-foot runway, it became the Grand County International Airport and an alternate landing site for the NASA space shuttle. Her parents stayed in town working as civilian airport employees for the FAA while raising

Wendy and her older sister, Megan. And they loved it.

Well, they could have it. The heat, the annual Eagles barbecue, the VFW hall, and the Grange. All of it.

She hated the endless summer evenings sitting on the porch swing with nothing to do but listen to Mariners games on a staticky AM radio station and dream of escaping the flat, boring town. Megan never left. She boomeranged back from Washington State University freshman year, married the hayseed who'd knocked her up. Megan and her husband were raising three boys. Which, from Wendy's point of view, held as much appeal as rinsing out your mouth with Clorox.

For reasons Wendy could never grasp, she'd always wanted to be a cop. Right out of high school, she enlisted in the army after receiving assurances from the recruiting officer that if she did well on the tests, she'd be assigned to their Criminal Investigation Division. After four years of active duty and some junior college courses, she figured she could pass the physical fitness and civil service exams for the Seattle Police Department. And she did.

A week after graduation from the academy, she was called into the chief of police's office.

She stands at the desk, the fresh rookie assigned to patrol.

The Chief says, "Close the door, please."

She does and returns to the desk. The Chief remains seated with a manila folder open on his desk.

"I've been reading your record, Student Officer Elliott...may I call you Wendy?"

"Yes, sir."

"Good performance in the Academy. Good enough for Internal Affairs."

"Sir?"

"I've been looking for a fresh face to be assigned to basically work undercover for Internal Affairs."

"Just what does that mean?" she asks in spite of having a pretty good idea.

"Means you'd be assigned to a unit we have reason to investigate. Say, Vice. While there, you'll do the work you're assigned, but in addition, you'll be conducting an investigation for us by looking into questions we have about other members of your team."

"In other words, you want me to spy on other cops?"

"That's one way to view it. The way we prefer to think of it is the cops we put on your radar may turn out to be the ones who shouldn't be on the force. Even the police need policing, sorry to say. What do you think, Wendy?"

She likes the fact that the Chief knows her name, but she also knows that IA investigators are often veterans only a couple years away from retirement. They can put in their final time and then leave the force without worrying about not being liked by the rank and file. Also, she wants to eventually make the Homocide squad.

When she hesitates, he adds, "Says here," with a nod at the folder, "you want to work up to Homocide. That true?"

"Yes, sir."

"Well, then…give us four to six years of good undercover work and I'll see to it you end up where you want. We have a deal?"

"You have an assignment in mind, obviously. What is it?"

He sits back, closing the file.

"You're young, statuesque, and blonde. You have a face that can be hard. And I don't mean that as an insult. At the moment, we need someone to be assigned to the Vice squad. But you didn't answer my initial question. You want in?"

She doesn't like the idea of ratting out fellow officers, but the Chief has a point. Someone has to police the police.

"Yeah, I'm good for it."

The Chief smiles, holds out his hand.

"Welcome aboard, Officer Elliott."

They shake hands.

The Chief says, "Officer Travis Hunt is your husband, right?"

She and Travis were married halfway through their time in the Academy.

"Yes."

"Good. That's perfect cover if he's your primary contact. As of now, you're off patrol and reporting to him. Officially, however, you're now assigned to the Vice unit. After we're done here, you can walk over to meet your superior officer. You okay with that?"

"No problem."

That was the same time her marriage started sliding sideways.

She and Travis had assumed that because they were both cops they'd understand their hectic schedules and the emotions the job sucked from them. But it didn't work like that. Under the daily stress, they quickly lost patience for each other's quirks and began arguing. In the end they blamed their failed marriage on job-related stress instead of other possibilities, like their inability to compromise to get along. Wendy called him an anal neat freak. He viewed her as a slob and would go ballistic if toothpaste wasn't squeezed from the end of the tube or if a fresh roll of toilet paper wasn't in the john before the old one ran out.

Little things accumulated, becoming fodder for more resentment and bigger arguments. Rather than scream at her during blowups, Travis simply shut down and wouldn't talk. This cold shoulder would go on for days until they eventually drifted back together, neither one assuming responsibility for the disagreement. It seemed to be during those times of zero communication she needed him the most, so his neglect of her hurt worse. It didn't come as a surprise when, after one of those blowups, Travis suggested they separate. She agreed. And that was that. But they still liked working together and were good at it.

The three-year anniversary of their divorce passed just last month, she realized.

The car felt comfortable enough to get into, so she climbed in, fired the ignition, and backed out of the parking space. Another car was already waiting to take the spot.

Wendy turned up the volume of the FM station to drown out the constant din of radio traffic from the police radio. She tuned it to the local country-western station. Just another vestige of life in Moses Lake. As a teenager she hated country music, seeing it as *so* not cool. But during the divorce, when some lyrics assured her things could be worse, she grudgingly had to admit to a certain closet enjoyment in the pissing and moaning about other people's tough times. A kind of roots thing, she guessed. Yet she made a point of not letting her friends know she listened to shit kicker music. It didn't fit the image she wanted to portray in her life on this side of the mountains.

Waiting for the traffic light to let her escape the sweltering parking lot, she thought about Bobby Ditto again. Seemed like the more she learned about him, the more she was convinced he was involved with Lupita's disappearance. She had no tangible evidence yet, only her gut feeling of being on the right track. Boynton just verified it.

Now she had to prove it.

Chapter 12—Hong Kong

LUCAS WAS UP before the wakeup call. He showered, checked out, and headed to the airport early, hoping he might be able to catch an earlier flight. There wasn't one.

He used the lounge computer to check his email, but there were no new messages. Then he went to the Seattle Times web page and typed Andy's name in the search line. He hesitated, unsure if he wanted to see the answer, but pressed enter. A few seconds later "No Match" popped up, leaving him with a sense of relief.

After checking his luggage through customs, Gerhard headed to the departure gate but saw McRae in the departure area. He stopped. The last thing he wanted to do was get into another pissing match with the bastard. If McRae saw him, that would surely happen. And if that happened, Gerhard might slip and say something he'd regret. The one thing he'd learned in this life— thanks to his time in the army—was to walk away from confrontation because if he didn't, it usually ended badly.

He also intuitively knew McRae was smarter than he was. Maybe not in street smarts, but in other ways. And he didn't want McRae asking him tricky questions.

Gerhard stepped into a bookstore and browsed the magazines, picking out a *Popular Mechanics* for the flight home. He was certain McRae would be flying first or business class, meaning he'd go through the front gate. He'd wait until McRae boarded before taking the rear gate to the coach section.

Once the heads were back safely where they could be disposed of, there was nothing that son of a bitch McRae could do about it.

Chapter 13—Seattle-Tacoma International Airport

AFTER CHECKING THE suitcases to make sure the suitcase containing the heads hadn't been tampered with and the seals remained intact, Leo Gerhard hefted both locked aluminum cases onto a luggage cart.

Fucking Customs.

Those agents weren't supposed to open them, but ever since ICE became part of Homeland Security, you really couldn't trust those yo-yos anymore. They did all sorts of crazy shit in the name of national defense.

This being a routine trip, he should be able to just zip through as long as the paperwork appeared in order. Except this time he felt a little twitchy. For a couple reasons. Partly on account of the Chinks being the ones to sign off on him in Hong Kong. Never trusted those slants. They'd fuck you over for a quarter and never think twice about it. More than that was a nagging suspicion that somehow McRae had enough juice with the authorities, maybe on account of being some big shot doctor, to cause him grief. If McRae pissed and moaned load enough, might be that immigration would give him a closer look. Then again, he was carrying good paper. Fuck McRae.

He knew he was being paranoid, but still…

Especially with Bobby ranting about that female cop. He could kick himself for leaving the Suburban in that alley. Fucking *No Parking* signs all over the place. But parking in that area sucked, and besides, it was going to take him only a few minutes.

What were the odds?

Should've known. Bad luck being pretty much his life story.

He filed into the customs line and watched more travelers fill in behind him. Glanced around for McRae but didn't see him. He probably didn't bring more than one carry-on bag, so the bastard wouldn't have to wait for luggage like he did. McRae. Fucker worried him. Had that nervous, squirrely look about him. The moment he got back he'd have a talk with Bobby. No way was Gerhard going to let him underestimate McRae. He had a feeling about McRae, and it wasn't good.

A troublemaker is what he is.

And he needed to make sure Bobby understood that. Bobby was smart, probably the smartest guy he knew. Except for chess. When it came to chess, they were equals. And he bet that if they ever kept track, he won more games than Bobby. But when it came to gut feelings about people, Gerhard figured he was the better of the two.

Gerhard approached the booth and handed the immigration officer his paperwork. He checked to make sure it was all there: the departures from Sea-Tac and Hong Kong. The special papers.

The guy flipped through them with a bored expression, stamped Gerhard's passport, and handed it back.

"Nothing to declare?"

Gerhard shook his head.

The agent looked at the papers again.

"Bring the suitcase into the other room, and let's have a look."

Gerhard hesitated, wondering if it was possible for McRae to have already stirred up the cops, but knew he couldn't very well refuse to be inspected.

"Certainly, Officer."

Gerhard followed the officer into a small side room used for this type of inspection and wondered...

Why this time?

Most of the time they didn't inspect. He set the Halliburton on a small table, and the officer inspected the security tape covering the latches by the Hong Kong authorities. The tape stuck like hell, making it impossible to remove or open the case without cutting through it.

"Open it, please."

Gerhard glanced around for a box cutter, saw it on the desk, slit the tape and opened the suitcase. He was sweating now. How detailed would the guy check? But, he reassured himself, the papers would look good.

Inside, the dissected heads were wrapped in blue-green surgical towels. The officer glanced down at the individual packages, then back at the papers. "Unwrap one, please."

Gerhard swallowed, selected a bundle that wasn't Baer—just in case this was being videotaped—and carefully pulled away the towel exposing a disembodied head. The jaw had been disarticulated during one of the dissections and the nose had been pushed to the side. Gerhard realized it was the one McRae made such a scene over.

The officer said, "I've seen enough. Wrap it up."

Gerhard stifled a sigh of relief and replaced the towel, closed the Halliburton, thanked the officer, and left the room wondering...

Why the fuck did someone want to look this time?

It never ceased to amaze him that customs never bothered to check the suitcase's contents. They simply accepted his word that what left Seattle matched what came back in. McRae had that part right. Gerhard could fly out of Sea-Tac with a suitcase full of human body parts and return with a load of dead cats, and no one would know. Yeah, but there was always the chance they'd check.

All it took was getting caught once, and you were fucked. From then on they'd check you every time—if they even let you continue. So far, Gerhard's record was impeccable.

Gerhard continued through the baggage claim area, out through the sliding glass doors to catch the shuttle to long-term parking, unable to shake the feeling of being watched. He glanced around for someone paying too much attention to him but didn't see anyone. He then noticed a Port of Seattle cop walking his way.

Where the fuck is the shuttle?

The cop sauntered past just as the shuttle rounded the corner and came into view.

At the long-term parking, Gerhard transferred the cases to the trunk of the black Chrysler and headed to Seattle. Forty minutes and McRae's buddy's head would go up in smoke.

Like all the international flights Lucas took to Sea-Tac, the United 747 docked at the South Terminal. Lucas followed the zigzag route to the immigration arrival lounge where he took a place in one of the rapidly enlarging lines for US citizens.

With only a carry-on, he bypassed baggage claim and went straight for customs where an agent waved him through without a word. Then he rode the subway to the main terminal and called Laura's cell. As planned, she was waiting in the nearby lot.

He headed out to the passenger loading zone to wait. Despite having been gone only a few days, he looked forward to seeing her. Returning home was always the best part of each trip.

Lucas checked his watch—1:04 PM on Friday. No matter how many times he'd been to Asia, it amused him to arrive an hour before he departed. It was as if he had just gone through some sort of time travel.

He reset his watch to local time and waited. Long international flights left him feeling grimy, fatigued, and thankful the plane didn't crash or blow up from a terrorist bomb. Though the experts claimed air travel was safe, Lucas never felt at ease.

Lucas recognized Laura's silver Volvo station wagon swing into the curb lane and slow. Grabbing his wheeled carry-on, he waved to catch her attention and wove through a throng of travelers boarding a bus to the downtown hotels. After dumping the suitcase in the backseat, he climbed in the front and shut the door.

Laura said, "Welcome home," and pulled away from the curb.

"Missed you." He remembered how they used to kiss when he returned from a trip. Long gone, those days. Now she was already checking traffic and accelerating into the left lane. He sat back to watch her drive. She still looked good after twenty-one years of marriage. Luxurious brown ponytail adjusted just so out the back of a foofoo white ball cap. A trim five-foot-seven-inch frame. She hadn't put on weight after the pregnancy, nor with the subsequent years, like so many people do. Kept the gray out of her hair and always made sure she looked put together before leaving the house.

"I'm meeting Carol at the spa, so I'll just drop you off. Your flight was ten minutes late."

That figured. Funny the pall only a few words can cast on a mood. Just minutes ago, he'd been looking forward to seeing her. But that seemed to be the byproduct of the memory of better times. Now, face-to-face, the rancor of their pending divorce made him not want to be in the same car as her.

Where did things go so wrong in their relationship?

He doubted she was involved with someone. If that were the case, the signs would be different, he believed.

Years ago, when Lucas returned from a business trip, they'd hurry home to enjoy sex. No longer. Laura's libido vanished as the other symptoms of depression became apparent. Making matters worse, their sex life had become an off-limits subject, one that Laura refused to even discuss, leaving him even more frustrated. To him, sex was an important part of loving the other person. To have it unilaterally amputated from their relationship left him feeling alienated and, well, angry. And sometimes it felt like neither of them seemed capable—or perhaps even desirous—to fix their problems. As if it would be too much trouble.

He asked, "You get hold of Andy?"

She hesitated too long before answering. It was a sure sign she was scrambling to figure out how best to lie.

"I called his condo a couple times but only got the answering machine. When I tried his cell, I got an out-of-network message."

Yeah, shit, she hadn't even tried.

Which, given the intensity of her dislike of Andy, didn't surprise him. Lying about it did. But what could he do? Nothing. Certainly, he couldn't challenge her story. Her attitude toward Andy was a battle he'd surrendered years ago.

Lucas sighed, dug out his cell phone. This time of day, Andy would already have left the office to work out at the Athletic Club. He tried the office number anyway and got the standard recording about not leaving any trade instructions because the timeliness could not be assured. Next, he tried Andy's cell and reached the synthesized message that the Verizon customer was out of the service area. That could mean anything from the phone being shut off to having lunch on Mars.

He decided to unpack, shower, then go out and find Andy himself.

Chapter 14—Ditto Funeral Home

ARMS LOOSE AT his sides, Bobby Ditto leaned against a reinforced concrete support column waiting for the steel garage door to start clanking up with that loud metal on metal screech the maintenance guy never seemed able to fix. Had his ankles crossed in a pose he thought looked extremely cool if anyone happened to notice. Dressed in corporate casual: chinos, a lightweight navy polo shirt, and Top-Siders sans socks. Always fantasized the life depicted in Ralph Lauren ads—to glow with the subtle patina of old money. Instead of leaning against a bare concrete column, he should be leaning against a granite column on his mansion's front steps and circular flagstone drive.

Why couldn't he have been born into money?

The luck of the draw, he supposed. He'd had the bad fortune to grow up in a working-class neighborhood. Instead of a father with an undertaking business on the first floor of the family home, his dad should've come from a family with enough power to keep him out of jail if he piled up the Benz after too many Heinekens with his school buddies.

He should be enjoying the privileges of a Florida winter home and a Nantucket beach house for those times he needed a break from his plush Manhattan co-op and the rush of the city life, living off a trust fund with a seven-figure income regardless of whether or not he chose to work at his father's brokerage. He threw the cigarette into the drain.

What the hell was taking Gerhard so long?

He'd called from the car, giving an ETA of ten minutes. Meaning he should be here by now.

Fucking Seattle traffic.

Parallel rows of concrete columns ran the length of the floor, which made some parking spots a bitch to get into. But the good news was this section was totally isolated from the adjacent larger basement area, making it perfect for transporting bodies. For reasons he never could understand, dead bodies always seemed to spook people.

He heard the motor catch, followed by the metallic grind as the heavy door started up. The distinctive grille of the black Chrysler nosed in. Ditto moved away from the column and waited for Gerhard to park and pop the trunk.

Gerhard stepped out, arched his back, arms stretched above his head. He stayed like that a moment.

"Come on, let's get these taken care of."

Ditto went to the trunk.

"What's wrong?"

"Customs. They stopped me to check the shipment."

Ditto looked in the trunk for the suitcase with a discreet DFH Inc. Sticker next to the handle, the one that carried the specimens. Lifting it out, he examined the seals and saw the slits. As far as he was concerned, turning those heads into unidentifiable ash couldn't happen soon enough. Then maybe the crazy recurring vision of Detective what's her name would stop haunting him.

"What exactly happened?"

"Nothing, really, but it fucking freaked me."

Gerhard hefted the remaining suitcase from the trunk, closed and locked the lid before following Ditto to the elevator.

"Tell me exactly what happened," Ditto said, stepping into

the cage.

He poked the first-floor button. The door closed, and they started up as Gerhard explained in his whiny voice.

When starting Ditto's Budget Funeral Services, he invested in an Ener-Tek IV Cremation System. He loved that particular model because it had relatively quick throughput, taking only seventy-five minutes or less per body, allowing for up to fifteen cremations in eighteen hours. But hell, no one could be *that* busy. More importantly, the Smoke-Buster 190 feature eliminated airborne particulates and odor from the cremation process, making it environmentally sound.

What's not to like?

The unit was large, almost ten feet high, eight feet wide, and twelve and a half feet long, and front loaded. Ditto punched a button. The square, recessed front door opened noiselessly, exposing the firebox. What a beauty. It was already fired and ready to go.

Ditto watched Gerhard throw the suitcase on a stainless-steel dissection table and unsnap the locks open. Inside were four bundles in black Hefty garbage bags. He unrolled all four, then unwrapped the surgical towels covering the heads and set them aside.

Suddenly, Gerhard turned toward him and said, "Yo! Heads-up."

Bobby saw a head come flying across the room, caught it, faked left before doing a one-handed jumper through the furnace opening.

A regular fucking Brandon Knight.

"Three points," Gerhard yelled, then pumped a two-hander rocket from behind the table.

The head sailed toward the furnace, hit the front just above the door, fell to the floor with a thunk, rolled to a stop at Ditto's feet. A woman, her hair salvaged for wigs, her face now indistinguishable from the dissection.

Ditto scooped it up, shoved it through the opening.

"Rebound. Two points."

Gerhard took another shot, this time making it.

"Swish!"

Laughing, Ditto pushed a button, closing the door, cutting off the heat entering the room. No sense keeping it open any longer than necessary, what with the cost of air-conditioning. For a moment he watched through the small tempered glass window as the heads were engulfed in two rows of gas flames. He felt relieved now that the evidence was gone.

Ditto and Gerhard took an extra couple of minutes inspecting the suitcase, making sure it was spotlessly clean. All that remained of any evidence were the damp surgical towels and wrinkled garbage bags. Gerhard balled the bags and dropped them into the waste. The towels went into a bucket of weak Clorox solution to denature any residual DNA. The towels would be washed and reused. He seriously doubted that lady cop would be back with a search warrant, but you could never be too sure.

Finished cleaning up, Ditto smiled with satisfaction. Maintaining a neat work area was another trait learned from Dad.

"Well, that takes care of that," said Gerhard.

Despite the huge sense of relief at watching the heads incinerate, Ditto was not completely at ease. Nagging doubt still troubled him.

"It takes care of any evidence, but if you're right, McRae might still try to cause a stink. We don't need anyone looking at us."

Gerhard nodded.

"You can count on it. He threatened as much."

Realistically, Ditto knew there was nothing McRae could do at this point. Still, he hated the specter of any lingering threat, no matter how small. The Tigers and Red Wings served as perfect examples of why you should never underestimate your opponent's tenacity. Tenacity too often prevailed. He couldn't count the number of times he'd watched a comfortable lead evaporate into a defeat. Relaxing your guard was just asking the other team to regroup and win. Never ever let up. Not until the game is over. Squash them.

So this McRae...no way could he allow even the slightest threat to remain. And the only way to eliminate the threat was to eliminate the man.

Earlier today he'd Googled McRae, searching for every bit of information he could find. Then, for good measure, he'd driven past his two-story house in the Magnolia neighborhood in northwest Seattle.

Ditto handed Gerhard a slip of paper.

"Here's his address. Have a beer, relax a bit, maybe even nab a few hours shut eye, then drive over. Find a way in. See what you can figure out in case we have to, you know..."

He nodded at the oven.

Chapter 15—Magnolia Neighborhood, Seattle

BY THE TIME Lucas removed the key from the front door, Laura was halfway down the block, not having bothered to wave goodbye.

Welcome home.

He watched the Volvo round the corner and disappear. He'd forgotten what it was she was going to do. Meet one of her girlfriends, maybe. Was that one of the problems? Not paying as much attention to what she said, his mind too busy with other things?

With a mixture of sadness and frustration, he carried his suitcase inside the modest two-story remodel that had originally been a one-level rambler. The upstairs master bedroom provided a southeasterly view over multiple layers of rooftops to the downtown Seattle skyline. The panorama wasn't as grand as the multimillion-dollar homes two blocks away on Magnolia Boulevard, the first tier above the bluffs, but he loved it. Seattleites appreciated views regardless of limitations.

He went to the phone and called all three of Andy's numbers. No answer.

Go over to his condo?

If he was there, he'd answer.

So, what next?

He sat down at his desk and thought about that for a moment. Initially, he intended to go over to Andy's condo, but now that he thought about it, that wasn't likely to yield much because he'd not be able to get past the doorman. Besides, it wasn't unusual for Andy to take a three- or four-day vacation with his latest girlfriend. Or maybe he'd gone to Las Vegas to play with the hookers. He did that once in a while. Probably shouldn't get too worried unless he didn't show up for work on Monday.

Lucas unpacked, tossed his few dirty clothes into a wicker hamper, and removed his safety razor from the shaving kit before replacing the kit in his bag. Then he stowed the bag on the top closet shelf. He tripped, showered, dried with one of the oversized bath towels Laura liked so much, put on black jeans and a black T-shirt. Didn't bother with socks or shaving.

He padded down the hall to the small guest room that doubled as a home office. On one wall hung a framed black-and-white poster from *Casablanca*, the one with Bogart leaning on a café table with an almost empty bottle of booze touching his right hand. It brought to mind the line, "You played it for her and you can play it for me."

He settled into the rolling chair and started the small CD player. Albert Collins started singing about not being drunk.

For a moment he studied Josh's framed high school graduation pictures. His son had inherited Laura's nose and eyes. From Lucas he'd inherited persistence. Now he lived in an apartment with two other students on the other side of the mountains at Whitman College as an economics major. Lucas shook his head.

What do you do with an economics degree?

Business, well, that was pretty obvious, but economics? He'd never mentioned these doubts to Josh, believing instead that what really mattered was for Josh to do whatever fulfilled him and gave his life purpose. Economics seemed to do that.

Lucas missed having him around, even if only for Sunday dinners. He would prefer him closer at the UW or even Seattle University, but Josh claimed the huge UW campus made him feel intimidated and insignificant. So, after touring several West Coast schools, he opted for the family feel of Whitman. At least he wasn't 3,000 miles away at some East Coast school.

Lucas debated calling Trish, Andys ex. Far as he knew, she was the only one Andy listed as an emergency contact. He dreaded talking to her because she'd always resented him. Never understood why exactly, but suspected she held him partially responsible for Andy's self-destructive behavior. As if Lucas could've made a difference. Sure, he'd talked with Andy about it numerous times, but addictions were impossible to change with only words.

Reluctantly, he dialed Trish's number. She picked up after the third ring.

"Hello, Trish. Lucas."

"What do you want?"

Great.

"Just got back to town and haven't been able to reach Andy. Have you talked to him recently?"

"No."

Figures.

"Ah, how long since you talked to him?"

"Why?"

"Like I said, I haven't been able to reach him. I was wondering if something was wrong."

"Like?"

"I don't know. An illness, maybe."

"The world should be so lucky. But if Andy had a problem, he'd call one of his girlfriends, not me. He knows better. That's it? I have to run."

"Okay, well, thanks. Good-bye."

Lucas stared at the phone, wondering what to do next. Had

to do something.

Lucas pushed through the front door to Andy's condominium building and entered the lobby.

The doorman looked up from behind the counter, asked, "May I help you?"

Lucas didn't recognize the man and assumed he was a temp for one of the regulars who was either ill or on vacation.

"Dr. McRae to see Mr. Baer."

"Is he expecting you?"

"Yes," Lucas lied.

The doorman put the phone to his ear and dialed. Then started drumming the eraser end of a yellow pencil on the granite counter.

After thirty seconds he hung up, said to Lucas, "He's not answering."

"That's strange. He's expecting me. Did you see him go out?"

"No."

"Have you seen him during the past couple days?"

"Dr. McRae, we're not allowed to give out personal information."

"I'm just asking if you've seen him. That's not personal."

The doorman returned an icy stare.

"Anything else I might help you with?"

Lucas trudged along First Avenue wracking his brain for another place to look or call. Nothing came to him. This was Saturday and if Andy took one of his girlfriends on a trip, he might not be back until Monday. He'd go nuts waiting until then.

The diffuse uneasiness in Lucas's gut returned, but this time he knew what was causing it. Before leaving for Hong Kong, he'd signed out of the office for ten days of vacation when he got back. He and Laura planned on visiting friends at their weekend cabin at Black Butte Ranch in Oregon. But he couldn't very well leave now. Not until he found Andy. To say Laura would be pissed about it would be a gross understatement. Well, it couldn't be helped.

A need swept over him—not a want, but a soul-wrenching need—to see Josh and do something simple, just the two of them, like share a meal. He dialed Josh's cell and waited for an answer, visualizing his son frantically rummaging through his rucksack for the phone.

Josh answered, "Hey, Dad. Back from Hong Kong already?"

"Got in about a couple hours ago. You free for lunch tomorrow?"

"Guess so. Why?"

"Thought I'd come over, see how you're doing. That fit your schedule?"

"What's wrong?" Josh sounded alarmed.

Aw, man, was it that apparent?

The last thing he wanted was to upset him.

"Nothing. So, it's okay to come?"

"Not unless you tell me what's up."

"I'll tell you when I get there. Noon? Your favorite place?"

"Okay."

Lucas hung up and began rehearsing ways to explain to Laura. No matter how carefully he chose the words, she'd never understand.

Chapter 16—Magnolia Neighborhood, Seattle

GERHARD SAT BEHIND heavily tinted windows watching the front of McRae's house. He'd parked the black Chrysler across the street and down one lot to appear as if he were visiting a neighbor. He knew the tinted windows made it impossible for an observer to tell if anyone was inside, much less see well enough to provide a description. Sure, some nosey Neighborhood Watch asshole might jot down the license number of an unfamiliar car, but he'd switched to bogus Montana plates, something he should've done that night with the fucking Suburban. And that one, it turned out, had been a spur-of-the-moment opportunistic catch. Which, in retrospect, was really stupid.

He watched a Volvo station wagon turn onto the street and slow as it approached McRae's driveway, then turn in. It stopped while the door to the double garage opened, then went forward to park beside an Audi.

Gerhard was out of the car, trotting across the street, timing his move.

The garage door started down. He hesitated, out of range of

the car's rearview mirror, before hunching down and stepping under the closing door without triggering the safety beam, between the driver and the Audi. He ended up hidden underneath the German car's rear bumper. The garage door motor stopped groaning a second before the car door slammed. Then he heard footsteps slap cement followed by the thunk of another door closing. The steps had been quick and light like a woman's.

Minutes later the garage went black as the door light timed out. He smelled concrete and motor oil, heard the ticking of a cooling car while waiting for his eyes to adjust to the dark.

His butt cold from sitting on concrete, arms warped around knees, Gerhard catnapped as the hours ticked slowly by. Having familiarized himself with the garage, he was now positioned in the spot least likely to be seen if someone opened the door from inside the house. Sporadic sounds came from inside, but these diminished over time until finally he heard only the occasional creak of cooling joists.

He stood and waited for his legs to come back to life before pulling on disposable exam gloves. After flicking on a tiny Maglite, he carefully made his way to the interior door, put his ear to it, and listened for sounds from inside. There were none.

He tried the doorknob. Unlocked.

Then he was in the kitchen, looking around. Enough streetlight angled through windows that he didn't need a flashlight.

Fuck a duck, what luck!

A purse and key ring sat on the kitchen table. The ring held a car key, one that looked like it could be for a locker, and a Schlage. The last one had to be for the house. From his pocket he pulled a wad of clay and folded it over the key and came away with an impression good enough for a locksmith. After putting the key ring back on the table, he left the kitchen to explore the rest of the house.

Gerhard stood at an open bedroom door listening to the soft snores of two people, thinking if McRae turned into a real pain in the ass, this was an excellent way to quickly and quietly take care of him, no problem. He pointed his finger like a gun, thought, *Pop, pop.* All done.

He crept down the stairs and out the front door.

Lucas awoke with a start, aware of something wrong. He sat up in bed, careful not to disturb Laura. To his shock, he detected the faint odor of formalin, the embalming fluid, something he hadn't encountered since medical school. The nebulous dread congealed into fear. He reached for the phone to call 911.

This is stupid.

Instead, he slid out of bed and edged to the door to the hall.

Nothing.

At the head of the stairs, he looked down to the first floor, saw only familiar shadows in the weak streetlight through the windows, the house deathly silent. With the lights out, he went downstairs, checked the doors. Locked.

Still, he couldn't shake the feeling of something wrong, that someone had been inside.

Chapter 17—Applebee's, Walla Walla, Washington

LUCAS FIGURED WALLA Walla was about as far as you could get from Seattle and still be in Washington State. It hugged the Washington-Oregon border in an area rich with wineries.

Lucas was up, showered, and out the door by five-thirty wolfing a breakfast sandwich and sipping a grande latte from a downtown Starbucks before hitting the 1-90 interchange and heading east toward the Cascade Mountains, the navy Audi A6 on cruise control three miles above the speed limit and his iPod blasting Albert Collins, Freddie King, and a raft of other serious blues players on the car stereo. He sang along to Collins's *Master Charge* while blowing past North Bend, the sun in his eyes.

Figured four to five hours each way with maybe an hour for lunch and he'd be back in time for dinner. Josh, as much as he loved his dad, couldn't sit still for a conversation much over sixty minutes. Even that was pushing it. The kid got restless easily. But so had Lucas at that age.

After Snoqualmie Pass, he nudged the A6t a hair past seventy-five, the highway patrol thinner on this side of the mountains. Eventually he left I-90 to cut down through Yakima and Pasco, the synthesized GPS voice constantly reminding him which exits and turns to take. The first time he used the GPS, he named it Maddie and wondered if the voice was 100 percent synthesized or modeled after a real person's voice. The best thing about Maddie was she never got angry if he missed a turn. She just recalculated.

Stopped once for another coffee and recycle the first latte, topped off the tank, and was off again.

He rolled into Walla Walla, took Plaza Way, and parked facing the front of Applebee's. He'd made it with time to kill.

Lucas was already in a booth waiting when Josh walked through the front door, army surplus rucksack over his right shoulder. His son's face lit up as soon as their eyes met.

He slid out of the chair to hug, said, "Great to see you, son."

They hugged each other tightly and as they released, Lucas looked him over, making sure he seemed well and fit. Josh had on a black T-shirt, olive cargo pants, Converse tennis shoes.

"You look good, Josh," he said, patting him on the back.

"So do you, Dad."

They slid into their respective seats.

Josh pushed away the menu, having memorized it more than a year ago. Lucas had already decided on a cheeseburger, figuring screw the cholesterol worries. At least for this visit.

Josh looked down at his hand while unrolling the paper napkin and freeing his flatware.

"What's going on? You and Mom getting a divorce?"

"What?"

"Well, that's what's coming, isn't it?"

"What makes you think that?"

"I'm not an idiot."

"No, seriously, why would you say such a thing?"

"Well, duh, it's clear you guys aren't all that happy together."

"That obvious, huh?"

Josh averted his eyes and started curling and uncurling one corner of the place mat.

After a few moments Lucas cleared his throat.

"You're right. That wasn't really a question. And yes, we've talked to a lawyer about it. Just not sure exactly how this is going to play out. I'm still hoping we can resolve things with a marriage counselor."

His son met his eyes.

"I hate to say anything mean about Mom, but she hasn't been herself lately."

Not so long-ago Lucas would have automatically defended Laura, especially after a remark like that from Josh, but this was interesting.

"In what way?"

"Aw, jeez. You know. She's constantly pissed at you. And me. At the world, really."

He's right, Lucas admitted.

He just hadn't considered her in quite that light. Which was sad because she was no longer the woman he'd married.

Did she think the same of him?

Had he changed that much too? He must have changed, but the question was how much? Organisms react to stimuli. Change doesn't occur in a vacuum. And that begged the question: What was driving her personality change? Him or did it come from within her? It was so easy to shrug it off as depression, but was it totally?

Why wouldn't she see the psychiatrist he'd suggested?

He wished she would, but that was something he couldn't force her to do. Whichever, he desperately wanted back the woman she used to be.

"I think she's depressed."

Josh shook his head and kept fiddling with the place mat.

"She doesn't seem depressed to me. She seems, I don't know, nervous or something."

"She is. But there's a form of depression in which agitation is a major part of the problem."

Josh stared at him.

"It's called agitated depression. What's unusual about your mom is she's a little younger than what's typical. It's seen more often in elderly people. But that's what I think she's got, and that's why I want her evaluated by a psychiatrist. She won't go."

"Why not?"

"I don't know. Maybe she's afraid."

Silence.

The waitress appeared, ready to take their order. Both ordered cheeseburgers and Cokes.

After she left, Josh asked, "You never answered my question. You're not getting a divorce, for sure?"

Lucas shook his head.

"Thought I said, we've contacted a lawyer."

"What does that mean exactly?"

"We haven't formally filed. But I have to say, it's not looking good."

"Then why'd you drive all the way over here? I can't believe it was just to have lunch. Something's bothering you. What?"

For a moment Lucas sat back to admire his son. Josh had Laura's canny ability to read people that Lucas lacked. Laura was intuitive, making decisions from a few facts.

In contrast, Lucas gathered and weighed as many facts as possible before reaching a decision. Not to the point of extreme, but to the point of feeling informed. The other way seemed so impulsive.

"Guess the only way I can explain it is I have this feeling that something's not right. It's making me uneasy. So," he shrugged, "I just need to be with you for an hour."

"*Need* to be with me?"

"Yeah. That's how it felt."

Josh paled.

"Oh, shit, you're not, like, dying, are you?"

So much for tact.

"No, no…nothing like that."

Lucas sighed, raked his hand through his hair, and started in with, "When I was in Hong Kong, I had this really crazy experience."

He told Josh about seeing what looked like Andy's head and now being unable to locate him by phone.

"Did you call the cops to see if there's a missing person report on him?"

"See, that's where I'm having a problem. I'm not sure anyone would even know he's missing. Or care. Much less file a report."

He told Josh about his phone call to Trish.

"What about work? If he doesn't show up, won't someone start asking questions?"

"Maybe."

Andy's problem had spilled over to the office, resulting in a couple warnings from HR to knock off hitting on some of the secretaries and using the work computer for viewing porn. Sure, Andy made good money for the company, but it would tolerate only so much before dropping the hammer.

"What are you saying?"

When Lucas didn't come up with an immediate answer, Josh said, "Tell me. It's something more than that, isn't it?"

Lucas sucked in a deep breath and decided to include the part about the run-in with Gerhard in Hong Kong.

"You know about Andy's problem, don't you?"

"What? Keeping his dick in his pants? Who doesn't?"

"It's an addiction. Just like an alcoholic struggles with drinking, he doesn't have a lot of control over it."

Josh gave a dismissive wave.

"Yeah, yeah, whatever."

Lucas elected to press on rather than defend Andy. Truth was, he'd long ago tired of defending him.

"Part of his problem is risk taking, which includes being in the wrong place at the wrong time. Usually with a hooker."

Or a couple of hookers together. Andy had once suggested they do a group thing with a few girls. Lucas declined.

"So, he screwed himself to death?" Josh said.

"No, I'm worried that…" Lucas found it more difficult to explain than he'd anticipated. He swallowed. "Maybe…maybe he was murdered."

There! Finally said it for the first time.

Josh seemed puzzled.

"Why tell me? If that's what you think, why not tell the police?"

"Because I can't be 100 percent sure it was him." Soon as the words were out, Lucas realized he'd left out a crucial part of the story, so he explained how the head had been shipped and that Gerhard denied it was Andy.

When he finished, Josh asked, "And you believe this dude Gerhard?"

"Absolutely not. He's lying. I know he is."

"Well, if you think this Gerhard or DFH had anything to do with Andy, all the more reason to talk to the cops."

"No. I'm not saying they killed him. But obviously, they ended up with his body. So, they'd have to know something. At the very least, where it came from. The only information Gerhard gave was denial. And that makes me all the more suspicious he's hiding something."

"You really need to talk to the cops."

"I plan to. If Andy isn't at work tomorrow."

Their burgers arrived. Josh lifted the top bun and dressed the melted cheese with mustard and catsup.

No longer hungry, Lucas nudged aside his plate, the greasy smell making his stomach churn.

Josh started fiddling with the place mat again.

"Tell me something."

"What?"

"Something I've never understood. Mom hates Andy. Trish hates Andy. In fact, I can't think of one of your friends who admire the way he screws around with women. But you and Andy have been best buds for years. What's that all about? I mean, what is it between you two?"

Lucas sucked another deep breath and sat back. Neither he nor Andy had ever told a soul about the incident that had silently bound them for years.

"Let me tell you a story…"

Chapter 18—Twenty-Five Years Earlier, Seattle, Washington

LUCAS SITS NEXT to Andy on the timbers at the end of the dock, bare feet dangling an inch above the smooth water of Lake Washington. The back of his thighs feel the scratchy surface of the rough-hewn boards grayed by weather and spotted with seagull shit, the type he knows will inflict serious splinters if he's not careful. The distinctive smell of warm shallow lake water permeates the summer air. Lucas isn't sure what causes the odor, maybe algae or the green slime coating the submerged creosote-impregnated pilings or something entirely different.

Shorts, T-shirts, flip-flops, and no homework. Each of them clutching an emerald-green bottle of Heineken stolen from Andy's dad's stash.

It's approaching dusk. They're at Andy's parents' unpretentious home at the north end of the lake, but still within the city limits. The kind of house that costs a small fortune in property tax each year because it's on fifty feet of waterfront. The lots were all built two generations ago, the houses crammed so close together you can hear the neighbor's TV when the windows are open.

Andy elbows Lucas and nods at the ski boat tied to the neighbor's dock. Yellow and sleek, big honking Mercury outboard weighing the stern. Just bobbing next to them, begging to be run full throttle on the open lake.

"Sweet, huh?" Andy says.

"Sweet," Lucas agrees.

He imagines the feel of the hull skimming the water, wind whipping his hair, miles of lake passing in a flash. They've been skiing in that boat before.

Andy studies the neighbor's house.

"Think the Coles are home?"

Lucas glances over his shoulder to look. The downstairs patio sliders are shut, and the sliders to the upper deck are also closed. No lights on, either.

"Doesn't look like it. Why?"

"Thought maybe we could borrow the yellow monster for a few minutes."

Lucas doesn't like the sound of that.

"You mean ask permission?"

"No."

Lucas licks his lips and stares at the house again. He's torn. What a perfect evening to be out on the water. But taking the boat without permission...he's not so sure about that.

"Oh, man, I don't know. I mean, that's his baby."

"We'll be careful. And it'd be for only one quick spin. We'll bring it right back. They won't even know we used it."

Lucas can feel the thrill of not only being out on the lake on such a beautiful evening but the thrill of doing something entirely radical. Something they'd never do in a hundred million years. Excitement boils up inside. Part of him has to do it, yet another part doesn't dare. It goes against every stitch of his fabric. But isn't that some of the allure? Besides, summer was ending, meaning they'd soon be back in school, not that that made it okay, but he felt so restless...

Andy says, "C'mon. Don't be a pussy."

The pussy threat. Lucas has never really bought into that one. But he stands, still not sure if Andy is honest-to-God serious.

Aw, man, Andy is heading down the dock now.

He *is* serious. Lucas brushes the dirt off his shorts and hurries to catch up.

Andy and Lucas both know that during summer Dr. Cole keeps the boat key clipped to a Day-Glo pink float in a footlocker by the lower sliders. Along with three or four orange life jackets.

How many times have they seen him reach in there for the key?

Next thing he knows, they're flying along the shoreline, Lucas driving, the overpowered Merc screaming. Andy taps Lucas's shoulder. Lucas looks over at him, sees his mouth moving but can't hear a word over the noise. He leans closer.

"What?"

Andy cups his hands, yells, "Slow down!"

Lucas imagines driving Miss Budweiser in the annual Seafair races, chewing up the course in first place. Andy points ahead.

"Lucas!"

Lucas looks. Directly ahead, coming up fast, is a huge concrete pylon for the floating bridge. Lucas jerks the throttle back and spins the wheel, but the boat can't turn fast enough and the port side slams into the piling.

The impact throws both boys to the deck. For one dazed moment they stare at each other before Lucas realizes the boat is severely damaged, maybe even sinking. Luckily, they'd been smart enough to toss in two life preservers but foolish enough to not be wearing them. They're on the deck.

"Here." Lucas tried to hand one to Andy but realizes his arm isn't working right. Then the pain hits, and he notices the weird angle between his elbow and wrist.

"Oh, shit! My arm's broken."

Andy is clipping on a life preserver and glancing around.

"Jesus, man, we have to get out of here. The boat's sinking."

"I can't go in the water. I can't swim with it like this."

He hears his own voice tight with panic. Lucas frantically

glances around.

Shit! Fuck!

The boat is definitely taking on water. So much so, bailing isn't even worth the effort.

Kneeling in the cockpit, Andy points off to his right.

"Shit, shit, shit. Look!"

Lucas looks. A Seattle Police boat is bearing down on them, blue light atop the cabin flashing.

Andy screams, "Lucas, hold on, this is going to hurt."

Andy scrambles over to him with the other life preserver, slips Lucas's good arm through, then grabs Lucas's broken one and a second later the preserver is on him.

Lucas wants to vomit from the pain. Not only are they in deep shit for stealing a boat and undoubtedly totaling it, but two months earlier, after passing their MCATs, he and Andy applied to the UW medical school. Dr. Cole, the owner of the now sinking boat, is not just an assistant dean there; he heads the admissions committee. They are totally screwed, blued, and tattooed.

"Lucas, c'mon, let's get out of here."

Lucas looks around although he knows the area well. To the north, across the ship canal is the UW campus and looming Husky stadium. To the south, on their left, condos and apartments line the shore. With the police arriving from the east, his only escape is to head for the condos. Being a strong swimmer, he could usually make the bank easily. But with his arm broken.

"But—"

Andy gives him a reassuring smile and a shove toward the shore.

"Go. Get out of the damn boat."

Then they're in the cold lake water, Andy pulling Lucas as he tried to swim with one arm.

Andy says, "Just breathe and let me pull you. Let the life preserver keep you up."

Andy pulls him to safety.

Chapter 19—Present Day, Applebee's, Walla Walla, Washington

JOSH LEANED FORWARD, slack-jawed, a half-eaten burger in both hands. That was unusual for him. Usually he scarfed down burgers almost as fast as his father.

Finally, Josh laughed.

"I can't believe it. You and Andy actually did that?"

"Believe it. We did."

"So, like, what happened?"

Lucas's face burned with embarrassment.

The story was bad enough, but to be telling it to his son...well, shit.

"It's obvious, isn't it? We got caught. I'm still not sure how I ever got accepted to med school after that."

"But what about Andy? I never knew he applied to med school. This is news to me."

"Med school was what his parents wanted Andy to do. Not him. Never was into it. He applied simply to make them happy. He figured if he ended up having to go, he'd never do a residency. Instead, he'd go on to get an MBS and become an administrator, maybe a medical director for a hospital or a biotech company.

Business was really his calling."

Josh sat silently for a moment.

"Wow, so Andy saved your life?"

"Yeah, probably."

"You ever tell this story to Mom?"

"Yeah, once, but it didn't make any difference. She can't see the good things in him."

Chapter 20—2200 Block, Second Avenue, Seattle

WENDY PARKED THE unmarked Caprice in a passenger loading zone, flipped down the visor with the police sign rubber-banded to its underside, and killed the engine.

So far, the majority of her day had been spent digging up information on Robert J. Ditto and the Medical Education and Research Company of Seattle. To her disappointment, other than two speeding tickets, Ditto had no police record. He was divorced, held an honorable discharge from the army, owned a legitimate business, paid taxes, and was a licensed mortician in Washington State. Personally, he owned no vehicles. DFH Inc., on the other hand, owned three. The black Suburban seen in the alley around the time Lupita disappeared, a black Chrysler, and a BMW. She assumed the first two were for business and the last one for Ditto's personal use.

DFH Inc. employed ten, including Ditto, the CEO. He owned 100 percent of the business. She ran every employee's name through the law enforcement databases and was again disappointed to strike out. She thought about the disappointment and wondered if she'd lost her objectivity on this case.

Was she trying to build a case that simply didn't exist?

But she reminded herself, if there was no case, why had Ditto lied about the Suburban? Besides, what about Boynton's accusations that he was shipping more material than was reasonably possible? That was the thing really driving her.

She'd called around to ask sources about the body parts business in general and their opinion of DFH, Inc. specifically. Professor Boynton apparently had several things correct. A huge, lucrative market for bodies and body parts existed and Ditto seemed to be doing a good business with it.

By all accounts, Ditto's company was successful, if not envied, by his competitors. Ditto had developed a reputation as a smart businessman who paid attention to details and nurtured his company. Everyone emphasized Ditto's canniness in creating a budget cremation company. Apparently, it was a niche no one had previously exploited because the profit margins were too big to consider discounting.

As for the body part business, Boynton had that right too: no one understood how Ditto was able to meet demand. But no one echoed Boynton's suspicions, and she wasn't about to ask. No telling how fast that might work its way back to Ditto, tipping him off to her "inquiries."

Wendy found it difficult to understand how a person might want to be a mortician and spend a career with dead bodies. Sure, everyone needed a job, but embalming, burying, and cremating the deceased?

You had to be a little fucked up, right?

And if that wasn't creepy enough, what about shipping arms or legs or other body parts all over the world? You have to have a freaky, kinky mind to be into that shit, no matter how well it paid.

But the biggest question of all, the one Boynton raised, was how did Ditto get his hands on enough product to keep growing and sustaining the business?

The obvious answer nauseated her.

Until learning of Ditto, she'd worried the missing girls might be victims of another I-5 or Green River Killer. The problem with that theory was that none of their bodies ever turned up. Now, with Ditto in the picture, the answer to that was easy; he could be harvesting their body parts, then cremating them.

She climbed out and locked the car. Ahead, on the corner of Second and Blanchard, was the remodeled Crocodile Café. The original Croc was an icon from Seattle's contribution to the grunge music scene. After it closed, the property was bought and reopened.

Wendy used the Second Avenue entrance. Just inside the door, she stopped to look around. About halfway down the room three Hispanic males occupied a table, two on one side, the other with his back to her, all wearing the baggy banger clothes that made it easy to hide weapons. Like it was some kind of regulation uniform.

She made eye contact with one. He muttered something, and his two homies pushed back their chairs and drifted off to another table nearby.

He was Luis Ruiz, Lupita's brother. If not for the ragged scar on his left cheek, the misalignment of a poorly set broken nose, and a couple amateurish gang tats, he might be handsome. Instead, at the age of twenty-three, he was a poster child for the wear and tear of gang life. Since his sister's disappearance, he looked even worse. Dark circles rimmed both eyes, and his face sagged from fatigue. Not knowing where Lupita was or if something had happened to her was destroying him. Wendy knew he held himself responsible for her disappearance. Then again, they both knew the risks of the sex trade.

Years ago, Lupita and Luis's parents died in a warehouse fire at work, leaving the two teenagers without family or money. Having been born in the United States, they were citizens despite their parents having been illegal immigrants. This left the kids limited choices: either return to Mexico to track down relatives they'd never even met or find a source of income. Luis had been hanging with a gang, but there wasn't much money in that unless you were dealing drugs, which he didn't want to do. Lupita knew a couple of older girls who turned tricks. Without other skills, prostitution became the quickest way to earn enough money for the two of them to survive. She hated the work and was saving money to pay for school. Luis didn't like his sister being a prostitute but had little choice. So, in return, he and the other gang members made sure some pimp didn't try to corral her or that she didn't get started on heavy drugs. They took care of each other.

Wendy took the chair opposite him and leaned forward, forearms on the Formica tabletop.

"How you doing?"

He answered, "Find out anything?"

Her drive over had been one internal debate on how much to disclose. She'd settled on divulging pretty much all, reasoning that with his street connections he might be able to dig up additional information on Ditto. Granted, it was a long shot, until you considered that Luis knew she was tracking other missing prostitutes. It was a small world on the streets, so you never knew what kind of information his network might yield.

"Maybe. But you need to understand it's not much," she said, knowing he wanted any scrap of information she could give.

She filled him in on the black Suburban seen in the alley a block from the video store where Lupita solicited. She purposely didn't mention the business DFH handled and her nagging suspicions about Ditto.

Luis asked, "Who owns it?"

"Guy by the name of Bobby Ditto. Word has it he's sometimes called Bobby-Bobby. Any reason you should know him?"

Maybe Ditto or one of his employees frequented the girls in the area or the store, meaning there could be an explanation for the vehicle being in the area.

"Uh-uh. But believe me, I'll nose around, see what I can learn."

"Do that. But don't discuss details with anyone. Don't let on why you're asking." She paused. "That's it for me. How about you?"

"Nada."

Wendy reached over and squeezed his hand.

"Keep at it. Sooner or later we'll get a lead."

"Lead? We both know she's dead by now. Shit, I just want the motherfucker who took her. If this Ditto's involved, he's a dead man."

Chapter 21

LUCAS SLID OUT of his car, stretched both arms over his head, and arched his back. For several seconds he stayed like this, allowing muscles to unknot after long hours of driving. It was a long trip to Walla Walla and back. But it had been worth it to see Josh. Also, he felt vaguely vindicated, having always sensed that Josh frowned on his unwavering friendship with Andy. At least his son now seemed to understand. And this made him feel better. Too bad Laura didn't see it.

When Laura had first expressed her hatred for Andy, Lucas explained how Andy saved his life in hopes of justifying their deep-seated friendship. But, unlike Josh, Laura chalked up the incident as only one bright moment of an otherwise degenerate life. Andy's addiction blinded her from appreciating his good points.

Lucas and Andy are riding their bikes along a neighborhood street when a loud bang causes all of Lucas's muscles to jerk. He hears laughter. Kids' laughter. They stop to see what's going on. Three older boys—maybe 15 years old—stand on freshly mown lawn, their backs to the street. There is a stake driven in the ground with a large tabby cat tethered to it with a ten-foot black nylon cord. The cat yowls and claws at the air. The boys are just out of the cat's reach. One boy, wearing heavy gloves, grabs the cat, presses it hard against the ground while a second boy binds a large firecracker to the tip of its tail with electrical tape.

"Hey, stop that!" yells Andy.

The three boys stop, turn to Andy and Lucas, surprise on their faces.

It only takes a second before the biggest one, the one with the heavy gloves, scowls, says, "Says who?"

The air suddenly goes eerily still. Lucas glances at Andy, wondering if he's nuts, if he realizes those older guys are bigger and stronger and can beat the shit out of them. All three of the other boys are looking at Andy, daring him to mouth off at them.

"That's cruel," Andy says, with a nod toward the cat.

The leader says, "So what? What are you going to do about it, dickwad?"

"That's someone's pet. It doesn't deserve to be tortured or killed."

The leader takes a step toward Andy, the move sending a jolt of adrenaline through Lucas's arteries. Lucas takes a deep breath and glances at Andy. Andy stands firm, eyes blazing right back at the leader.

The other two boys step forward to back up the leader, who seems to sense their approval without moving his eyes from Andy's face. The leader continues straight over to Andy, their faces now only a foot apart. The other two boys close ranks to either side of him.

"Know what I think?" the leader says. "I think you're a pussy."

Andy doesn't wait to say a thing, just hauls off and smacks the guy in the nose as hard as he can. Blood squirts everywhere. The other two guys start swinging.

He and Andy, bruised and bloodied, make up a cover story on the bike ride home.

Lucas walked around Laura's Volvo to the kitchen door, pressed the switch to close the garage door, and waited to make sure it started down before entering the kitchen.

Laura sat at the table, the *Seattle Times* spread before her. She leaned back and crossed her arms.

"Well, well, well. The traveler returns. How's Josh?"

Her icy tone and body language made it clear that Josh's well-being wasn't tonight's main topic.

He played along by saying, "He's fine."

Hungry and thirsty after such a long drive, he went straight to the cupboard, withdrew a glass, and filled it with cold tap water. He felt her eyes on him.

"How was your day?"

"Fine."

Lucas cringed.

Okaaay.

"What's for dinner?"

"When you weren't back by six-thirty, I assumed you ate something on the road. I went ahead and made a salad."

He opened the fridge, found a thigh and a drumstick of leftover roasted chicken. It'd do. He shoved the chicken in the microwave to warm.

"I'm having a martini. Want one?"

"No, thanks."

He mixed the drink in an oppressive silence broken only by the rattling of ice in the shaker. Disregarding the olive, he poured it into a cocktail glass, dumped the cubes in the sink, and upended the shaker in the drainer. Took a sip and turned to her.

Laura feigned interest in the newspaper.

"What?"

She looked up.

"I didn't say anything."

"I know you didn't. That's why I'm asking what's wrong."

"I notice you're not packed."

"Right. I'm not."

"And why is that?"

"You know why. We went over it, and I'm sorry, but I have to find out about Andy."

She shot him a look of disgust.

"I don't believe it. We've had this trip planned for at least two months."

"Feel free to go if you want, but I thought I made it clear. I have to find out what happened to Andy. Maybe even file a missing person report with the police. I can't help canceling. Two months ago, when we accepted the invitation, I didn't anticipate seeing Andy's head on a stainless-steel tray in Hong Kong."

"Goddamn it. It *can* be helped. All you have to do is pack some clothes, jump in the car, and go. It's that simple." Laura stood, hands on her hips, and yelled, "What you're really saying is that you don't *want* to go. That's the issue, isn't it?"

He took a deep breath, then a sip of his drink, trying not to let her push his buttons.

"For Christ's sake, something's happening to Andy. It needs to be looked into. Who else is going to do that? No one."

"You don't know for certain if anything's happened to him."

Had she heard nothing he said yesterday?

"Yes, I do."

"What? You think *maybe* you saw his head in Hong Kong? For the love of God, give me a break. What are the odds of that?"

The odds were irrelevant.

As far as he was concerned, he couldn't rest until he knew for certain.

"Helllllloooo. He's a pervert. That's why he doesn't have that many friends. He's alienated every one of them. How many times has he gotten STDs from seeing hookers? Answer me that."

How many times had they beat this particular issue to death?

And just like all the other discussions, this one would end up the same, with neither of them agreeing with the other's point of view.

"Go if you want, but I'm staying. At least until I have some resolution on this. It's not negotiable."

Lucas grabbed the plate of chicken and the martini and stormed to the guest bedroom.

Chapter 22

LUCAS SLAMMED THE guest room door. Too hard, he realized, like something a spoiled brat would do. He flushed with embarrassment. He wasn't acting like his usual don't-get-fazed self. He also realized he no longer gave a damn what Laura thought of him. Which made him feel sick with regret over the way their marriage was turning out. His parents divorced when he was thirteen, and he vowed that would never happen to him. Now look at him.

He stood by the door, considering whether to go back downstairs so they could try to talk through it again.

But her mind was made up and so was his, so why bother?

The impasse saddened him further. Mostly because he saw no way out of this spiraling decline in their relationship. Maybe it was best to just let things cool down before discussing it any further.

He dropped into the chair and turned on the small TV they kept in there. A Mariners game was on. Two outs occurred before he realized he didn't know which team was up, what inning it was, or who the opponents were. He was like an Alzheimer's patient the nurse had planted in front of a radio. He picked up the drumstick, took a nibble, but was tasteless and he wasn't really hungry after all. With a sigh, he shoved the plate aside.

Ah, but the martini...

It went down so easily that he contemplated another. But that would mean a trip to the kitchen and possibly encountering Laura again.

Screw it.

Lucas went to the guest bathroom, showered, then slipped in between the sheets and picked up a book from the bedside table. John Sanford, one of his favorites. He opened the book to the first page and started reading but couldn't seem to process the words. He started the page again, the same result.

He clicked off the lights and lay on his back, hands clasped behind his head, trying to let his mind drift.

But all he could think about was how miserable their marriage had become.

It wasn't that they argued frequently.

They just seemed to be drifting along, heading in different directions. His practice fulfilled him almost as much as watching Josh develop into a young man. He loved watching football in the fall and baseball in the summer, reading books, backyard barbeques, and an occasional island vacation when they could afford it and when he had the time, which was a lot less than most people he knew.

She, on the other hand, no longer enjoyed sex, watching sports, socializing with old friends, or going to the movies. Rather than vacation together, she preferred trips to a California spa with a girlfriend and the only books she read now were the ones endorsed by someone like Oprah or Dr. Phil. Which was fine, but it left them with little in common.

He'd tried talking with her about the state of their marriage, but she wouldn't discuss it and bristled at the suggestion they see a therapist, much less the psychiatrist he recommended she see.

For the first time in their twenty-one years of marriage, they were in the process of lining up divorce lawyers. Yeah, sure, the idea had previously flitted through his mind in the heat of arguments. But nothing like this. This was a seriously-considering-calling-the-lawyer level of thought.

It frightened and depressed him.

What were the possible options?

Continuing to live in increasing bitterness was intolerable. Especially if Laura wouldn't seek help.

These thoughts swirled around his brain until sheer exhaustion carried him into a black, dreamless void.

When Lucas awoke, Laura was already out of the house. He had no idea where she'd gone.

After a fried egg sandwich, Lucas took a mug of black coffee to his study. Once more he tried Andy's cell, home, and office phones. No answer. He thumbed through his address book looking for mutual friends. He couldn't think of any.

Laura was right: Andy's behavior had alienated a lot of people.

It wasn't easy staying friends with him.

Andy always seemed to leave a Sasquatch-sized footprint on everyone's life. He remembered when they were about thirteen and Andy developed an insatiable appetite for porn. Andy jerked off obsessively, to the point Lucas joked he was at risk for developing calluses on his dick.

Andy tried to put a lid on it but couldn't manage to

After they married, Andy introduced Trish to porn. Initially she went along with it to please him, but rapidly grew tired of feeling demeaned by it and put an end to it.

Andy began seeing prostitutes and ended up busted a couple times by Vice squad stings. Trish dealt with the embarrassment of bailing him out and finally leveled an ultimatum: stop seeing hookers or else.

When Andy told Lucas about it, he claimed he wanted to stop and admitted tremendous shame, pain, and self-loathing over his actions. Lucas gave him a pep talk and convinced him to join the sexual equivalent of Alcoholics Anonymous. Other than that, what else could he say? It was difficult for Lucas to empathize with Andy's struggle.

Andy curbed it for a while but then went right back to the prostitutes.

Regardless, he decided to wait until tomorrow, Monday— on the off-chance Andy had gone somewhere for the weekend— and if he didn't show up for work, he'd contact the police and file a missing persons report.

That was, if he couldn't find Andy before then.

Chapter 23—Monday Morning

IN SPITE OF it being a vacation day, Lucas rolled out of bed early after spending a second night in the guest bedroom.

He quietly showered and ducked out of the house without waking Laura. Figured she was still home since the master bedroom door was closed when he passed by on his way downstairs. It had been open when he'd holed up for the night.

Hell of a way to live a married life, but he wasn't quite sure how to turn it around. Maybe after this Andy thing is resolved, he'd give it another try.

But as long as Andy remained center stage, Laura wouldn't be rational.

Andy's routine was to be in his office by the six-thirty opening bell of the New York Stock Exchange. So, Lucas decided the best place to start looking for Andy was his office.

Gerhard watched the Audi back out of the garage. He slid down in the seat so any quick glance in his direction would make the car appear driverless. The A6 accelerated down the street with Gerhard following, making sure to leave enough distance between them to not be quickly noticed on this sparsely traveled residential street. Monday morning McRae should be heading to work up at Swedish Hospital. Or at least that's what he and Ditto had figured. We'll see, Gerhard thought.

The elevator doors opened onto the twenty-seventh floor of the small brokerage firm that Andy worked for, releasing Lucas directly into the reception area.

A trim woman in a well-tailored blazer with a blonde ponytail and a Bluetooth headset in her right ear smiled at him from behind a richly stained wood reception counter.

"May I help you?"

"I'm one of Andy Baer's clients. He's expecting me."

"Ah, well then, we have a bit of a problem. You see, he's not in yet."

Lucas checked his watch.

"That's strange. I have a seven o'clock with him."

He waited for a reply, but she sat there with an uncomfortable expression.

Lucas made a show of looking at his watch again before asking, "Is Mary in?"

"Just a minute. I'll check."

She scurried off in the direction of Andy's office, seemingly relieved to be able to hand him off to someone else.

To his left, a small conference room with picture windows provided a majestic panorama of downtown Seattle and Elliott Bay with Magnolia Bluff, the Space Needle, and Queen Anne Hill as a backdrop. A pair of good binoculars would probably allow him to see his own roof.

Mary appeared to his right.

"Dr. McRae, how are you?"

The receptionist quietly took her seat behind the counter and busied herself answering an incoming call.

He said to Mary, "I'm trying to find Andy. Is he in?"

She cocked his head.

"You say you have an appointment with Mr. Baer?"

"Yes."

Mary frowned.

"Strange. I don't see it on his schedule."

"Maybe he didn't put it down."

"Yes, that's possible, I guess." Mary glanced around. "Perhaps you should come to his office, and I'll get Mr. Singh to speak with you."

She started toward Andy's prized corner office, a symbol of his success as a broker, which, in turn, was a reflection of his personality and excellent judgment. He never churned accounts and always followed his client's tendencies whether aggressive or conservative. And for whatever reason, Andy never made sexual moves on his female customers.

Mary opened the office door and ushered him in. Large windows with stunning views to the north and east, a large desk, matching credenza, a navy couch, two chairs for visitors, navy carpet. Lucas recognized Andy's brass banker's lamp and the silver framed wedding picture of Trish. He'd kept the picture after the divorce in hopes of an eventual reconciliation. It never happened, and even after she remarried the picture stayed on his desk. The sight saddened Lucas. The recessed overhead lights were off, giving the room a cold, unused feel, as if Andy's spirit had completely vanished, leaving behind only material markers that he'd once worked here.

"Please have a seat. I'll ask him to join you."

A thin, bald, Indian or Pakistani man in a pinstriped charcoal suit stepped in, hand extended. He looked to be in his mid-forties.

"Dr. McRae? John Singh." They shook hands. "What may I do for you?"

Lucas decided to stick to his plan.

"I'm not sure you can do much of anything. I'm here for a meeting with Andy."

"If it has anything to do with your account, I can certainly be of assistance in his absence."

"No offense, but it's more of a personal nature. Estate planning. So, I'll wait to discuss it with Andy."

Singh closed the door, turned on the ceiling lights, and swept an open palm toward the small couch.

"Please. Have a seat." He turned one of the visitor chairs to face Lucas. "Mary says you're not only one of Andy's accounts but a personal friend."

Lucas remained standing.

"Right. We've known each other since grade school."

Singh sat down and crossed his leg, then straightened the crease in his pants.

"I'm not sure what to tell you. Mr. Baer hasn't been here for the past ten days, so it's unlikely he will be here for your meeting."

Lucas decided to sit after all.

"Do you mean he's on vacation?"

"No. He just didn't show up in the office the week before last nor any day since."

Lucas felt growing concern and dread.

"That's not like him. Did he call in sick?"

Singh shook his head.

"He just didn't come in. He hasn't called anyone here in the office, either."

Lucas felt his jaw muscles tighten in frustration.

"Anyone try calling him?"

The comment seemed to perturb Singh.

"Our HR policies are not the issue here. Your brokerage needs are. If I may be of assistance, fine. If not, well..."

Lucas sat back on the couch to make the point he wouldn't be dismissed so easily.

"Here's the deal, I'm concerned about Andy. I haven't been able to contact him for the past week." Which was stretching the truth. "That's why I'm concerned. It's not like him to just take off. You should know that. Did anyone here make any attempt to contact him, find out why he didn't come to work? Maybe check the hospitals?"

Singh pinched the crease in his pant leg again, pulling it

straight.

"We assumed his family would do that."

"He doesn't have any family," Lucas said flatly.

"It's more complicated." Then Singh seemed to consider these last words for a moment. "If you and Mr. Baer are as close as you claim, then you must obviously know of his, ah, problem?"

"You mean with sex?"

"Precisely." He paused. "He constantly was using his office computer for viewing pornography. He'd been warned, but that didn't seem to stop him. As a consequence, we were on the verge of letting him go when this happened. We simply assumed he realized what was about to happen and decided to move on. And that was fine with us because it negated the need for a termination hearing."

As if that exonerated them for their lack of concern. To say nothing of the lame reasoning. For Andy, starting over again would mean he'd have to jump ship to another brokerage house. To do that, he'd surely take as many accounts as possible with him. And Singh would certainly know about that. Lucas didn't buy the explanation.

Singh added, "He'd been warned several times. If he hadn't been such a good producer, well..."

Lucas stopped by Mary's cubicle on the way to the elevator and asked, "Know if Andy was dating anyone in particular at the moment?"

"No, not really."

Something in her voice made him probe.

"But?"

"Well, there was this one woman he called a lot."

"You happen to have her name?"

Mary cast a guilty glance around them before typing a few computer commands. She quickly wrote on a yellow Post-it and discreetly handed it to him.

"You didn't get this from me."

Chapter 24

LUCAS HANDED THE parking attendant a twenty-dollar bill and waited for five bucks in change. Incredible. Fifteen dollars for less than a half hour. At the early bird special rate too. The diagonally striped guard arm jerked once before smoothly angling up, allowing him to nose the A6 over the crest of the ramp and into thick Monday morning traffic.

He headed north on Fourth Avenue, debating what to do next and whether or not to call Andy's girlfriend or call so early. He decided to go ahead.

If he woke her up, so what?

He needed to exhaust every possibility before going to the police. He looked for a place to pull over so he could make the call and saw a free stretch of curb a couple blocks farther up the street. He drove there and parked but left the engine running.

Gerhard waited for a clot of pedestrians to clear the crosswalk before he could turn right when he noticed McRae's A6 exit the parking lot onto Fourth Avenue. Fucking streets didn't allow curb parking, so he'd been forced to circle the block and hope to hell he didn't miss him. Luckily, he didn't. Able to turn now, he accelerated around a Metro bus and made it through the next intersection as the light turned yellow.

Lucas unfolded the Post-it and re-read the name Margo Hadler. He didn't recognize it. Then again, Andy didn't mention every woman he dated. For that matter, she could be an active client.

Shit, he'd forgotten to ask Mary about that.

He dialed.

"Mr. Baer's office."

"Mary, Lucas McRae again. This Hadler woman, is she one of Andy's accounts?"

Mary hesitated before saying, "No."

"A girlfriend?"

Her tone carried a hint of embarrassment, as if there were something more to say.

"I'm not sure. It's just that they exchanged a lot of calls."

He considered asking point-blank if she was hiding something but decided against it.

"Okay, thanks. Sorry to bother you."

Well, that settled it. And would make it easier.

He sat back in the seat to rehearse his lines one final time, but decided he'd mostly have to improvise, and dialed. A woman answered after five rings.

"Ms. Hadler?"

"Yes."

"My name's Lucas McRae. I'm a longtime friend of Andy Baer."

She said nothing.

"I haven't been able to reach him and was wondering if you've been in contact with him recently."

"Who gave you this number?"

It was a simple question. One he should've predicted but hadn't. He didn't want to get Mary in trouble for passing him her name. Especially if this violated a privacy policy, which he suspected it did. Sticking to some truth was the safest strategy.

"I found your number on a piece of paper in his office."

Well, sort of.

"And why were you going through his office?"

"He hasn't been there for ten days. No one knows where he is. I was hoping maybe you might know something to help us," he said, making it sound as if he were officially investigating a disappearance.

She hesitated.

"I haven't heard from him in a few weeks."

"When was the last time you saw him?"

More hesitation.

"Well, we only actually met in person twice. We usually just talk on the phone."

Aw, shit. It snapped into focus.

"Through SAA?" he asked, without really thinking.

Another pause told him he was correct. He knew he just hit a nerve. SAA, the sexual addict's equivalent of Alcoholics Anonymous.

"Yes," Hadler admitted in a voice steeped in guilt.

Lucas felt like shit for even calling but figured the damage was already done, so why not see if there was anything she could add?

"I'm worried about him and simply trying to find out what's happened to him. Is there anything I haven't asked that you think might be important?"

This time she didn't hesitate.

"No."

He got the message.

"Thanks. Sorry to have bothered you."

Lucas sat in the car wondering was there anything else to do before filing a missing person report with the police. That step seemed so...final.

What if Andy came back tomorrow from Vegas?

How would it look to have gone to the police? Especially with Andy's record of being arrested by the Vice detail.

And what about Hong Kong?

If Lucas did go to the police with his suspicion, wouldn't it be a good idea to know something more about the supplier? What was the name? DHL? No, that was the overnight freight company...DFH.

He pulled up Google on his Droid and entered the name.

And was shocked to discover the company was in Seattle.

He merged back into traffic, heading for the foot of Queen Anne Hill and DFH, Inc.

Fuck. Gerhard picked up his cell, thumbed speed dial.

Ditto answered with a simple, "Yeah?"

"I lost him."

"What happened?"

"He pulled over and stopped in a bus zone. No way could I stop without being spotted, so I had to drive around a couple blocks on account of all the one-way streets. By the time I got back, he was gone."

"He heading to the hospital?"

"Didn't look like it. So, what you want me to do?"

"Let me think on it. Don't like it, him not going to work."

Chapter 25—DFH, Inc.

"HELLO, DR. FLEMING," Ditto said into the phone. He swiveled the black leather executive chair toward the window and leaned back. "Bob Ditto. Just following up on that last shipment. Everything to your satisfaction?"

DFH, Inc. had supplied Steve Fleming, a neurosurgeon in charge of several microdissection courses, an order for five preserved heads a month ago. It was a point of pride with Ditto to personally make these routine follow-up calls in the belief that customer satisfaction was an important key to business growth.

"Yup, everything was perfect."

"You'd let me know if anything isn't up to your standards, wouldn't you?"

"Absolutely. I mean it when I say it was top-rate material."

Ditto felt pleased and relieved.

"Okay, then, I won't bother you anymore. Just making sure."

"Uh, it's good timing you should call."

Ditto didn't like the sound of that, like it was a prelude to bad news. He sat upright, drumming his fingers on the edge of the desk.

"Yeah?"

"I know this is unreasonably short notice, but another supplier backed out of a commitment for the congress next month. Five heads. All fresh. I just hung up the phone with the course organizer. Boy, oh boy, is he steamed. Guy's frantic too. Already the class is fully enrolled, so he can't very well cancel it. I told him I'd look into it. You think you can handle that? I mean, fresh and all?"

Ditto started pacing, running his hand over his head. The Congress of Neurological Surgeons. Jesus, a supplier's wet dream. Problem, of course, was inventory.

"They have to be fresh? I mean, is that negotiable?"

"Can't say for sure, but fixed would be better than nothing at this point."

"No problem. Consider the order covered."

"Jeez, that's terrific. I owe you one."

Fucking straight you do.

"No, you don't owe me; I owe *you*. You're bringing me business."

"You're not upset with me, going to someone else first, are you? This is a huge order. I wasn't sure a company your size could fill it. Understand?"

"No problem." *You two-faced asshole.* "Glad I can be of service."

"Thanks so much. All I can say is you're a lifesaver."

Bobby hit the off button and sat staring at the phone in his hand. Their first order from the Congress of Neurological Surgeons. That was huge. He'd been working on nailing that account for years. Any other time, he'd be turning cartwheels down the hall. But Christ, five heads, fresh if possible…what a goat fuck! The timing stunk.

Why couldn't the damn prima donnas be satisfied with preserved heads? So what if the tissue elasticity wasn't exactly perfect? What difference did it make? Wasn't it the anatomy that counted?

Well, shit, he couldn't lose this job. If he did it right, he could sew up this account for all their future needs. But unless five people kicked the bucket at precisely the right time—which was about as likely as Hezbollah befriending Israel—he was going to have to procure them. Or rather, Gerhard would. That usually would not be a problem, but the detective's interest in the Suburban was making him very nervous. This wasn't the most opportune time, but he saw no alternative. The risks of procurement were always high. The last thing he wanted to do was push them even higher.

He settled back into the chair to think. They'd have to be careful. And, of course, avoid the hookers. The detective seemed too involved with them.

"Mr. Ditto."

Startled, he swiveled the chair around. Stella, the receptionist, stood in the doorway, arms crossed over her matronly chest.

"What's wrong?"

"There's a man out front. Dr. McRae. He insists on talking to you. I told him you were in a meeting, but he made a scene."

A bolt of rage zapped him. McRae was the cause of this present fucked-up situation. No, on second thought, that wasn't entirely correct. McRae may have known the guy whose head was used, but he couldn't prove a damned thing. The real threat came from that cop, Edwards or Elliott or whatever the hell her name was. And that would blow over sooner or later if he just hunkered down in the foxhole and hung tight.

Smiling at Stella, he calmly replaced the phone in its charger and stood.

"Did he say what it's about?"

"Something about a missing friend."

"Well, then, we can't have someone worrying about a missing friend, can we? Send him back."

Funny, Ditto thought, his tendency to form a mental image of people after either listening to their telephone voice or hearing a story about them. Weirder still was how wrong those images usually turned out to be. McRae, for example. A good example, in fact. His only image was from Gerhard's comments. Instead of being large, the man coming through the door was maybe five ten, one hundred and sixty-five pounds. Giving the impression of someone wiry and quick. Short brown hair, with bright hazel eyes that appeared intense. Well, shit, intense is what he'd want if looking for a neurosurgeon. But it was not what he wanted from someone searching for a missing friend.

Ditto offered his hand in an attempt to appear friendly and relaxed, a person with nothing to hide.

"Dr. McRae."

McRae shook it.

"Robert Ditto. Have a seat," he said, pointing to one of the chairs in front of his desk. "What may I do for you?"

McRae eased down into the chair. Ditto did likewise behind his desk.

McRae said, "I was in Hong Kong last week at a surgical demonstration. One of the specimens, a head, looked exactly like someone I know. Now he's missing. I'm trying to determine if that was him or not. You know, to sort of settle things if it was him."

Ditto nodded compassionately, slipping into his well-honed funeral director mode.

"Yes, I'm aware of your concern. Mr. Gerhard called me about it at the time. He also was quite concerned. While he was on the phone, I personally checked our records. Your friend, his name is Baer, if I remember correctly."

"Yes. Andy Baer."

"The donor of that particular body was not your friend Mr. Baer. If Mr. Gerhard didn't pass that information on to you, I apologize. What's more, I'll make a point to have a word with him. That's unacceptable."

McRae shook his head.

"Andy and I've been tight since grade school. There is no mistake about this. It *was* Andy's head in Hong Kong."

Ditto tried for a look of deep sympathetic concern.

"How can you be so certain?"

"Can you just prove to me it wasn't?"

Ditto thought about it a moment. McRae was upset and convinced it was Baer.

What could persuade him otherwise?

"Doctor, come here. Let me show you," he said, motioning to the computer screen on his desk.

As McRae came around to stand beside him, Ditto moved the mouse to kill the screen saver. With McRae looking on, he called up their tracking database and entered *Baer* in the last name field.

No such name appeared on the screen.

"See?" said Ditto with a nod.

"Then whose head was in Hong Kong?"

"I'm very sorry, but I'm not allowed to divulge that information."

"Why not?"

Ditto feigned surprise.

"You of all people should ask? There are myriad reasons," he said, slipping in a word he hoped would impress the fucker, "but it all boils down to one simple principle: confidentiality."

What he wanted to do was stand up and deck the little prick.

"Confidentiality?" McRae asked incredulously. "The man's dead. His face was clearly recognizable. Other than releasing his name, you're not divulging anything not already known."

Ditto raised both hands in surrender and dropped back into the soothing tone learned from his father.

"Please calm down. I'm sure you're required to uphold similar confidentiality standards in your practice. They're called HIPAA rules, aren't they?"

"That's correct. But those rules have limitations. They don't obstruct practice to the point of operating on the wrong patient. If your records indicate that head was someone else's, then your records are wrong."

"Let me assure you, we know the correct identity of our

donors. Mr. Baer was *not* the man whose head you saw in Hong Kong. Are we clear on this?"

"Hey, humor me. Check it again. Okay?"

Ditto thought the best thing to do was just end the interview and get the prick out of his office before things turned ugly.

"No. I checked our records last week when Mr. Gerhard called, and I just rechecked them now. The man you saw is *not* your friend, and that is final. I can see you're upset and I'm sorry. But this is all I can do for you. Please understand."

McRae stood perfectly still except for clenching and unclenching both fists. After what seemed an excruciatingly long time, he pointed at Ditto.

"You're lying. I know you're lying. This isn't finished."

He turned and stormed out.

Chapter 26

DITTO REMAINED BEHIND his desk watching McRae leave the office.

Go after him in an attempt to soothe his frustration?

No, the way he looked, he was locked into a mind-set not easily changed by a few kind words. Especially when he believed he was right. Besides, Ditto had enough trouble controlling his own rage.

Instinct warned that what he needed to do right now was remain calm, assess the situation, and prepare for contingencies. In that order. He knew what he had to do.

He opened the small built-in wet bar refrigerator and removed a chilled bottle of Starbucks Frappuccino. Mocha flavor, his favorite. Shaking it, he returned to the desk and settled in to think. A moment later, he walked out of the office looking for Gerhard.

And found him pushing a broom in the cremation room.

Of the many things he liked about Gerhard's work was his obsession with keeping the place neat. Which was fine with Ditto. About the time Ditto started using street people for parts, he'd decided not to trust a janitorial service to clean the offices. Too much risk. Instead, he and Gerhard did all the cleaning. And that turned out to be good for the morale of his few employees, like Stella, the receptionist. Wasn't every job you saw your boss waving a Swiffer over a desk or replacing toilet paper in the latrines.

Ditto glanced around to make sure he and Gerhard were the only ones in the room, then closed the door.

"We have a couple problems."

He explained about McRae's visit.

Gerhard listened intently, nodding occasionally but not interrupting.

After Ditto finished, he said, "I warned you that bastard would be trouble. Didn't I tell you."

It wasn't a question.

Ditto started to say something, thought better of it. Gerhard had an annoying habit of always reminding him when something turned out the way he'd predicted.

"Yeah, yeah, you were right. Time to move on. Thing is, I want to make sure we're overreacting. Don't do something foolish. What do we know for sure?"

"He knows his friend's missing."

"So?"

"So he goes to the cops, says we know what happened to him."

Ditto nodded.

"So what? We deny it was him. Hell, we have the papers to show he's wrong."

Gerhard nodded slowly, apparently mulling something over.

"Got a point, I guess, but the thing is, he's the kind of guy who doesn't take no for an answer." He continued to think some more. "Okay, how about this...he figures out a way to prove he's right?"

"See, this is where I don't think we agree. I don't see it."

Except Ditto knew that, in spite of his lack of formal schooling, Gerhard had an uncanny ability to sense a threat when other people were oblivious to it. That's what kept him out of trouble with his job. Well, except for the Suburban. What a royal fuck up that had been.

Gerhard thought some more.

"What if he has connections we don't know about, with the FBI or something?"

Huh. Now there was something he hadn't considered.

He knew about the Seattle Police, but the Feds? But what were the odds? Fuck the odds. This whole clusterfuck had gone against the odds.

Ditto said, "Good point. So, what do we do about it?"

His way of shifting the actual task to Gerhard.

Gerhard nodded at the cremation oven.

"Sounds like a good job for Old Smokey."

Ditto shook his head.

"No, we can't just have him disappear. That's too close to his buddy, especially if he's gone to the cops. Let me think about it."

Gerhard resumed examining his fingers.

"Seems to me this is the sort of thing when you need to tap your source and find out what they know. That's what good intel's all about. Having the advantage."

Yeah, but Ditto suspected that if push came to shove, his connection, the cop, would cut him loose to protect himself, claim he knew nothing, and leave Ditto dangling in the goddamned wind.

Allegiances went only so far, no matter how much money you ponied up. And it frustrated him to no end that the only hold he had on the guy was money.

Ditto nodded.

"I'll call him, but it's possible he might not know everything she's working up."

"Meaning?"

"Word is, she's suspicious that more than one hooker disappeared. She's worried another Gary Ridgway is working the area."

Several times over beers he and Gerhard had discussed Gary Ridgway, the Green River Killer. Ditto believed Ridgway killed whores for some crazy weird sexual gratification thing and then discarded the bodies. Discarded them. That was what really rankled Ditto. Man, talk about a societal parasite. Too bad he and Gerhard never knew Ridgway's identity before the cops nailed his ass. They would've made him pay for such waste. They would've taken him off the street and put him to some good use. In Ditto's opinion, this was Gary Ridgway's scorecard:

Targeting hookers: plus one point.

His reason for targeting hookers: minus one point.

Discarding the bodies: minus ten points.

Bottom line: guy was a fucking loser.

"So?" Gerhard asked.

"The thing working against her is nobody's found a body yet."

Gerhard grinned.

"And they never will."

Fucking Gerhard, always completing thoughts.

"That's not the point. If McRae suddenly disappears, well…"

Let Gerhard finish that one too.

Gerhard sucked a tooth for a moment.

"I'll think on it too. Between the two of us, there's got to be a way to eliminate McRae."

Excellent. Ditto relaxed a bit. Gerhard was good.

Until the bad luck with the Suburban, he'd never made a mistake. He'd come up with a good way to take care of the problem without pointing a finger at DFH, Inc.

"There's one more thing."

Ditto told him about the order for five fresh heads.

Gerhard curled his fingers, inspecting his perfectly manicured nails again.

"Shouldn't be too difficult. I'll start working on it tonight."

Ditto figured on building up an inventory of fresh heads by flash freezing each one immediately. Like any other tissue, it wouldn't keep indefinitely but would last long enough to be in excellent condition when thawed before the meeting in thirty days. Flash freezing was a trick he'd learned from Alaskan fishermen.

"Know I don't need to say this, but until this blows over, we need to be extremely careful. No working girls. Understand?"

Gerhard had a special vengeance for hookers ever since ending up with a very bad case of an STD at sixteen. Ditto didn't quite recall the details other than the infection required extensive treatment.

Dumb shit didn't use a rubber, and the stupid hooker didn't have sense enough to demand one.

She was probably too strung out to care. That's what you get when you go around dipping your wick in a cesspool.

"No problem."

Already Ditto felt better. He had faith Gerhard would get the heads *and* take care of McRae.

Everything might just work out.

Chapter 27—West Precinct, Seattle Police Department

LUCAS APPROACHED THE Northeast corner of Eighth and Virginia and stopped, realizing he hadn't organized his story well enough.

He thought through it once more, refining a few parts for clarity. Satisfied, he started up the shallow concrete steps to the West Precinct, a low steel and concrete building of a utilitarian design that made it difficult to estimate how many floors were aboveground. Maybe three. It was a model of urban defensive construction at its best, probably able to withstand pretty much anything short of a direct nuclear blast. And maybe even that. He opened one of the heavy glass doors into a sparsely furnished granite lobby, crossed about ten feet of polished floor to a stainless-steel counter and greenish-tinged bulletproof glass. There was no one else in the lobby.

The glass partition slid open, a uniformed cop behind the counter asked, "May I help you?"

"How do I go about filing a missing person…"

Complaint? Report? What?

"Adult or child?"

145

"Uh, adult."

"Just a moment."

The cop shut the window before walking away.

A moment later the cop returned and opened the window, handing Lucas a sheet of paper with printing on both sides.

"Fill this out. Give it back to me when you're done." Then he said almost as an afterthought, "Anything suspicious about the disappearance?"

Yeah, just about everything, including his head showing up in Hong Kong.

"That's the thing. I'm not sure."

The cop seemed more interested.

"What's that supposed to mean?"

Realizing how bizarre the story might sound, he stuck to his plan of starting with an explanation of possibly seeing Andy's head at a medical meeting, how it was supplied by DFH, Inc., how Andy was now missing, and how Bobby Ditto refused to reveal the true identity of the person who the head belonged to.

When he finished, the cop gave him a dead-eyed look.

"Stay here. I'll be back."

Wendy was removing her purse from the bottom desk drawer, getting ready to leave the office, when an officer appeared at her cubicle saying, "Sergeant, you still interested in seeing all missing persons reports, or just females?"

"Why? Got something?"

"Yeah, but it's not female."

She set the black leather bag on her desk.

"I'm listening."

As the officer told the story, she realized he was officially punting the case. If she blew it off and the missing Joe Public turned out murdered or living in Mexico with a cool twenty-five million of embezzled funds, fingers would point at her instead of him. In the next breath, the officer mentioned DFH, Inc., and her interest went off the charts.

Was this some ploy dreamed up by Ditto to force her to do something stupid?

This seemed almost too coincidental to be coincidence.

Standing behind the protective glass a few seconds, Wendy studied the man filling out the report in the lobby. He looked like your average clean-cut, middle-class citizen. At least that would be her professional assessment.

Her personal assessment was: *Lord have mercy. He's hot.*

"Sir?"

Lucas looked in the direction of the voice and saw a woman holding open a door-sized section of wall. Until now he hadn't recognized it as a door, which was obviously the intent of the architect.

She motioned him over and held out her hand.

"Sergeant Wendy Elliott."

She was stunning and sexy but every bit the professional. Lucas caught himself staring. She wore black slacks and a black blouse, blonde hair banded into ponytail. On second appraisal, she might be a bit too tall. Perhaps her face was too hard. Still, he was totally taken by her.

"Lucas McRae."

She said, "Follow me, please."

As she walked away, his gaze dropped to her ass.

Had to admit, nice.

Wendy proceeded along a hall through another door, stopped at a cubicle, swiped a metal chair from her neighbor for him, and took the swivel chair behind the desk. Legs crossed, she leaned back and folded her arms.

"Tell me about your missing friend."

No wedding ring, he noticed.

He walked her through the story point by point. By the time he finished, she was frowning, forcing him to stop in mid-sentence.

"Something wrong?" he asked.

Wendy's mind flooded with various thoughts, all fighting for dominance. But the one bugging her most was: *Why do I know the name Andy Baer?* It had a ring of familiarity. It was important.

"Your friend's name, it's Andrew Baer?"

"Yes. Why?"

"Just a sec."

She turned to her computer, brought up a database, entered the name. Two hits immediately popped up, sending a jolt of adrenaline through her. She blew a low, slow involuntary whistle, her mind zinging but on an entirely different tangent now.

McRae leaned forward, angling for a shot at the screen.

"What?"

"And you saw the heads you used were supplied by DFH? The same company that's over by Lake Union?"

He studied her.

"Exactly."

Electricity crackled through her limbs. She wanted to jump up and run into Redwing's office, throw this new information in his face, and demand a search warrant for Ditto's Suburban. She started to brush a strand of hair from her face but realized it was in a ponytail today.

"Want a cup of coffee?" she asked, figuring it was a good excuse to take a few minutes to organize her thoughts.

After stuffing a dollar in the coffee fund can, Wendy carried two Styrofoam cups back to the interrogation room where she'd parked McRae instead of leaving him alone at her desk. The break had allowed her to put her thoughts together.

Two people had disappeared around the same time.

Coincidence? Maybe.

But Baer frequented prostitutes and Ruiz was one. And her gut couldn't ignore the possibility.

As a Vice decoy she'd busted Baer, an admitted sex addict, twice. Odds were, unless he received serious professional help, the arrest wouldn't stop him from going right back to picking up the ladies. Taken alone, that link between Andy and Lupita was pretty weak until you factored in the DFH angle. The logic for that went like this: Baer's head turned up in Hong Kong via DFH. In addition, a black Suburban registered to DFH was identified in the immediate area where Ruiz was last seen. You'd have to be an idiot not to see the connection.

The problem, of course, was not having a single piece of tangible evidence. And it was a stretch. As it stood, even a first-year public defender would blow holes in her argument. Then again, Wendy might be able to sell it as sufficient probable cause for a look at Ditto's vehicle. *That* would be worth something. That would be a start.

She offered McRae a cup and asked, "Mind if I record this?"

He shook his head. She took that as assent.

Recorder turned on, she walked him back through his story, stopping to clarify a point or probe a little deeper. He appeared to be an excellent witness. Had a solid story, didn't waver, didn't allow inconsistencies, came across as persuasive, and most of all, had no reason to fabricate the story. It really didn't get any better than this.

By the time she'd exhausted her questions, she was even more convinced this had something to do with Lupita's disappearance.

How to prove it?

Redwing would say everything was circumstantial.

Wendy said, "I'll look into this further."

"There anything I can do to help?"

Now there was an appealing offer. She smiled.

"Now that you mention it, where does Mr. Baer live?"

He pushed out of his chair.

"Why don't I take you there?"

Chapter 28

ANDY LIVED IN a high-end twenty-seventh-floor steel and glass building in the center of downtown. A prime location, providing easy access to Pike Place Market, movie theaters, assorted retailers.

Lucas opened the street door for Wendy and stole another head-to-toe glance. He followed her into the small but elegantly appointed lobby. Marble floors, designer furniture, tastefully displayed Asian art, muted thick carpet, windows that masked most street noise. It was a cocoon of serenity and good taste that immediately told anyone who didn't belong here to have the good grace to turn around and leave.

A doorman in a navy blazer and gray slacks watched them enter from behind an L-shaped mahogany desk. Lucas recognized him as Larry.

Wendy flashed her police ID.

"Sergeant Elliott, Seattle Police. We're here to see Mr. Baer."

Larry picked up a cordless phone, checked a list under a glass desk protector, and dialed. After listening several seconds he clicked off.

"Sorry, but Mr. Baer doesn't answer."

"Does that mean he's out?"

Larry's expression remained neutral.

"It means he's not answering."

Wendy pressed on.

"That's the point. He's been reported missing. When was the last time you saw him?"

"Can't really say, a week, maybe more. Residents can come and go directly from the parking garage without coming through the lobby."

"In that case, we'd like to have a look at his condo."

He frowned.

"Sorry, ma'am. That's against policy."

Wendy's tone hardened.

"Let me make this clear. This is a police investigation. Please do not try to impede it."

"Makes no difference. I can't let you in."

Wendy asked, "What if he's there dead on the floor?"

Unfazed, Larry shook his head.

"Sorry. Those are the rules."

Lucas stepped in.

"Larry, you recognize me, don't you?"

"Dr. McRae, isn't it?"

"Right. You know I'm a close friend of Andy's, don't you?"

"Sure, but—"

"I know your job is to protect the homeowner's privacy, and I appreciate that. But this is a little out of the ordinary. He's missing. Understand?"

"Tell you what. I'll go up and check his apartment while the two of you wait here."

Wendy said, "We'll go with you."

"No. One step from this lobby to the interior of the building, I'll file a complaint. Are we clear?"

Lucas resented it but wondered what level of security he'd expect if he lived here. Larry did have a point.

Larry returned in less than five minutes, said, "He's not at home."

Wendy asked, "Did everything look okay?"

"Meaning?"

"Did you actually set foot in the unit and check every room?"

"Yes."

"See any evidence of a disturbance? A fight? Something like that?"

"Everything seems in order. He isn't there."

Lucas thought of another angle.

"What about his car? Is it in the garage?"

"Don't know but I'll check. The garage is a common area, so you can come with me."

Larry pointed to the empty stall.

"His car's not there."

Another thought popped into Lucas's mind.

"When you checked his apartment, you didn't happen to look in the closet or bathroom to see if it looked like he went on a trip?"

"No, I didn't, but he would've notified us if he intended to be gone more than a couple days."

"You have an extra mailbox key?" Lucas asked, remembering that when Andy intentionally left for more than a few days, the staff stacked his mail on his foyer table.

Checking his mail might give some idea how long he'd been gone.

"I see where you're going with this, but no, we don't. If the resident wants us to, they leave their key with us. Otherwise, we don't keep a copy. Too much risk in that."

"Thanks."

Wendy turned toward the door, gave Lucas's sleeve a tug.

Out on the sidewalk Wendy pulled a cell phone from her purse, dialed, and after a few words was apparently put on hold.

"What're you doing?" Lucas asked while trying not to stare.

"Running a check on Baer's car. Never know. Might've turned up somewhere. Maybe an accident."

A minute ticked by, the two of them standing on the sidewalk, street traffic and pedestrians flying past in both directions, neither one saying a word. Lucas wondered what her story was, how she became a cop, did she like it, what her favorite food was, if she'd been married. If so, was she divorced or widowed with three kids? A million little things all suddenly important to know.

And it made him stop and wonder why he wanted to know. Sure, he was attracted to her, but so what? No harm in admiring a woman, was there? Yeah, but there was a difference between admiring and becoming interested in her personal life. A big difference.

Wendy started talking again, thanked the person, folded the phone, and walked away, apparently lost in thought.

He caught up with her.

"Where are we going?"

"Back to your car. Then you're going to drive us over to the impound lot."

"His car's there?" Lucas didn't want to believe it. Or rather, the implication.

"That's right. It was impounded a little more than ten days ago. Towed from the parking lot of a porn shop on Aurora."

Wendy picked up her pace, her pulse pounding at her temples. Just one more coincidence, one more piece to shore up her suspicions. What she didn't tell McRae was that Ruiz cruised for johns at the same store, and it was only one block from where Ditto's Suburban had been noticed.

Finally, she had enough for a search warrant.

And once she had it, she'd wipe that smug expression off Ditto's face. Intuition told her the black Suburban was the key to busting this case wide open.

Chapter 29

THE IMPOUND LOT was two blocks from the south end of Lake Union—an area under development by Vulcan, one of Paul Allen's business ventures.

It surprised Lucas that the lot still existed, considering how much money the lot would sell for.

A high cyclone fence topped with razor wire protected not much more than an oil-stained patch of dirt and gravel and a small clapboard shack of flaking gray paint and cars. He figured the only change the place endured during the past fifty years was more oil on the ground, which was probably the reason Paul Allen hadn't snapped it up.

Too expensive to detoxify the land to EPA standards.

Andy's BMW 5 Series baked in the sun with a thick coating of dust over midnight-black paint.

The sight saddened Lucas.

Andy had always kept the car spotlessly detailed. It served as just another bit of evidence that something had happened to his friend.

Wendy grabbed his shoulder.

"Don't touch it. No one puts a finger on it until it's been completely gone over."

He watched Wendy walk around it, first inspecting the exterior, then looking through the windows. Satisfied, she slipped on latex gloves and tried the driver's door.

"Unlocked," she muttered, opening the door.

She leaned in, examined the interior, then did the same with the other three doors. Finally, she popped the trunk.

Finished, Wendy spoke to the lot attendant, then motioned for Lucas to join her as she started for the front gate.

Lucas caught up with her.

"What now?"

"How about a lift to the precinct?"

"Then what?"

"What do you mean? That's it."

"But—"

But what?

He had no argument. He fastened his seat belt but didn't fire the ignition.

"You're holding something back."

Wendy wedged her back between the door and seat to study him.

"You've known Baer how long?"

"We grew up together. Why?"

"Then you know he frequents prostitutes?"

Lucas gave a sarcastic laugh but immediately realized how that might sound.

"I know. It cost him his marriage."

"Yeah? Well, just so happens I met him a couple times. I worked the streets as a decoy. You know, get some john to proposition me, settle on a price, call in the troops. I busted him. Twice."

"Oh."

He couldn't see where this was going.

"What I'm about to tell you is off the record. Okay?"

"Yes."

Wendy brushed at a hair.

"I got to know several of the girls. It's not a nice life. It's hard. Risky. Not one of them wanted to be out there turning tricks, but they all had their reasons. Most of it out of their control. Or out of their ability to control.

"Anyway, I got to be good friends with this one girl. Lupita was saving up to become a beautician. Turns out she went missing about the same time your friend did. That by itself could be nothing more than coincidence. But the thing is, she wasn't just standing on the street waiting for cruisers. She had this thing going at the porn store where Baer's car was towed. It was her way to screen johns a bit more than leaning in their car window to ask if they wanted to party. She'd hang around inside the store pretending to browse, the whole time checking who came in. If she saw a likely candidate, she'd follow them out, offer to watch the porn with them."

"You're thinking she might've picked up Andy?"

"No idea. But I know the approximate time she went missing and the fact a black Suburban owned by DFH was seen in the area at that time. Adds up."

"You saying what I think you just said?"

"There are way too many coincidences for this to be a coincidence. I got interested in the vehicle because I was trying to find out what happened to Lupita. So, I talked to Ditto. He denied it'd been out of the garage that evening, and I know for a fact it was. I know it was in the neighborhood. I have to ask myself, why is he lying? Maybe I'm just suspicious by nature, but I want a closer look at it. I appreciate your help, and because I know how worried you are about your friend, I'm sharing this with you. But at this point none of it involves you. Understand?"

Lucas said nothing.

"I'm serious. I know your concern is Andy. Believe me, I'm looking into it. So, thank you very much for taking me to Baer's place and here."

"But—"

"I find anything about Baer you'll be the first to know. We

clear on this?"

Well, at least somebody is taking it seriously.

"Yes."

"Okay, then." Wendy pointed at the ignition and mimed turning a key. "How about getting me back to the station?"

Chapter 30

WENDY SAID TO Lieutenant Redwing, "Here's what I've got."

He tilted his chair back, clasped his hands behind his head, and listened without interrupting. When she stopped talking, he rubbed the side of his nose a moment and straightened up.

"Is that it?"

She didn't like the sound of that, as if he were minimizing the links she'd so carefully put together.

"Yes."

"Come on. That's not exactly what I'd call a compelling argument."

"Were you even listening?" She held up a finger. "Baer's car is found in the same video parking lot where Ruiz is known to have solicited. The day before that—the same day Ruiz goes missing—Ditto's Suburban is identified half a block away. A week later Baer's head shows up in Hong Kong courtesy of DFH. I mean, hey, what's not to like? Sure, it's circumstantial, but you can't deny it's a compelling argument for going over that vehicle."

"Looking for what exactly?"

Wendy felt her blood pressure rise and struggled to keep from sounding angry. Pissing Redwing off wasn't going to help her cause. She owed Ruiz her best shot. Letting her ego ruin it wasn't going to happen.

"For starters, how about blood?"

"What?" Redwing pointed at her. "You telling me what you just outlined is evidence of a crime? Compelling enough for a warrant to search that Suburban? Get real."

Why was he pushing back so strongly? It didn't feel right.

Intuition warned her not to rise to the bait. Something was going on she didn't understand.

"That's not what I'm saying. I don't know that he has committed a crime, but here's what we do know. Two people are missing: Ruiz and Baer. You at least agree with that?"

"So *you* say."

Wendy shot him a look.

"Maybe this is the reason we're out of synch here. They're both missing. That's a matter of record. Want a copy of Baer's missing person report?"

"No need. But keep in mind how many of those reports end up false."

She balled and unballed her fist.

"For the sake of this discussion, can we agree they both have a missing person report on file?"

"Point made."

"Next point is that Baer's head showed up in Hong Kong. Far as I could determine," she said, "there is no record of him being sick or in an accident. That being the case, how do we explain that?"

Redwing leaned forward on the desk.

"Here's where we don't agree. How can you be so sure it was Baer's head over there?"

"McRae's known—"

Redwing cut in.

"—Baer for years. You said that earlier. But there's no proof, and I'm not about to simply take his word on that one. People look alike. That's why there are cases of mistaken identity every damn day."

He was right.

McRae claimed it was Baer's head, but how could he be absolutely sure?

After all, he'd mentioned jet lag and fatigue, both of which can result in weird perceptions. Dead people look different from live ones. Even live people can be dead ringers for someone else. Moreover, other than he seemed to be a trustworthy person, she had no real reason to believe him. Then again, it was hard to see why he'd fabricate such a story.

"Maybe I don't have proof of that specific point. At least not yet. But unless I'm mistaken, this is an investigation, not a trial. All I'm asking for is a warrant to have that vehicle inspected."

"Yeah, you made that exceedingly clear. In return, I'll make myself equally clear. No dice. For me to ask for a warrant, I need damned solid compelling evidence a crime's been committed. If Ditto takes issue, we're talking civil rights blowback you wouldn't believe. We can't start using Gestapo tactics and impound personal property just for our amusement." He paused to study her. "Anything I just said make one bit of sense to you?"

She decided it was best not to answer.

Redwing said, "Didn't you say that both Ditto and the courier told McRae it wasn't his friend in Hong Kong?"

"Yes."

"For just a minute, sit in my chair and take an objective look at your argument. We have two conflicting stories, Ditto's and McRae's. One from the supplier of the head, the other from a person who, upon seeing it became so emotionally upset he had to leave the room. Given these facts, which version should we believe?"

Wendy blew out a long breath, then sucked in another.

"I'll give you one thing: I have nothing evidentiary. But I interviewed both parties. My gut says to believe McRae. Why? First, because he has nothing to gain by lying. Second, Ditto *is* lying, at least about the Suburban."

"Fuck." Elbows on the desk, Redwing cradled his temples in both hands. He stayed like that for several seconds. He shook his head and sighed. "Let's say it *was* Baer's head in Hong Kong. Where's your link between Ruiz and Baer?"

"DFH."

"Based on?"

"That's why I need a shot at the vehicle."

"We've just gone full circle." Redwing looked up at the ceiling. "Okay, here's what I'll do. I'll ask around, see if I can get a sympathetic ear. Check back with me in the morning. This may take some finessing."

Goddamn right I will—I'll be back in front of your desk first thing.

Wendy stood, smoothed the front of her pants.

"Thank you, sir. I appreciate it."

Chapter 31

BOBBY DITTO WALKED the son and daughter-in-law of a terminally ill eighty-year-old man to the DFH reception area when his cell phone began vibrating against his leg. A discreetly as possible, he slipped it from his pants pocket enough to peek at the screen.

Redwing.

Another lesson Dad taught him was to always remain calm, reassuring, and unhurried when dealing with customers. After all, these were very trying times for the soon-to-be deceased's loved ones, especially if they were signing up Mom or Dad for one of his premier cremation packages.

Putting the phone to his ear, he said, "I'll call you right back."

He disconnected without waiting for an answer.

He rested a reassuring hand on the son's shoulder and with sad eyes said, "I'm terribly sorry, but this is an extremely urgent call. Could you possibly excuse me?"

"Oh, certainly," the man said almost apologetically.

Ditto extended a warm hand and an even warmer sympathetic smile.

"I appreciate your patience. If I can be of service during this trying time, you can always reach me here."

"Thank you so much for making this easier for us."

Ditto gave a hint of a bow and backed away, turned and walked briskly toward his office. As soon as he had the door closed, he dialed the number. It was picked up before the first ring completed.

Ditto said, "I'm back."

Redwing said, "Did you get the Suburban taken care of?"

Are you fucking crazy? Only an idiot would've ignored it.

Ditto said, "Roger that. I had it completely detailed yesterday. Looks brand new."

"Do it again. Now. Have them pay particular attention to the interior. Vacuumed and scrubbed. And I mean vacuumed and *scrubbed*. You don't want to take any chances, and I can't delay this forever."

Ditto checked his watch. The place over in Fremont stayed open late. He'd pay triple for them to do it tonight and then again in the morning. He could run it over himself with Gerhard following in the Chrysler. If they were already closed, he'd scrub and vacuum the fucker down himself.

"Thank you. Consider it done."

"And one more thing. You told Detective Elliott the vehicle wasn't out of the building that night. Why?"

A chill settled in the depth of Ditto's gut.

"I don't have a good explanation. I wasn't about to admit to something I didn't have to. Why?"

"It was parked in a no parking zone, and a patrol car ran the plates. It's a matter of record it was there. The point of this little conversation is that Elliott knows damned well you lied. You realize the danger this puts you in?"

Shit.

"Just make sure there's nothing in the vehicle you don't want there. Do I need to explain further?"

Chapter 32

LUCAS WATCHED THE garage door roll down, choking off daylight, bathing everything in only weak fluorescent light from the underside of the whining ceiling motor. He dumped the car key in his pocket and put his hand on the door to the kitchen but hesitated, dreading another confrontation with Laura. Was there any way to preempt it? Something he might say? Seeing no way to dodge it, he opened the door and entered the kitchen.

Laura sat in the nook with sections of the *Seattle Times* scattered haphazardly on the table. She tossed him her unmistakable look of irritation.

"Hello," he said, making a beeline for the liquor cabinet.

A drink would help get through this.

"Where have you been?"

A sarcastic reply flashed through his mind. Which he swallowed, figuring there was no point in fanning the flames. But it served as just another symptom of the escalating friction between them.

"I'm having a scotch. Want one?"

"I asked you a simple question."

There was that tone again, making it sound as if he committed an egregious sin by not answering. He squelched another sarcastic response and opened the cabinet, pulled down the bottle of Green Label purchased at the duty-free shop in the Hong Kong airport.

"Was that a yes or no on the offer of a drink? I couldn't tell."

Laura slammed her palm on the table.

"Goddamn it. Are you purposely trying to provoke me? Because if so, you're spot-on."

He turned to face her.

"I was at the office catching up on paperwork. Before that, I was at the police department filling out a missing person report on Andy. Now about that drink. Yes or no?"

She slumped back against the cushion, staring at him with undisguised hostility.

He returned his attention to the counter, filled a glass with ice, added scotch, figured what the hell, and added an extra splash. Finished, he turned to her, raised his glass.

"Cheers."

Laura was still holding the same expression, eyes boring into him. As if he didn't get the message the first time.

"What?" Lucas asked innocently.

Which was uncalled for. He knew damned well what the issue was. Or at least what the issue *du jour* was. The real, more comprehensive issue was complex, having compounded layer upon layer over years of marriage. *Baggage* was the term some of the telepsychologists termed it. He immediately felt lousy for provoking her and was about to apologize.

But she unloaded on him.

"You spent one of our vacation days—one of the few days we have together—catching up on office work? And you wonder why this marriage isn't working."

He set down his drink and held up both hands in surrender.

"I spent only a couple hours before coming home. The rest of the time was working on the Andy thing. Want to hear what I found out?" he offered, trying to defuse the situation with a distraction.

"No, I don't want to talk about Andy." Laura shook her head. "Andy's been a thorn in the side of this marriage since the first day I realized what a slimeball he is. Despite knowing how I feel, you continued to have him over to the house and flaunt your friendship in front of my face. And don't give me that bullshit about how he saved your life. That doesn't make up for the fact he's a misogynist."

"He's not a misogynist. Far from it. And you know it."

"All I know is how badly he mistreated Trish. It's unconscionable."

Even though he suspected she threw that statement out just to press his buttons, it had the desired effect.

"That's enough. I think Andy's dead."

"Why? Because you *think* you saw his head in Hong Kong? Give me a break."

Lucas splashed more scotch over a fistful of ice cubes, grabbed the rest of the three-day leftover fried chicken from the fridge, and headed for the guest bedroom.

He found himself thinking of Wendy.

Chapter 33—Downtown Seattle

BOTTLE IN HAND, Gerhard staggered in the dim light along a debris-strewn alley. He stopped at a recessed back door of a furniture store and with an audible sigh wearily sat down, wedged his back against the door and shoulder against the jamb.

He hugged the half empty bottle of cheap wine with both arms as if it were grand Bordeaux. Breathing deeply, he let his chin slowly drop to his chest. He knew the moves well from watching his father slowly commit suicide with progressively shittier and shittier booze in greater and greater quantities until his liver called it quits.

He sat like this, pretending to be almost asleep, while waiting for what he knew would happen in a few minutes. To pass the time and distract himself from the cold concrete against him, he let his mind wander. He wondered how his mom was doing since checking in with her by phone last week. And made a mental note to call first thing in the morning. She now lived with her eighty-two-year-old sister in Flint fucking Michigan, the only place he could think of that ranked worse than Detroit as one of the world's most unlivable shit holes.

Gerhard picked up the obnoxious odor of layered stale sweat and dried urine before he heard the scrape and crunch of someone stepping on broken glass. His own three layers of shirts were equally rank, just a different body odor. Perfect for these missions. And he kept the lot well ripened by carefully storing them in a black garbage bag the moment he returned to DFH. His routine was to disrobe, store the clothes, then shower to wash off this fucking smell. What made matters worse was their itchy, dirty feeling against his skin.

There was a gentle tug on the bottle.

He hugged it tighter, slurring, "Hey, hey..."

Then he slowly raised his head, pretending it required great effort to focus on the shit bag now sitting next to him.

"Just a little taste?" the man asked while offering Gerhard the butt of an unlit filtered cigarette. "Trade."

At least give the guy an ounce of credit, offering a trade like that, even if it was only a fucking worthless one like this. Most of the time these useless parasites just wanted, wanted, wanted, wanted, not even thinking of quid pro quo.

Gerhard grabbed the butt and in the weak light inspected the stained filter, as if it'd been hours since his last nicotine hit. The piece of shit butt had been pulled into some semblance of straight but had only a few puffs remaining. Hardly worth it. Assuming it would even light. Which was highly debatable.

And another thing. What had this dirt ball done for it? Nothing more than bend over to pick it out of a gutter. Big fucking deal.

This was the thought that sealed the deal for Gerhard, the thing that made this dirtbag the right one for the right reasons. He always needed a good reason to despise his victims, otherwise the job was meaningless.

Gerhard grunted, carefully set the cigarette butt in his lap, handed over the bottle, and busied himself searching his own pockets for a light.

The man unscrewed the top and guzzled the liquid.

Greedy bastard too. They all were. Just another validation of his choice.

Gerhard asked, "Got a light?"

"Nope."

The asshole sucked down another long drink.

"Hey, hey, lighten up. A taste is what I said, not the whole thing."

The man took a third large gulp before handing back the almost drained bottle.

"Well, shit, my brother, that's all I took. A taste."

"Motherfucker, you didn't have to get all greedy on me. Shit."

Gerhard wrapped his arms around the bottle. They sat like that for a few minutes, not talking.

The dirt ball moaned, muttered, "Shit, my gut..."

He then tried to push up but couldn't seem to get his legs to work right. He grunted while pressing a hand against the brick wall for stability, his breathing becoming more labored with each breath. Through the shadows Gerhard saw a flash of panic in the shit bird's eyes.

Gerhard glanced up and down the alley.

Good, there was no one else around.

His victim muttered, "Fuck."

The word barely audible.

"Here, let me help you."

Standing, Gerhard grabbed the man's shoulders, turned him into the doorway, and let him take his place on the cement stoop. Then he folded the man's body up, facing the door, so it looked like just another street bum sleeping it off. He could feel strength ebb from the bum's muscles with each weakening heartbeat. Working quickly, he removed the man's filthy raincoat and draped the tattered raincoat over the dying body. Then stepped back to admire his work. Perfect. No one would disturb him before he returned.

With headlights off, Gerhard bounced the black Chrysler over asphalt chuckholes deep enough to expose the alley's original bricks. He braked beside the doorway and body, slipped the transmission into park, letting the motor idle. He dragged the dead body over to the car and scanned the alley one more time. If someone approached and asked what he was doing, he would explain that he was trying to get the guy to a hospital.

Not a soul in sight.

He popped the trunk and muscled the deadweight into the car, carefully closed the lid. It locked with a muted click. Then he made sure to collect the bottle and dump the residual fluid over garbage sacks in a neighboring Dumpster. Soon as he got back to DFH he'd carefully rinse it out before tossing it in the recycling bin.

Then he was off again, no sweat—except he would've preferred the Suburban.

The decapitated body lay on stainless steel, feet splayed to either side in the awkward way a corpse could manage. The table, a real beauty, had a half-inch ridge along the border to contain fluids. It sloped four degrees toward the foot where a drain emptied via black rubber hose into another drain in the cement floor. A retractable rubber hose with a chrome shower nozzle dangled from the ceiling.

First thing Gerhard did after cutting of the dirt ball's clothes was rinse the body with cold water which only slightly lessened the gag-me stench. Incinerating the clothes also helped. Even after doing all this, the fucker still stunk like hell.

Gerhard wore a disposable "bunny suit," goggles, and rubber gloves because you never knew what diseases lurked in these dirt balls. But as bad as they were, nobody was as contagious as the whores. AIDS, hepatitis, drug-resistant TB—you name it; they had it. Just one more reason to take them off the streets. Which, if you looked at it objectively, was a real public health service. And just another reason to be careful to minimize the spatter. Dead people don't bleed more than gravity allows to leak out, but there was always splatter. Especially when using the band saw to detach the head, which was already removed and wrapped in cloth and in the quick freeze.

He had XM radio tuned to music from the Forties. His favorite for working. Big band shit like Glenn Miller, Benny Goodman, Lionel Hampton. He loved those guys. Loved them almost as much as the black-and-white World War II movies he watched. He sometimes wondered why he was attracted to those years, especially seeing that they happened before he was even born. Maybe it was because life appeared to be purer then, what with everybody putting their shoulder to the war effort, everyone focused on a common goal of fighting Japs and Nazis. Not the chaos you have nowadays from terrorism and the fear of natural disasters.

Gerhard sat on a rolling stool, the shit bag's arm draped over the edge of the table, working on the fingernails. He would have them perfectly manicured before detaching the arms to eventually be used in a demonstration somewhere. They were already earmarked for a meeting of orthopedic surgeons. Next to him stood a small stainless-steel Mayo stand with a basin of soapy water, clippers, a pick, and buffer. After washing the hands, he always cleaned and clipped the nails into perfect shape. A good manicure was a thing of beauty.

Ditto didn't require him to put so much work into the nails, but there was something about a corpse's fingers that he couldn't allow to be dirty. To him, fingernails and toenails were an index to personal hygiene, a reflection into the person's inner self.

There was something fascinating about fingers. You never knew what skills they contained. They could be short and stubby or long and elegant, nimble or klutzy. Play a virtuoso violin or break rocks with a sledgehammer. Their touch could be soft and caring or calloused and crude. It was, well...fascinating.

It reminded him of reruns of *What's My Line?* The object of the game show was for the weekly panelists to guess contestants' jobs within a certain number of questions. Wasn't easy either because the producers went out of their way to dredge up really weird shit, like the only guy in the world who did nothing but inseminate polar bears. The first thing the panelists did was inspect the contestants' hands because they gave away so much information about the person.

Hands were more important than people thought. Hell, lose one and see how well you do. It's probably more disabling than losing an eye or an ear or a kidney. Lose both and you're totally fucked. Can't even wipe your own ass. Imagine what kind of a fucked-up deal that would be.

Gerhard began whistling *In the Mood* along with Glenn Miller's band.

The round military clock on the tile walls showed 1:32 AM. The time really didn't matter. Soon as he finished, he'd grab a bite, then sack out. He preferred it this way, "free-ranging" his circadian cycle. Sleep when needed and be available when the job demanded it. And he was being paid well too.

Life was good.

Chapter 34

WENDY MARCHED STRAIGHT to the DFH receptionist's desk and locked eyes with the woman. Ah yes, time to slap that smug smile off Ditto's lying face. She'd fantasized about it the entire drive here.

Walk in, hand him the warrant.

Take that, asshole.

She wasn't sure what bugged her more—knowing he lied to her about the vehicle or that goddamn superior attitude he radiated. Like he was smarter than everyone else. Arrogance was what it was, and she hated that. Not over-the-top Hannibal Lecter style arrogance of self-appointed intellectual superiority.

She figured Ditto for a simple greedy, self-absorbed, cunning businessman. If you considered his line of work, he had to be careful. But 99 percent of the time arrogance got you in trouble because you ended up thinking you were smarter than those who hunted you, and you made mistakes. This time it was the Suburban that would be Ditto's undoing.

Wendy was convinced he'd used that vehicle to transport his victims and the crime techs would find incriminating evidence in it. You couldn't just go around plucking people like Ruiz off the street and never get caught. Yeah, now she was going to shove the warrant right up his ass without any K-Y Jelly. She smiled at the visual of a rolled-up warrant sticking out of his butt.

"May I help you?"

She flashed her ID.

"Detective Elliott to see Mr. Ditto."

"I'm afraid Mr. Ditto is busy at the moment."

Of course he is.

"When will Mr. Ditto not be busy?"

The receptionist didn't bother checking the monitor or an appointment book, just returned a flat-eyed stare.

"Oh, he's busy. All day."

"In that case, I'm here to impound the black Suburban registered to this company. Just tell me where it is and I'll have it picked up."

She recited the license number from memory.

The woman stood, swallowed, and glanced down the hall.

"One moment. Maybe there's a way he might tear himself away to speak with you."

Face etched with concern, Ditto hurried down the hall toward the reception area, his secretary hustling to keep up. He was dressed casually in gray slacks and a pale blue button-down dress shirt. No tie. Penny loafers. Black hair slicked straight back. His goatee and moustache were perfectly trimmed.

Ditto glanced around as if making sure the area was free of clients before saying.

"Stella said you intend to impound the Suburban?"

"That's right. Here," Wendy said, handing him the warrant. "Where is it?"

He unfolded the paper to read it with a smile hinted at the corners of his mouth.

"I don't understand. What could you possibly want with it?"

"I thought I explained that last week."

Ditto glanced at his receptionist, then back at Wendy.

"No, not really."

It gave her the impression this was an acting job, put on for his receptionist's benefit.

Wendy said, "Did you ask around, see if any of your employees had it out the night in question?"

"Yes. Exactly as you requested. But no one admitted to it. Still," he paused to stroke his goatee, as if seriously thinking about it, "I suppose it might've been used without being signed out."

"So, where is it?"

Ditto's confident smile returned.

"Over at Fremont Detailing." He made a big deal of checking his watch. "He, it should be ready to be picked up by now. Want the address? Might want to use them sometime yourself. They do a very thorough job."

"It was just detailed?"

"Yes, of course. We always keep our vehicles spotless. They represent our business. You know, first impressions and all." Ditto started to turn and go back to his office but stopped and added, "I'll call, make sure it's paid in full. Just let me know when you're ready to bring it back so I can make sure the garage is open. Is there anything else I might help you with, Detective?"

"Yeah, there is something else."

You smug son of a bitch.

"I need copies of the records for the heads used in Hong Kong last week."

Ditto held up the warrant.

"Nothing in here says squat about records."

He was right. It didn't.

How did he know without even looking at it?

Wendy forced a smile at the receptionist and Ditto.

"You've both been very helpful. Thank you."

Chapter 35

WENDY SAT ON concrete steps facing the circular Seattle Center Fountain, Key Arena behind her. In front of her, Memorial Stadium loomed beyond the changing skyward sprays of water from hundreds of pressurized jets choreographed to the theme from Kubrick's *2001: A Space Odyssey*.

The warm temperature had lured a group of young mothers here. They clustered on a bench, chatting animatedly, keeping one eye on their squealing barefoot children who were running random patterns through the artificial rain from the fountain.

Wendy held an untouched Starbucks iced latte. It served as more prop than drink. It was tasty but contained enough calories to blow her entire day's allotment.

Travis was late. Typical. Always had been, probably always would be.

Then she saw him approaching, also holding a white Starbucks cup. Tall, lanky, sunglasses, denim jeans, black T-shirt under a black leather bomber jacket.

Shit, he looked good. Too good.

But he always had. Even when they were married, and she knew he was sleeping with other women.

"Still looking good, kid."

He settled onto the bench beside her, leaned forward, elbows on knees, both hands holding the cup, forming a triangle.

Wendy was still admiring him.

"Nice shades. What are they, Porsche?"

He couldn't suppress a grin.

"Yep."

That was another thing about Travis. Buying accessories he couldn't afford. But he always had a sense of style. She could never quite decide if he bought things that looked good on him or just had one of those faces that made everything look good.

"What's up? Got something for me?"

She turned to him and was immediately hit by a rush of anxiety. She'd requested the clandestine meeting because of wanting a good dose of reality testing. She needed to talk to someone she could trust, and Travis, her direct report in Internal Affairs, was that person. Was she crazy? How would it sound, this first translation from suspicion to words? But she had to bounce the ideas around with him. She scanned the area for someone watching, which she knew was paranoid, but working IA undercover while assigned to another detail did that to you. She looked at her shoes.

"Bear with me on this. It's circuitous and has nothing directly to do with our investigation. Okay?"

"Yup."

"For six months, maybe longer—I don't have the means to check—there's been a bump in the number of working girls missing. Maybe even some other kinds of street people. It's hard to tell."

Wendy assumed he realized what she meant—that those were the people least likely to be reported.

"And?"

"I got this nudge in my gut. It tells me some of them shouldn't be missing."

Travis turned toward her a bit more, his eyes shielded by the shades.

"People go missing every day. Especially the kind you're referring to."

"The *kind?* You can say the word. Prostitute."

"Sure I can. Prostitute. It's just you get so damned defensive about it."

"That's not the point here."

"Then what is the point?"

"I know some of these girls. They were friends when I was on the street, so I know there's no reason for any of them to get up and leave. And there are no missing persons reports on several of them."

"What are you implying? They've been murdered?"

She was thankful he didn't sound cynical.

"Yeah. Exactly. Like maybe there's another Gary Ridgway in the area."

He nodded slightly, sipped his coffee.

"Any bodies to show for it?"

And there it was, the major stumbling block to her theory.

"No. Not yet. But remember, they never did find all the ones Ridgway admitted to, even after he showed the King County cops where he'd dumped them. Things happen. Animals eat them, bones get scattered or covered with brush or are in an area never noticed. In his case, there were other missing girls he never admitted to—now cold cases—and still other missing girls never accounted for."

"But some of those Ridgway cases were over ten years old. Like you said, a lot of things can happen to a body in ten years. How long have your girls been missing?"

"Just a few months," she admitted.

Travis sipped his coffee again, said nothing, leaving her hanging out there feeling defensive.

She needed to shore up her position, so she told him about the string of coincidences, like Ruiz vanishing and about McRae seeing Baer's head in Hong Kong How a cop had run the DFH Suburban license plate near where Ruiz worked and how DFH had supplied the Hong Kong demonstration. Then she went into Boddy Ditto and how he denied the Suburban had been out of the building the night in question.

"The really troubling thing," she said, "is he had the vehicle detailed before we could inspect it."

Travis sipped his coffee.

"Meaning what?"

"Here's the thing. I don't trust the guy. Either he was incredibly lucky or maybe he has a friend in the department and got tipped."

There, that was out too. And she knew it would sound paranoid.

"A snitch?"

"Yeah."

"Go on, I think I interrupted you."

She went on to explain DFH's business in detail.

She told him about her interview with Professor Boynton and said, "He raised some very interesting questions, like how he gets so much material to be so successful."

"What are you saying? He's a Gary Ridgway?"

"Crossed my mind. I mean, with the Suburban and all…"

Her phone rang. She dug it out of her leather purse, checked caller ID, and felt the chill of another coincidence. Lucas McRae. She stuffed the cell back in the bag and let the call roll over to voice mail.

Travis asked, "Let me see if I got this right. You're saying Ditto is killing people for their bodies?"

"Yeah, that's the bottom line."

Travis thought about it.

"I have to admit, when you tell the story in that sequence, there's a faint ring of possibility to it. Problem, of course, is there's nothing whatsoever to back up your theory."

"But it's a possibility, right?"

He shrugged.

"Anything's *possible*. But why tell me about it? Why not

someone in CIB?"

He referred to the Criminal Investigations Bureau, which was command structure for the Missing Persons Unit.

Wendy realized she'd missed the other important point.

"What if Ditto's snitch is somehow linked into someone in CIB?"

Travis's eyebrows rose.

"Have someone in mind?"

"No. But the point is Ditto not only knew the vehicle was going to be inspected, he also knew the limits of the search warrant."

She realized she'd left out that part, so she circled back over it.

"Thought you said he read it?"

"Nah, he just glanced at it. Never really read it."

Travis shook his head.

"Haven't changed a bit. Still paranoid, aren't you?"

"Don't start in with that. Thing is, Ditto *knew* I didn't have a warrant for any records. He *knew* before ever looking at it. How could that happen if he wasn't tipped?"

"How can you be so sure?"

See, that was the problem with intuition. You knew things without having to deduce them.

Wendy replayed the scene in her mind, looking for whatever it was that caused her impression.

"He was too calm. Here's a guy with no criminal record who's got a cop wanting to impound his SUV. That's make the average citizen very nervous, maybe even make them call a lawyer. Not this guy, no way. He *knew* the exact limits of my warrant. No, he had to have prior coaching from someone."

"Maybe he just got lucky, took a guess. It happens, you know."

"No. There's something hinky with Ditto. I know it."

Travis smiled at her.

"Then prove it."

"Easy to say, but I can't see how. I've been over this a thousand times now."

"This guy McRae, anything more you can get from him about the head?"

How many times had she considered that too? She'd even gone back over the interview three times, and there was nothing there.

"Don't think so." Then again, it'd be nice to see McRae in person again, even if only professionally. "But I'll go over it again with him, just for drill."

Travis patted her knee, ready to stand up, but then seemed to think of something.

"Instead of someone in CIB, why not someone outside of it? To explain the warrant business."

"You mean like the judge?" She hadn't thought of that. "I made the request through Redwing, and he said he went straight to the courts."

"Sure, but someone had to fill out the paperwork."

She hadn't really considered that either. But it didn't make sense.

"I don't know…doesn't feel right."

He smiled.

"Based on?"

Was he mocking her?

"Gut."

"Right or wrong, gut feelings are based on observation. If you're so convinced, then there's got to be something in there." Travis pointed at her head. "What is it?"

He was right. Something floated just below consciousness, just out of grasp, but she couldn't connect with it.

When she didn't answer, Travis stood and squared his sunglasses just so.

"I know I don't need to tell you this, but if you're right about someone in the department, this could get dicey. You still in it for the long haul?"

She nodded, relieved that he hadn't been mocking her a

moment ago.

"I'll try to cover your back as much as I can, but that's limited." He leaned over, kissed her forehead. "Be careful."

Watching him walk away she was struck with fresh regrets over not having been able to make it as a couple.

Soon as he was out of sight, she dug out the cell to return Lucas's call.

Chapter 36

LUCAS SAT AT the kitchen table flipping Wendy Elliott's card over and over between his fingers, wondering if he should phone to ask if she's found out anything new. She said she'd let him know if that happened, but sometimes people got busy and forgot promises. At the time she seemed sincere and genuinely interested in looking into it. Andy's disappearance, but everyone knew cops were overworked. They probably assigned her a new case every few days.

How could he expect her to keep pushing on Andy's case when others were piling up?

Then again, there was the squeaky wheel phenomenon. If he wanted her to find out what happened to Andy, he had to bug her.

He listened to her cell phone ring until it clicked over to voice mail. He decided to leave a message.

"Hey, this is Lucas McRae, Andy Baer's friend. Just checking in to see if you've found out anything since we last talked. Please give me a call one way or the other."

He recited his number twice before hanging up.

Lucas dumped the phone back in its charger, propped his butt against the counter, and thought back to earlier this morning. Laura was already on her second cup of black coffee when he came into the kitchen. They didn't say much to each other, just went about their business like two strangers in a supermarket checkout line, civilized but distant—both convinced of their own righteousness. Neither one willing to make the first move toward reconciliation for fear it would...what? Concede something?

That wasn't quite right, but close enough.

What he did know for sure was their marriage had been corroding for at least a year now and if something wasn't done to revive it, it would die. He held that thought a moment before realizing just how dangerously close they were to the tipping point.

It scared the crap out of him.

He didn't want to lose her.

Why hadn't he taken the opportunity to talk with her while she was having her coffee, before she left the house? He looked at the chair she always sat in. Where did she go? He realized he hadn't even asked where she was going and she hadn't offered. For all he knew, her bags might've been packed and stored in the car waiting for her. Would she do that? Calmly sit here drinking coffee and never say a word, and then up and leave for good?

Lucas ran upstairs to the bathroom and was relieved to find all her cosmetics, there along with her Lipitor and contacts case.

Try her cell?

And say what?

No. He'd wait for her to come home.

Still unsettled and anxious, he wandered downstairs to the kitchen. He poured another coffee and sat down to think. If he was unhappy with their marriage, she must be also.

It dawned on him that they always sat in the same place.

He moved to her spot and sat there, trying to imagine what she thought of him. He pictured a cup of coffee in front on him, maybe a newspaper on the table. Now he was Laura looking at the man she'd married. What did she see? What did she feel? Did she despise him? Well, he did work a lot of hours, so he was guilty of that charge. Had to admit he continued his friendship with

Andy even though she objected to it. He wasn't as social as she might like in the days before her depression set in. How about the times she wanted to talk about problems he thought were trivial, so he either cut the conversation short or didn't seem interested? She claimed he never said, "I'm sorry."

Probably none of these issues in isolation was a major issue, but taken together they certainly could be. Point was, he had to assume some responsibility for their problems and the path they were taking to divorce.

He thought about that a moment, trying to maintain her perspective. But found himself quickly becoming defensive. It wasn't true. Half the time he *was* the one who apologized, but did it really matter?

No. The important thing wasn't whether she was right or wrong about it. The important point was she believed it.

He decided to take the first step.

As soon as she returned today, he'd make a special point of saying "I'm sorry."

Maybe then they could sit down and start working things out. If she wouldn't seek marital counseling, maybe if they worked together on the issues, he could talk her into seeing a psychiatrist to deal with the depression.

Relief surged through him. Finally, he had a plan to try to reverse the horrible slide they were in. It didn't matter if he was right or wrong about the Andy thing, he would do whatever it took to get their relationship back on track. He felt a giddy with relief.

The phone rang and he answered.

"Hey, McRae, Wendy. Got your call. Unfortunately, no news is bad news. I haven't made a bit of progress. In fact, it looks like I might've hit a dead end. At least for the time being."

He was floored.

"Dead end? What does that mean?"

"I can't see anything more to do. But I'll keep the case in mind."

Lucas was at a loss for words.

Silence.

"You're giving up?" he said, unable to believe she would let it go so easily.

Just a moment ago he'd been thinking how committed to the case she seemed.

"Not entirely. Something comes up, I'll sure as hell follow up on it. All I'm saying is it's off the front burner for now."

"No! I can't accept that. You can't just walk away from this. Andy is a missing person. Isn't that your job, finding missing persons?"

"Simmer down. I understand how you feel. I don't feel very good about it myself, but there's only so much I can do."

"Bullshit. There must be something else."

"What about the Ditto angle?"

Wendy said, "That's not going anywhere."

"But..."

Arguing would yield nothing, Lucas realized.

He also knew that this would not be the end of it. He'd personally see to that. How many times had he heard about the one person who constantly nagged the cops until they ultimately solved a case? The squeaky wheel thing again. If he let Andy's case sink into the cold case files, it would never be solved.

She'd hear from him again and again and again until something was done. But today Laura was his priority.

Chapter 37

LUCAS SLAMMED THE phone on the kitchen counter. For a moment he just stood there, looking at the kitchen sink, replaying the conversation.

"Fuck!"

Standing here simmering wasn't going to accomplish anything.

What he needed was a distraction, something mindless that would burn off the frustration tying him in knots. He stalked through the house, noticing a burnt-out ceiling bulb in the storeroom, that rat nest of wires behind the TV equipment he always intended to organize. On and on. All things that would need tending to if and when the house was sold to settle the distribution of assets after the divorce.

No, those were tasks better left for another time.

Right now, he needed something physical and frustration free. Something that would take hours and require physical activity. Ideally, something you wouldn't want to do in cold weather. Aw, of course, the garage. Perfect. One of those shit jobs you knew was there but never got around to doing. Probably because it was a shit job. Also because you knew the results were as fleeting as organizing the clothes in your closets.

The back wall was contiguous floor-to-ceiling storage closets that constantly became repositories for partially empty cans of old paint, broken rusty gardening tools, three piles of tiles left over from the bathroom remodel, an assortment of unidentifiable mechanical parts, one shelf crammed with plastic containers of various car cleaners. And, of course, the floor covered with years of decaying leaves blown in during fall winds. Every damned closet needed cleaning and reorganizing.

Happy to have a consuming project, Lucas changed into jeans and a sweatshirt. iPod fully charged, he started in. First, he backed out his car and parked it on the driveway.

Next, he hauled out every article in all three closets, dumping them into rough piles to be sorted later. He swept the floors and cleaned the shelves. Finished with that phase, he stood back to admire his work, knowing it would be only a matter of weeks before it reverted to similar disarray. On the other hand, he'd find a lot of junk to be taken to the dump or recycled.

Then came the job of sorting the piles into new piles. He briefly considered using the lawn for one but figured it would be less damage to the grass to keep the junk destined for recycling or the dump on the concrete drive. Everything else went back on the shelves.

By noon Lucas was starving, so he drove to Subway for a twelve-inch turkey ham, came back, and ate it sitting on the grass next to the driveway. The job, he decided, was a good distraction, having put his mind in a better place than this morning.

It took the remainder of the afternoon to reorganize the closets. Finished, he reparked his car inside the garage. The junk pile in the driveway blocked Laura's half of the garage and would force her to park in the driveway or at the curb when she returned home. First thing in the morning, he'd use her Volvo to haul the crap away.

He was upstairs in the shower when he heard Laura come in. Butterflies stirred in his gut as he dried off.

Maybe he should start by inviting her out to dinner?

She'd like that. Maybe go to one of their favorite places over

Allen Wyler

at Fisherman's Terminal.

Lucas caught up with her in the kitchen, gave a cheery, "Hi."

She took a glass from a cupboard, filled it with cold tap water. She was wearing brown cargo pants and a beige safari-style shirt with epaulets, an outfit he hadn't seen before.

"How was your day?"

Laura took a long drink of water, set the glass on the counter.

"Fine," she said, then started toward the hall.

He held up a hand.

"Hold on a sec. I'm sorry I cancelled the trip, and I'm sorry we're having this disagreement about Andy. And I'm sorry we're at the point of seeing divorce lawyers."

She sighed and seemed to slump into some sort of resignation.

"We've disagreed about Andy from the day we married. That's nothing new. And as far as cancelling the trip, that's nothing new either. How about the trip to Seaside you cancelled so you could bail him out of jail?"

Forget defending Andy, pal. Change the subject.

"Back to the vacation thing. What can I do to make it up to you?"

Laura straightened slightly and crossed her arms.

"I already took care of that today."

"You did? How?"

Uneasiness burrowed into his gut.

"Carol and I are flying down to Cal-a-Vie for a week. We're leaving Sunday."

It took a second to register.

"The spa? The one outside San Diego?"

Carol was one of her friends she liked to go shopping with.

"That's right."

She sounded testy now, as if to say, so what?

Lucas blew a long breath through pursed lips, trying to stay calm. Carol loved the place. To him, it seemed like one of those

189

Southern California existential marketing marvels that claimed to instill total wellness through interweaving spiritual with physical health, ionic transfers through skin pores with seaweed wraps or mud or some such thing. Massage, meditation, soaking tubs, aerobics, aroma therapy, salt scrubs. You name it; they provided it.

Not to mention it was expensive as hell. The figure seven thousand dollars per week popped into his mind. Plus airfare. Which, booked this late, would be more than horrendous. They didn't have that kind of money to flit away on a whim. Or on vengeance.

Laura's pose became more defiant.

"What?"

The word sounded like a direct challenge.

He knew better than to mention the cost. At least for now. At the moment, that was the least of his worries.

"Guess I was hoping we could do something together."

Hands on hips, she narrowed her eyes.

"We were *supposed* to *do* something together. Go to Black Butter. Remember? But no, you chose to go play Bulldog Drummond instead. Answer me this. If you thought it really *was* Andy in Hong Kong, why didn't you just turn it over to the police and let them handle it?"

Well, shit, we went over this, what, a hundred times?

"Honey, I explained that. I couldn't be sure it really was him. Not with one-hundred percent certainty. And as soon as I found out he really was missing. I filed a report with the police. And as for notifying the Hong Kong authorities, what would they have done? Nothing. Especially since the supplier claims it wasn't Andy's head. So now the Seattle police are looking into it."

Yeah, shit, for what that's worth.

"And why did *you*," Laura said, jabbing a finger at him, "have to be the one to file the report?"

Hard as Lucas tried to remain calm, her tone was getting to him, like a sliver under a fingernail.

"We've been through this also. Who else was there to do it? No one. No one looks after him. I'm his closest friend. It was the right thing to do."

"I think you did it because everything is always about *you.* Your career, your work schedule, your practice. You, you, you. I'm sick of it."

"Okay, then, let's talk about us for a moment. I'm so sad about what's happening to us. This divorce. Is there anything we can do to try to fix things?"

Laura's shoulder sagged and she moved to the kitchen table and sat down.

"I'm sad too, Lucas. Our marriage hasn't turned out even close to what I imagined it would when we married. I even wish things were different. I really do, but they aren't. You have your life that centers around your practice, and I have my life that centers around my friends. We just don't have anything in common other than Josh, and he's in the phase of his life where he's moving away from us. So what is there left?"

"But what about the feelings we had for each other when we married? What happened to those?"

"We were younger then, Lucas. We saw life differently. We had dreams…they just don't exist anymore."

"Like what dreams?"

"A happy life together."

With that she got up and walked out of the room, leaving with an empty sadness.

For a moment, Lucas sat and thought about how sad their exchange made him. It also made the house seem small and foreign, like a place he didn't belong anymore. He wanted some dinner and to have a drink, but there was nothing in the ice box and he didn't want to have a drink and then have to drive somewhere.

When he went upstairs, the bedroom door was closed, so he went to the guest room, stuffed his wallet and keys into his pockets, and headed for his car.

Chapter 38

TWO BLOCKS FROM his house, Lucas curbed the Volvo, then slumped back against the seat, head against the rest. He massaged the muscle tension clamping both temples like a pipe wrench. The pressure built into a pounding headache.

Shit.

Their conversation had gone completely sideways, not even close to what he'd intended. And now he sat here stewing in a toxic brew of sadness, depression, fatigue, and anger. Anger was equally divided between Laura and himself. At Laura for booking the spa vacation just to spite him. At himself for having handled the situation poorly. But most of all, anger at having to defend himself for doing the right thing.

His headache began to loosen up. He glanced around to see where he was and recognized the neighborhood.

Now what? Too soon to return home.

They both needed time to cool off. The more he thought about it, maybe a week of massage and meditation might not be such a bad idea for Laura after all. It might just be worth the outrageous cost.

And as long as Lucas was totaling up injustices for the day, what about Wendy dropping the investigation? Frustration and anger percolated through his gut again. He couldn't let her do that. There had to be something he could do to keep it alive. On a whim, he picked up his cell phone.

He knew he needed to be extremely careful not to let his anger show through and piss her off.

A moment later Wendy answered.

He said, "Sorry to bother you this late in the day, but I've been thinking about Andy. Got a couple minutes to talk?"

"Sure," she said, sounding noncommittal yet interested.

"Tell you what. I'm headed downtown and it's getting late. If you're not busy, may I buy you a bite to eat?"

"Actually, I'm almost home, and I really don't feel like driving all the way back to town." She hesitated, as if thinking something over. "To tell you the truth, dinner does sound good." Another pause. "You willing to drive out to the north end?"

"No problem."

"There's an Olive Garden near Alderwood Mall. Why don't you meet me there in, say, forty-five minutes?"

Wendy Elliott was waiting in the vestibule when Lucas opened the cut-glass door. She wore tight denim hip huggers and a black tank top that showed off well-toned biceps. She carried a lightweight black leather jacket over one shoulder. He fantasized a tattoo on the small of her back, maybe a butterfly or something symmetrical. She seemed the type, the tough sexy look all rolled into one package. And he was amazed to still find her incredibly attractive, especially seeing how this particular look wasn't his preference. Until now.

Well, that wasn't entirely true, was it?

He'd been drawn to her from the moment he'd seen her.

"Table for two?" asked the hostess.

The hostess seated them, handed out menus, and asked for drink orders.

"Glass of chardonnay," Wendy said.

"Why not make that a bottle," Lucas added.

They started with small talk—the drive out, the weather, anything but Andy.

A waitress returned with their bottle of Kendall-Jackson and two glasses, poured, asked if they'd decided on their orders yet.

"I'll take your chicken Caesar," Wendy said without looking at the menu.

Lucas hadn't looked, either.

"A pepperoni pizza with mushrooms," he said, figuring odds were they had it. The air smelled of garlic bread and olive oil, and the background clatter was loud enough he had to listen carefully to hear her.

The waitress departed, leaving them in awkward silence.

Lucas asked, "So what made you want to become a cop?"

Wendy took him through a bullet point life history. Growing up in Moses Lake and how, unlike her sister who attended Washington State University to major in pregnancy and now lived with three rug rats and a husband down the street from her parents, she had wanted to be elsewhere.

"I wanted out," she said. "I wanted to get away from the blistering summers and small-town atmosphere. Solving mysteries intrigued me ever since I read my first Nancy Drew. Sounds silly, huh?"

He shook his head, fascinated.

"No, not at all. Go on."

"My parents used to limit the amount of TV we could watch. Thirty minutes a day. That was it. Didn't matter if it was the news or the Mariners. What happened was I ended up in my room reading most of the time."

Wendy paused, smiling, a light blush on her face.

"Know what I'd do some Saturdays? I'd ride my bike to the post office and memorize mug shots. You know, the FBI's most wanted. Then I'd spend the afternoon lurking around the mall playing undercover agent, checking out shoppers. Never caught one of the bad guys, but that wasn't for lack of trying. A neighbor of ours was a K-9 officer."

She blushed again before continuing.

"I was so conniving. It's embarrassing now that I look back on it. I purposely made friends with his German shepherd so I could get to know him. Once I did that, I conned him into letting me ride with him on patrol. I'd ask questions about police work. I'd stay out as late as I could. He seemed to like having someone care about what he did and taught me a lot. Even now, one of my favorite TV shows is *Cops*."

She paused to sip wine.

"Senior year in high school I signed up for a stint with the army. Dad never said a word, but I know he would've preferred me to go air force. Thing was, the army said they'd guarantee me a spot in CID and the air force didn't. Man, you should've seen it the day I told everyone what I'd done. We were all sitting at dinner when I dropped the bomb. Dad was so cool. He said he didn't mind, just as long as I was happy. Not Sis. She couldn't believe it. Thought it was unnatural or something. She couldn't understand why I didn't want to start a legacy of babies. *Legacy*. That was her exact word."

She laughed.

"Mom was totally disappointed. She came right out and asked why I didn't want to do better. Become a nurse, or if law was really that important to me, become a lawyer. To this day she still doesn't get the difference between solving mysteries and practicing law. Mysteries are intrigue; law is flat-out boring. I can't imagine sitting at a desk for hours poring over all the small print. Worse yet is criminal defense work. Spending all your energy trying to find ways to squirm some two-bit guilty loser out of taking responsibility for his actions. Look at the O.J. Simpson case. How can you justify that kind of crap?

"There's no similarity between law and justice," Wendy continued. "That was one of the reasons I hated working Vice. The way the laws are written, the girls are forced to take unacceptable risks. I get sad and angry just thinking about it. My ex—he's a cop too—and I used to argue about it all the time. He believes the girls are just lazy. But even if you look at the ones who aren't into drugs—which is a minority, I know—most of them really don't have other options. At least none they know about. Christ, I get worked up talking about it. Anyway, getting back to the story, I went into the academy straight out of the army."

Lucas felt comfortable sitting here listening to her. Happy for the break from the arctic tension that radiated from Laura. In contrast, Wendy was warm and interesting.

"What about you? How does someone decide to be a brain surgeon?"

Ah, the perfect opportunity to focus on Andy.

He said, "Being a doctor was what I always wanted. Sort of like you. Andy almost became one but only because that's what his parents wanted. I mentioned we've been friends forever, didn't I?"

"Yes."

"Well, we went through grade school together right on through Stanford premed. Going to med school was just another thing we have in common."

"But he never went, did he?"

"No. His parents died in a car accident when he was twenty-two. After that, Andy went to business school." He shrugged. That part was true, his parents had been killed. "He probably would've done well in medicine. He has a huge heart and a great sense of humor. He's fun to be around."

Usually. When he isn't drinking too much.

She tore a piece of bread from a small loaf, dipped it in seasoned olive oil, and held it up while making a point.

"Yeah, but the sex thing got him in trouble. At least with the law."

"Yes, unfortunately."

She put a finger to her mouth while chewing.

"I told you, didn't I? I busted him twice."

Maybe it was the wine, but man, Wendy looked good.

No, it wasn't just the wine. She must've been a killer decoy. He could appreciate why Andy zeroed in on her. She probably racked up the squad's all-time arrest record.

Dinner finished, Lucas and Wendy headed for the front door, the place maybe only a quarter full of customers now with the early birds long gone. Then they were outside the front door looking at each other. The night was cooler than normal for August, and a chill in the air was slowly replacing the sun's earlier warmth.

She asked, "You up for another drink?"

His pulse quickened.

Was she coming on to him or was he reading too much into the suggestion?

"Sure." He glanced around the mall for a likely place but saw only retail shops. "Where?"

"I live a couple minutes from here. You can follow me," she said with a smile.

Wendy's unit was one of ten contiguous cookie-cutter two-level townhouses crammed into one block. Wood siding in various shades of brown paint to distinguish one unit from another. White trim around every window. She had only one designated parking spot directly in front of her door, which she took.

She came over to his idling car.

"Go find a spot while I turn on the lights."

By the time Lucas got back, her front door stood open and she was in the small kitchen area pouring wine. The interior was sparsely furnished. Not much more than a black leather couch, a laptop with external speakers, and a huge flat-screen TV already on to the Mariners game with the audio muted. Three large cardboard U-Haul boxes stacked in one corner.

He asked, "Just move in?"

"Those?" Wendy said with a dismissive wave. "Nah, been here a couple years. Never seem to have enough time to unpack them. Stuff from when I was married." She held out a glass for him and nodded at the TV. "I splurged on that."

Lucas looked more closely. A Sony, maybe fifty-four inches. Black with silver trim, high-definition, vibrant colors. It was the top of the eighth, the A's up by two. It figured. As usual, the M's pitching sucked.

"Have a seat."

He settled into the couch, and she nestled down next to him, right leg tucked up under her, knee barely brushing his thigh. The touch sent a tingle up his leg directly into his groin.

Lucas tried to concentrate on the game. Two on, two out, and the M's pitcher struggling. Then he was studying her profile, the angle of her jaw and a spot just below, the place on the neck where he loved to kiss Laura. A kind of erogenous zone for her.

Wendy turned slightly, caught him staring, and smiled faintly, the simple act of seduction.

Was it intentional?

"Let me take care of these," she said, moving both wine glasses to the floor next to the couch, then leaned in, brushing her lips against his.

Then his lips were touching that spot on her neck, kissing softly.

She tilted her head and put a hand on the back of his head, pulling him closer.

His chest filled with tightness. The sounds of the game were drowned out by the pounding in his ears. It had been too long since he kissed a woman who eagerly exchanged a long, slow kiss. He had her in his arms, alternating his lips between her lips and neck as her hand ran back and forth over his head, encouraging him.

Lucas awkwardly tugged at her tank top—she gently stopped him. To his surprise, she slowly peeled the tight-fitting garment over her head...

Lucas awoke uncertain where he was, turned, recognized her queen-size bed. Wendy was curled on her side, back to him, breathing softly. The soft blue glow of the clock radio showed: 12:31.

Jesus Christ, what have I done?

Laura's image floated in his mind. He felt guilty as hell. And rightly so. But he had to admit the sex had been terrific. Mostly, the lack of conflict that was so constant with Laura seemed refreshing. But he reminded himself, that can quickly change with increasing intimacy. Somehow the more you got to know somewhere, the more license there was for conflict.

Shit, what do I do now?

Get dressed and sneak out the door without waking her?

No. He didn't want to leave without saying good-bye, yet…didn't want to wake her to say it. Too late to go home now anyway, so he might as well roll over and try to go back to sleep.

"…will be the high today," bubbled the perky AM radio announcer.

Lucas opened his eyes.

Wendy, already showered and dressed in a blue pantsuit, came over from the mirror, hairbrush in hand, and killed the radio.

"I put out a bath towel for you and a razor."

The words held no embarrassment, regret, or judgment, just a statement of fact.

Then she added, "All I have is coffee. I usually grab a muffin at the 7-Eleven down the street."

Lucas was out the door heading for his car with guilt weighing down both shoulders like huge sandbags.

He kept thinking, *How could I have done that to Laura?*

Key in hand, he stopped at the car door, stunned with the realization he'd just gained a bit more insight into Andy.

Chapter 39

LUCAS'S VOLVO JUMPED on Aurora Avenue, old US Highway 99, instead of I-5 southbound. A slower route this way, but it gave him more time to think and sort out the many amotions zinging around in his brain.

Sitting back against the leather, he tried to calm the ten thousand volts that coursed through his nerves—had to keep from looking as guilty as he felt.

Get my shit together. I'm closing in on home.

Just a couple more blocks.

Another right turn and Lucas hit the brakes. Ahead of him, the residential street was choked with cop cars, two fire trucks, vans from at least two local TV stations, and clots of looky-loos.

Shit. They appeared clustered around his house.

A lightning bolt of dread struck.

Something's happened to Laura.

No, can't be. It's a neighbor's house. Has to be.

A uniformed cop stuck out a hand for him to go no farther.

Lucas became aware of the smell of burnt rubber and wood. A deep dread exploded inside, filling him with panic. He slammed the transmission into park, jerked up the parking brake, and was out of the car running toward his house, shoving people aside, noticing for the first-time debris and charred wood in place of the garage.

A strong hand grabbed his arm from behind.

"Hold it! You can't go there."

He spun around, swatted the hand away and yelled.

"Goddamn it, I live here. I have to find my wife."

Chapter 40

"IT'S A CRIME scene," Detective Jim Lange said to Lucas.

They sat in an unmarked cop car, Lucas in the back, on the side opposite Lange. Two communication radios, one bolted to the console and a handheld lying haphazardly on the front seat, intermittently broke squelch with various calls. The interior smelled of copy machine toner and stale coffee. Lucas wanted to vomit.

"But my wife's in there," Lucas pleaded for the hundredth time.

"We've been over that. No one's in the house. Believe me, we checked. Soon as the garage cools down, we'll check that too. But it looks like there was an explosion followed by a fire. You say your car was parked inside?"

"Yes."

Lange looked the same height and weight as Lucas. About five ten, one hundred and sixty pounds. Maybe a few years older judging by the crow's-feet behind slightly tinted lenses. Dresses casually in a navy polo and tan Dockers with his ID dangling from a neck lanyard.

"She wouldn't leave without putting out a note. I need to know where she it."

"Are you tracking anything I just said?"

Lucas wanted to vomit.

Lange said, "You didn't answer my question."

"What question?"

"Did you have anything explosive in the garage? Flammable liquids, gasoline, paint thinner, things like that?"

Lucas realized for the first-time what Lange was getting at. He looked around, saw the news trucks from the local network affiliates. What if Josh saw this on TV? Would he recognize the house?

A crab was clawing its way through Lucas's gut.

"Excuse me."

He pulled on the door handle, but it was locked.

"We're not done yet."

"Okay, but I have to call my son."

"What's wrong, Dad?"

"There's been a fire at the house…"

He ran out of words, his mind simply shut down.

"I'll be there soon as I can." Josh hung up.

Lucas looked at his phone for a moment before pressing the button to disconnect his end. He realized something was completely wrong in his world but couldn't wrap his mind around exactly what. Laura couldn't be dead.

Lange said, "You didn't answer me. We need your statement recorded properly. Will you come to the precinct to give one?"

Statement? What the hell for?

He couldn't seem to concentrate on what was being said to him.

Suddenly the nauseous foreboding from Hong Kong was back, only this time stronger. Much stronger. It started becoming clear…a car bomb. Laura was dead. What other reason would there be for the cops to consider it a crime scene? He felt weak and dizzy.

"Well? What's it going to be?"

Lucas tried to think but kept coming back to one thing: she's dead.

"McRae, I'm talking to you."

His brain started to work again.

He'd seen enough cop movies and TV shows to know he should ask, "Do I need a lawyer?"

Lange raised his eyebrows.

"Why? You done something wrong?"

Lange's tone sealed it.

Damned right he needed one.

Lange opened a solid-looking door, motioned Lucas into an interrogation room no different from the ones seen in countless TV shows and movies, except it didn't have one-way glass. This was the same building where he'd filed the missing person report.

Was Wendy down the hall? If so, did she know about this? Could she help him?

"Want something to drink? Coffee, Coke?"

"A Coke."

Soon as Lange left, he called his lawyer. The only lawyer Lucas knew was out of town, so his secretary transferred him to another attorney in the office.

Lucas was halfway through the story when she said, "You need a criminal defense lawyer. No one in our firm does that kind of work. I'll see who I can find. You said West Precinct, that's where they're holding you?"

Lucas waited in the room for Lange to return with a Coke. He desperately needed something to settle his stomach with the crab still clawing the hell out of him. He couldn't bear the thought of Laura being dead.

No, it was all a huge mistake. Laura was still alive. One of her girlfriends had picked her up, and right now they were doing yoga or aerobics or getting a massage. That could be why her cell phone was off.

Sure, that was it.

A cell phone might break the mood from all that new age music and incense.

But then why would he be here in a goddamned interrogation room?

Jesus, where was that lawyer?

Lange finally returned but without coffee or a Coke or the previously friendly smile. In fact, he looked serious as shit.

"Mind if I record this?" he asked in an offhanded way.

Alarms rang in Lucas's head. He glanced around for a microphone or camera but didn't see one so figured it must be hidden in the vents to put people more at ease.

"What about the garage? You find anything?"

"I'll repeat the question. May I record this conversation?"

A flash of anger ignited in Lucas's chest.

"Yes! Now goddamn it, what about the garage?"

Lange pointed to a straight-back metal chair behind a small table. Both the table and chair were bolted to the floor.

"When I have definitive news, I'll tell you. Now have a seat so we can record your statement."

He went through the business of stating the date, time, his own name and then asked Lucas to say his name and residence. This sudden formality did nothing but spike his anxiety. Then again, he saw no problem in answering such benign questions.

What harm would it be to admit his name and address?

Lange asked, "What cars do you own?"

A voice inside warned to wait until the lawyer arrived, that this was now edging into problem areas. But Lange probably had his DMV files and his VIN numbers, so the question might be aimed at evaluating his truthfulness.

He said, "An Audi and the Volvo."

"Is the Volvo your wife's?"

"Yes."

"Then why were you driving her car this morning?"

Lange's tone triggered a queasy feeling in Lucas's gut. Where was this headed and why? He saw problems with a truthful answer. The cheating husband kills his wife so he can be with his lover. He decided to stick close to the truth, but not every detail.

"I cleaned out the garage yesterday and piled a load of junk in the driveway. It blocked half of the garage, so when Laura came home yesterday, she parked in the driveway directly behind my car. When I needed a car this morning, I used hers."

Which, if taken at face value, was true. Just not quite the whole story.

Lange kept looking at him.

"For?"

Careful now.

The queasiness grew. He was treading into the lie quagmire and knew that once entered, it could suck him down, forcing lie upon lie until he'd lost all sight of his starting point.

What was he going to say? I was out last night sleeping with a detective from this precinct?

"I went out for a cup of coffee."

Technically speaking, this was the truth. Wendy had given him one.

Lange nodded as if appreciating the response.

What if Lange knew he'd been with Wendy? Had they talked? Was he trapped already?

"Mind telling me," Lange said, "where you were between the time you last saw your wife and when you returned to the house?"

"Why are you asking me this?"

"Thought I made that obvious earlier. There was an explosion in the garage while you were out in your wife's car. Your wife isn't accounted for and there's a body in the wreckage of what's probably your Audi. There's every reason to believe your wife was killed in the garage in the explosion. Can I make myself any clearer?"

"Not another word until my lawyer gets here."

Wendy was at the two-burner hot plate pouring a cup of overcooked coffee when she got wind of an interrogation in progress down the hall. Out of curiosity she ambled to the observation room and glanced at the video screen.

Oh, shit, now what?

Chapter 41

IN SPITE OF the irregular hours his work demanded, Ditto doggedly clung to daily routines. Up by seven, pack the coffee maker with Starbucks Kenya roast, listen to the local news while grunting out fifty push-ups, shave, spruce up the goatee, shower, dress for the day. Always in that order. Routines were what allowed a busy life to remain ordered and running smoothly while permitting you to concentrate on other things. Business, for example. Only the ditzy, fractionated people of the world allowed their lives to run haphazardly.

Maybe when he retired, he would allow himself the luxury of sleeping in occasionally. But he doubted it because, well, it just wouldn't seem right. Besides, his internal clock woke him at seven regardless of what time he went to sleep.

Ditto sat in his office with the door closed and his black leather executive chair positioned to comfortably watch the local news. He was waiting for one particular story. He leaned forward as the words "This Just In" flashed on the screen.

The picture switched to a reporter in a yellow KING TV Windbreaker holding a wind-screened microphone to his mouth. Behind him a chaotic array of emergency vehicles with flashing lights. Fire, police, a Medic One van.

"Thanks, Ed. What you see behind me is the residence in the Magnolia neighborhood where Seattle Police and Fire Departments are investigating an explosion earlier this morning that is thought to have taken the life of one person, apparently a woman."

A woman? Fuck.

"Police are saying the source of the explosion was a car. Why the car exploded is under investigation, but sources close to the case have said that the woman's husband has been taken to the West Precinct for questioning as a person of interest."

Ditto watched in stunned silence as the anchor assured viewers the news team was monitoring the situation closely and would break to the story the moment more developments were available.

How could that have happened? Gerhard had assured him...

He wiped his mouth and smoothed his goatee. Clearly an unanticipated turn of events. That McRae's wife became the victim was irrelevant. What was more relevant was that McRae remained alive and quite possibly even more of a threat than before.

But McRae wasn't a reasonable person.

Ditto picked up the phone and dialed Gerhard's line.

"I need to see you. Right now."

"Your lawyer's here," Lange said.

Lucas looked up at the doorway where a trim, tall, middle-aged man squinted behind fashionably narrow glasses. With shoes buffed to a gloss and a charcoal pinstripe Armani, he radiated a simple but emphatic don't-fuck-with-me aura. Lange's dour face told Lucas that this attorney probably wasn't a likely candidate for honorary membership in the police guild, making him a great choice and exactly what he needed now. Lucas stored away a mental note to thank whomever was responsible for the referral.

The lawyer stepped into the room, hand extended.

"Lucas McRae? Palmer Davidson." After shaking hands,

Davidson locked eyes with Lange. "What—if anything—has my client been charged with?"

Lange said, "Nothing. He's here to answer some questions concerning the explosion."

Davidson smiled knowingly.

"You haven't changed a bit in the last several years. I need some time to talk with my client in private."

Lange moved to the door.

"I'll be outside."

"No. We'll talk in the hall."

Lange gave him a bemused look. "You can talk in here."

"I said private." Davidson pointed toward the ceiling vent. "This is about as private as the Iraq embassy."

Lange frowned.

"He tries to leave, you'll both have big problem."

"Bite me."

Out in the hall, Davidson sidled up close to Lucas.

"All I know is what I heard on the news on the way over. What's going on?"

Lange stood about twenty feet down the hall, arms crossed, legs spread, watching like a military guard.

Lucas explained the events of the past twenty-four hours, including spending the night with Wendy. He figured everything needed to be out on the table. Davidson listened to the entire story before having him repeat it.

When Lucas finished the second time, Davidson said, "That alibis you for last night, but if the cause of the explosion is proven to be a car bomb—which seems likely with what we presently know—there is nothing in your story that would remove you from being the prime suspect."

Lucas's gut knotted so tightly it ached.

Wendy stood outside the interrogation room conferring with Davidson in hushed tones. Lucas had been one-hundred-percent truthful to his attorney in recounting his whereabouts last night and the reason for not being in his car this morning.

She saw his checks blush with embarrassment but didn't stop eye contact. That Lucas was with another woman the night before his wife is killed would not sit well with Jim Lange, the lead investigator on the case. The truth would have to come out, sooner than later. And it would cast more suspicion on Lucas than was warranted.

In answer to Davidson's question, she said, "There's not enough evidence at this point to determine if this will be considered a murder or accidental death. So, I doubt they'll hold him much longer."

"My priority is my client's safety and if he's right, if Robert Ditto is behind this, then he's still in danger. What should I do with him?"

She'd been wrestling with the same question.

"If you're asking where he'll be safe, you need to consider several issues. He needs to be readily accessible for additional interviews. I don't know what kind of support system he has around, but he's going to need help."

"He wants to leave, and now he's worried about his son being in the house. He called the kid to tell him to come home, and he wants to be there when he arrives."

Wendy thought about that a second.

"For a moment, Ditto knows the garage is a crime scene. The last place he wants to go is anywhere remotely near McRae's house. And as far as later goes, after things settle down, I'll make sure McRae hires some security if he can. Also, I'll make sure the cars assigned to that district keep a closer eye on that neighborhood."

Davidson returned to the interrogation room but left the door open. "Come on," he said to Lucas. "Let's get out of here. They can't hold you any longer."

"What time is it?"

"A few minutes past nine."

"Morning or night?"

"Night."

He stood on shaky legs, wondering what to do next. Laura was dead from a car bomb that had probably been planted when he was in bed with Wendy.

How could he have done this to Laura?

Yes, they were having their problems and had begun the long process of negotiating a divorce, but he was still married to her. He was a worthless specimen of a husband.

And how would that look to the police?

He knew that when a person was murdered, the police first looked at the spouse, then at people close to the victim. And what would they find? That on the night before the murder, he'd slept with another woman. If the cops began to look into his and Laura's relationship, they'd quickly find out they'd been in the first stages of a divorce.

Davidson pulled his arm.

"C'mon, let's get going."

Chapter 42

LUCAS LEANED AGAINST the passenger door, forehead on the glass, staring at the passing darkness as Davidson drove. God, what he'd give to turn back time one year knowing what he did now. How differently he would do things.

If only…

Lucas lets himself into Laura's apartment, closes the door, yells, "It's me."

"You're early. I'm still in the tub."

"Stay there, Calgon Girl. I'll be right in."

He sets the plastic bag of Chinese takeout on the counter, then carefully places the other bag next to it. From the second bag, he removes two champagne flutes and a chilled bottle of Veuve Clicquot with its distinctive orange label. He peels the price tags off the bottom of the flutes, rinses them out, polishes both with a dish towel, tears off the foil seal, and uncorks the bottle. His stomach churning with anxiety as he carries the glasses and sweating bottle into the bathroom where Laura is up to her neck in bubble bath.

She glances at the glasses and bottle, her eyes lighting up.

"You got your residency?"

He closes the lid to the toilet, sets the bottle and glasses on it, starts taking off his shoes and socks, throwing them into the bedroom.

"I got crispy walnut prawns, broccoli beef, Buddha's Delight, and brown rice. That okay?"

"All my favorites. What's the occasion?"

He starts on the shirt next.

"I thought I'd bring dinner over. You know…a quiet night at home, so we don't have to go out."

"My God, Veuve Clicquot. You can't afford that."

He tosses the rest of his clothes into the other room, pours two glasses, hands her one.

"Move over."

She slides forward and he slips in behind her, pulls her back against his chest, begins to cup, then drip water over her breasts.

"You know how much I care about you, don't you?"

She snuggles into him more, relaxing, her head under his chin, the scent of her hair in his nostrils.

"Yes."

"We're so good together…" He stumbles on the words because he wants them to sound right. "We have so much fun…we like the same things like movies and neither one of us like slapstick…it just feels so right."

"Lucas—"

"What I mean to say, is I love you, Laura."

"And I love you too, Lucas. But what's going on?"

He sips the wine to bolster his next words. For three restless nights he's thought about this moment, agonized over how to ask, wondering how she'd answer.

"What do you think about getting married?"

Aw, shit, that didn't sound right.

She squirms around to look at him.

"Is that a proposal?"

"Yes. I mean…it is."

She leans over to kiss him.

"Yes, Lucas, absolutely. Did you have any doubt?" She studies his eyes a moment. "Now tell me what's going on."

He's at a loss for words, overcome by the moment. He was so afraid she might not want to marry him. Finally, he says, I got UC San

Francisco."

She turns back around and nestles back against him.

"San Francisco, huh. Always thought that would be a neat city to live in."

He's struck again with the realization that the person, the woman he loved so much that night was now gone from his life forever.

My fault...responsible.

If only...

... he hadn't gone to Hong Kong.

... he hadn't worked too hard to build a practice.

... tried harder to be a good husband.

... insisted she get help.

... encouraged Laura to find part-time work when Josh started school. And if she hadn't wanted to work, maybe volunteer for something that resonated with her heart. Anything to enrich her life might have prevented such bitterness these past few years.

Lucas said, "Oh, honey, I'm so sorry."

"What?" Davidson shot him a strange look.

The realization of what had happened hit and brought him back to the present.

And the horror of seeing the smoldering garage came flooding back.

Davidson was right. Although the police investigation was only hours old, they all knew this wasn't an accident, an accident from cleaning out the garage. It was a car bomb intended to kill him, not Laura.

Any previous dislike for Ditto was now hateful rage. He wanted to find a gun, walk into DFH, and blow the son of a bitch's head off.

Wait, calm down. That would accomplish nothing.

There had to be another way...

This time, Lucas's street was no longer chock-a-block with blue flashing lights, smoke, and chaos, but the smell of charcoal and melted plastic lingered.

Lucas noticed Josh's Nissan parked at the curb, asked Davidson, "Just so I'm sure, you talked with Wendy...I mean, Detective Elliott, and she thinks it's safe to be in the house?"

Davidson pulled the car to the curb, set the hand brake.

"They believe that if the explosion was an accident due to flammables in the garage—which I'm not sure I agree with—there's no continued risk. On the other hand, if this is Ditto's work—which we believe is the case—he won't take the risk of coming here. At least for a while. So, yes, you're okay if you want to stay there."

Lucas's primary concern was Josh's safety. Followed closely by helping Josh through the heartbreak of losing his mother.

Josh might have been at the window because as soon as Lucas began to get out of the car, he came flying out the front door of the house, ran to Lucas with wet cheeks, and threw his arms around him. Lucas hugged him fiercely.

"Who is that?" Josh asked as Davidson pulled away.

"My lawyer."

"Your lawyer?"

Josh stood still, a look of dismay etched on his face.

Neither one spoke, for a long moment until Josh asked, "Mom's dead?"

"Yes, son."

Lucas started toward the house, knowing he had to pull it together for Josh's sake.

"I still don't understand. Why a lawyer?"

"Because the police wanted to question me."

"About what? It was an accident." Josh looked at him. "Wasn't it?"

Lucas's first reaction was to protect Josh from the truth. But there's nothing to gain from lying. He decided to tell him everything. Well, except for last night. He looked at Josh, thinking about the drive over, how he probably hadn't had anything to eat and Laura would've made sure he was fed. Most of all, right now, he wanted to take care of his son, then slowly try to explain what he thought was going on.

"We'll get to that. First, have you eaten anything?"

As the words came out, he thought about how trivial they sounded.

"No. I drove straight over. When I got here firemen were still going over things and I..."

His voice trailed off.

"I'll order pizza."

Even though the thought of food nauseated him.

After calling a neighborhood pizza joint that delivered, Lucas grabbed two glasses and the bottle of Green Label from the cupboard. While filling the glasses with ice, he began explaining.

He carried the drinks over to the table and handed one to Josh.

Lucas finished the story without mentioning that he spent the night with Wendy.

Josh sat silent, lips pressed tight in anger, fists balls of white.

The doorbell rang. Lucas jumped, thinking maybe Ditto realized he hadn't succeeded and was coming back...

Christ, get a grip. I ordered pizza.

He took a deep breath to slow his heart back to normal. Still, he glanced out the window to make sure before opening the door.

Lucas placed the open pizza box on the table, but Josh waved it away. Fine with him. The cheesy greasy smell made him nauseated. He closed the lid and moved it to the counter.

"It's over here if you change your mind. In the meantime, how about another?" Lucas asked, holding up his drink.

Lucas stopped to gaze at the label of the very same bottle purchased from the duty-free store at the airport. Hong Kong. And wondered if anything he did during that twenty-four-hour period caused Laura's death. The butterfly effect, some called it when taken to its extreme logic. If he hadn't pissed off Gerhard...

What if the explosion was nothing more than something he did while cleaning out the garage? The red gasoline container...paint thinner...a pile of rags... He felt sick to his stomach, thinking he'd never forgive himself if Laura's death was from some stupid mistake he'd made. Well, in a way it did. If he had never gone on that trip...would Laura still be alive right now?

At the thought of Laura dying in an explosion, tears welled up along his lower lids. He sniffed and swiped at them, but they only got worse. A moment later he was standing at the counter with tears streaming down his face. Josh got up, came over and wrapped his arms around him and hugged. Both men stood there crying and hugging.

Later, Lucas and Josh sipped scotch in silence, seeming mired in thought. He wondered what his son was thinking.

Did he hold him responsible? Was he responsible?

Josh broke the silence.

"I could move back here if you want." Which sounded more like an attempt to comfort Lucas than a sincere desire. "You know, transfer. I'm pretty sure I could transfer to the U, and it's not a bad department."

Lucas loved him for that. But Josh needed the experience of being on his own. He had a great start on life: a good job as a teacher's assistant, a girlfriend he adored, and inexpensive apartment shared with two compatible roommates. His professors knew him. And Lucas didn't want Josh here out of sympathy. But at the moment, they were totally controlled by grief and unable to think clearly.

He said, "I don't think either one of us should make any decisions for a while. Neither of us is thinking straight. For now, let's just try to get through the next couple days, then see where we stand. Okay?"

Chapter 43—Five Days Later, Saint Mark's Chapel

THE CLOYING SCENT of white morning lilies and incense thickened the chapel air. The oak pew felt as hard and unforgiving as the priest's voice. Lucas sat in the front row for everyone to see and sensed accusing eyes boring into the back of his head. Even if they didn't know where he was when Laura died, they knew he wasn't there. He knew where he was, and he hated himself for it. No need for him to go to hell. The fire of guilt charred his soul with each passing second. Regardless of who triggered the explosion, he, and no one else, bore ultimate responsibility for Laura's death. The guilt was bad enough. Missing Laura made it exponentially worse.

Laura's memorial service. No funeral. The medical examiner hadn't released Laura's remains because her death was under investigation, and he continued to be the prime suspect. And everybody here knew it.

Was there anything he would ever be able to do to atone for her death?

He'd talk to a priest if he thought it might help, but he wasn't religious.

That psychiatrist he wanted Laura to see, would that help?

Josh sat on his right, cheeks glistening, sniffing occasionally. Lucas hung his own head and dabbed his eyes with a Kleenex and held Josh's hand, squeezing it now and then, as much to comfort himself as his son. To Josh's right sat Laura's sister.

Lucas put his arm around Josh's shoulder and held him as tightly as he possibly could and silently swore that he would do everything humanly possible to protect and love him and not allow his anger at Ditto to place Josh in harm's way.

He thought of some of the arguments he had had with Laura over the past year, how trivial they now seemed. If he'd put as much effort into the marriage as he had in his practice, this never would've happened.

Which brought up DFH. And Ditto again. The man was responsible for planting the explosive in the car.

Would the police be able to prove his culpability? Was there anything he could do to help prove it?

Josh worked himself free of Lucas's arm and began massaging his hand. Lucas realized he'd squeezed him too tightly and patted Josh on the knee to apologize.

The congregation was singing a hymn. He had no idea which one or when it started. Another thought hit.

What if...?

No, it wasn't possible. Was it?

Lucas and Josh stood at the chapel door, shaking hands and thanking people as they shuffled out. He hugged Laura's teasy sister and kissed her cheek.

She whispered to him, "A detective called. Lange, I think. He asked about you and Laura..."

With eyebrows arched, she searched his face.

"Tell him the truth. I have nothing to hide," he said, then turned his attention to the next person in line.

He couldn't believe it; Andy's ex-wife hugged him and said, "I know you miss her. I do. She loved you, Lucas. And I know you love her."

It was the only warmth she'd shown him in years.

He noticed Wendy working her way forward. When she finally reached him, they shook hands.

She said, "I'm sorry for your loss."

He nodded and introduced her to Josh.

Then said to her, "I have an idea I'd like to talk to you about. Maybe tomorrow."

She nodded solemnly.

"Whenever you feel up to it."

She walked away as he greeted the next person in line.

After the chapel emptied, Lucas wrapped Josh in his arms and hugged, and for a moment they stayed like that, starting past the rows of empty pews toward the altar. This wasn't the same Episcopal church his parents forced him to attend as a kid, but the interior evoked the same hollowness in him as it had back then, as if he were supposed to feel something he couldn't. And he always marveled at those who could believe in their religion of choice and the comfort it seemed to give them. Or at least that's what people claimed. He wished it could give him some comfort now, but it didn't. He wanted to cry from the ache in his heart for Laura, but he also wanted to be strong for Josh.

Okay, so maybe there was a supreme power. If so, Lucas wasn't about to give it a formal name.

He believed when you die, you're gone, completely leaving behind only a decomposing body. Your legacy is only in the memories of the living. But at this moment, he wanted more than anything to believe in a heaven and that Laura was there. Most of all, he wished things had been different between them, that he'd been able to wrap his arms around her while telling her how much she meant to him. Instead, she left life with the bitter taste of a deteriorating marriage and the beginnings of a divorce.

Josh said, "Sure you'll be okay if I head back?"

They'd talked at length about whether Josh should stay or

return to school to classes, a girlfriend, and a part-time job.

Josh had said, "I need to get my head around Mom not being here. It'll be easier if I'm not in the house. It's so strange to be in my room and know she's not coming home. And the garage...it's..."

As much as Lucas wanted his son near him, he decided Josh knew how best to handle the grieving process. After all, it was only a few hours drive and they could talk on the phone.

Lucas hugged him, said, "I'll be okay."

Josh looked at him.

"You sure?"

Lucas nodded.

His son hugged him back.

"I love you, Dad. Call if you want me back. I'll be here as soon as possible."

They descended the few stone steps to the asphalt drive and started across the empty parking lot to where they'd parked both cars. Lucas noticed three males loitering at the far end of the lot. Low-hanging baggy pants, baggy shirts. They didn't seem to be paying him or Josh any attention, but their unexplained presence left him edgy, so he waited until Josh was inside his car, doors locked with the engine running, before he stepped away and waved good-bye.

Josh returned the wave and drove out of the lot.

Lucas checked to see what the bangers were doing. They were heading straight toward him.

Chapter 44

LUCAS GLANCED AROUND, saw no one else in the lot. Without trying to rush or show concern, he headed toward his car, thinking maybe he could make it before they caught up to him.

"Yo. McRae."

They know me?

He turned to look at them.

The lead guy pointed at him in that overhand-elbow-extended-from-the-shoulder sort of way.

"Hey, chill, man. Ain't gonna do you no harm."

The other two hung back as the lead guy pimp-rolled over and swung his hand out.

"Luis Ruiz."

A zigzag scar crossed Ruiz's left cheek, and his nose was never set correctly after being fractured. Shitty blue tats marred his right deltoid.

Lucas reached out, half-expecting to be embarrassed by some sort of complicated ritual shake. But Ruiz simply pumped his hand once and let go, very businesslike, but the move didn't put Lucas any more at ease. He hoped a cop would cruise by and take an interest.

"Do I know you?"

"No reason you should." Ruiz rolled his neck, like working out a kink. "Lupita Ruiz. That name mean anything to you?"

The guy sounded more inquisitive than threatening, and his body language was loose instead of hostile.

Lucas answered, "No. Should I?"

"I think so. She's my sister. Or maybe I should say *was* my sister. That's one of the problems. And the reason this should interest you. My sister dropped out the same time as your homie, Andy Baer."

For several seconds Lucas stood openmouthed, shocked this guy knew about Andy.

"How do you know that?"

"The cop, bro. Detective Elliott. She and Sis were tight."

He raised two fingers squeezed together.

It clicked. Lupita must be the missing prostitute Wendy mentioned. Lucas nodded slowly.

"What are you saying? There's a connection?"

"Don't know for sure, but here's what I do know. Your friend had a thing for girls like her. His car was found near where she worked. His head turns up in fucking Hong Kong, and a Suburban belonging to DFH was definitely seen in the area. I ain't no A student, but I sure as hell ain't stupid."

"How do you know all this?"

Luis Ruiz ignored the question.

"I need to find out what happened to her. Detective Elliott seems to think your friend's the key. And that Ditto's the man."

"I have no proof."

"You saw your man in Hong Kong."

"I *think* it was Andy, and I told the police everything I know."

The frustration and rage about the situation bubbled to the surface and he felt his jaw muscles clamp tight. He forced himself to loosen up.

"There's got to be away to find out what really happened."

"Christ, you don't think I've thought about this? I've gone

through everything I can possibly do hundreds of times, and believe me, there's not a damned thing more I can do."

"That's where you wrong, bro. There always something you can do. You just haven't thought about it long enough. Maybe I can help you."

"What can you do?"

"I don't know. We just starting to talk. But we know a couple things. One is the heads you saw in Hong Kong came from Seattle."

"We don't know where they came from. They were *brought* from Seattle, but Ditto denied the one I saw was Andy. What can I do about that?"

Ruiz shifted his weight and looked around.

"What you can do is think. Think back on anything that happened around the time your homie went missing."

"Why you so interested in what happened to Andy?"

"Because my sister went missing about the same time he did. What if they're related? Too many things give me strange thoughts about this. Too many coincidences." He shook his head. "Way too many. It's not fucking right. That's all I'm saying."

What could he say?

Frustration and anger at Ditto and the helplessness of the situation blinded him.

Ruiz handed him a folded slip of paper.

"This is my cell. You need help on anything, call. I'll do whatever to help. But my gut tells me that if we find your man, we find out what happened to my baby sister."

Chapter 45

"LUPITA WAS A good person. I got to know her well. We got close." Wendy shook her head. "No way she should be missing."

It was almost dusk. Earlier in the church parking lot Lucas had watched Ruiz and company walk away before he climbed into the Volvo and fired the ignition. He'd sat there thinking over Ruiz's words before calling Wendy on her cell. Now they sat in Lucas's car facing a six-foot galvanized fence intertwined with thick blackberry vines. Beyond that stretched a breath-stealing panorama of Elliott Bay and downtown Seattle stretching west to Alki Point. Wendy's car was parallel to his. At the other end of the parking lot a brood of Asian shutterbugs milled around a tour bus.

Wendy said, "Luis hated what she was doing. I mean, he isn't a model citizen himself. Nor is the gang he runs. But he really loved her. And he made sure she didn't get into the drug thing or any of the other occupational hazards."

Lucas nodded for her to continue.

"The impressive thing is that these two kids were able to survive on their own by living on the street after their parents died."

Lucas realized he was only paying half attention to her; the other half was zeroed in on Ditto, ruminating over what role he played in Andy's death. Or had he only brokered his body after the fact? Either way, Ditto was involved.

The question was: how to prove it?

Wendy said, "If we want to take down Ditto, we have to do it in a logical sequence. Find a direct link to him. And that just *has* to be Andy. Which brings us right back to where we started. Is there anything you can think of to prove whose head was in Hong Kong?"

"Jesus," he snapped at her, "don't you think I've been over that a thousand times?"

"I thought you called this meeting. If you want to leave, go right ahead."

He held up his hand.

"Sorry. It's just...I'm so goddamned angry I..."

Words failed him.

She softened.

"Apology accepted. Believe me, I feel your frustration. But one thing I've learned is to keep going back over things again and again, looking for something to help jog your memory. Can we do that one more time?"

Lucas really didn't see how that would help. Truth be told, he was sick of spending so much time discussing it. But he knew Wendy only wanted to help.

"One more time and that's it. I can't do this any longer."

She pulled out a small recorder from her purse.

"I appreciate it. Tell you what. How about this time we listen to the tape of your initial statement?"

"Wait!" His pulse accelerated. It was too obvious. Worse yet, it'd been with him all along.

How could I have missed it?

"I can do it. I can prove it."

Chapter 46

WENDY LOOKED AT Lucas with suspicion. "Prove what?"

"That it really was Andy's head in Hong Kong."

"How?"

"HDTV."

"Come again?"

A hundred and ten volts of excitement rippled through him, his mind running at warp speed, going back over the sequence of events that morning, making sure he had it right. Entering the room, walking to the table, looking to his right as he passed the rack of Sony equipment with the glowing blue lights and dials and the smell of warm electronics. They were recording *before* he removed the towel, meaning Andy's face must've been clearly documented.

"The dissection. They recorded the whole thing in high definition. Yes. It should be all there. Everything I just told you."

She stared at him.

"And now that I think about it, Andy had a scar…behind his right ear. When he was a kid, he had a bad case of mastoiditis and ended up having his mastoid cleaned out. There was a scar behind his ear. The camera over the table should be able to show us that.

Wouldn't that help prove it was him?"

She stared at him a moment longer before saying, "I hope you're not kidding. And if you're not, please tell me you can get a copy."

"I don't see why not. Jimmy said after he edited it he'd send a copy, so there's no reason I can't just ask for the unedited version. All we need are the initial shots that show his face."

Were they recording when the group using Andy's head turned the head to the side? And would the recordings be clear enough to look for the scar? Probably. So, yeah, that should be there too.

Wendy held up a hand.

"Hold on. Before we get too excited, let me think about this. We want to do it right. Not have any chain of evidence screwup. What was it? Tape or DVD?"

"I'm not sure. But I want to say DVD."

"Where is it?"

"Hong Kong. Jimmy Wong has it."

"No, I mean is the recording at the hospital or someone's home?"

"I don't know. The hospital, I suppose. That's where they recorded it. Wong intended to edit down the files to just the essential teaching parts."

Were the DVDs gone by now?

"Got a phone number, some way to contact Wong?"

Lucas had to think about that. The invitation to come to Hong Kong had come by mail, he remembered.

But did he still have it?

They'd exchanged a few emails, but again, they'd been deleted from the computer.

Could he find them?

"I don't know."

Chapter 47

LUCAS LEANED AGAINST the kitchen counter. Holding a copy of Won's emails in his left hand, the paper still warm from the printer, he picked up the phone in his right and used his thumb to punch in the long string of numbers for an international call to Wong's office. Wong's contact numbers—in Mandarin and English—were included in his signature on every email.

A female voice answered in Chinese.

Lucas asked, "Do you speak English?"

She answered, "Yes."

"This is Dr. McRae. I need to speak with Dr. Wong. It's an emergency."

"I'm sorry. Dr. Wong is in surgery. May someone else be of assistance?"

He left the message for Wong to call back as soon as possible and emphasized this was an emergency.

Wendy sat at the kitchen table in the same spot Laura favored for various tasks—reading the newspaper, writing letters, playing solitaire on her laptop—as if it were her desk. Lucas felt uneasy about Wendy sitting there but said nothing.

Wendy asked, "She say when he might be back in the office?"

"No. Just that she'd give him the message. When he's not available, he's usually tied up in surgery."

"Probably wouldn't hurt to email him too."

"Good idea."

Lucas picked up his Droid from the counter and started thumbing through the menu, searching for the contact.

A moment later, he was finished with the email.

He looked at Wendy, said, "I can't stand it, not knowing when he's going to call."

She nodded and fidgeted in the seat.

"You're not done."

"What do you mean?"

"We made a deal. You get me into Andy's condo, I let you tag along. We haven't been there yet."

Lucas phoned Andy's ex-wife, said, "Trish? Lucas."

"What's wrong?"

"I really need your help on something."

He explained what he'd seen in Hong Kong and that the police were now officially investigating his disappearance.

"What can I do?"

"The police need to look inside Andy's condo to see if there's anything that might help them find out what happened to him."

"So? Who's stopping them?"

"Until they justify a search warrant, the doorman won't allow them in."

"That's unfortunate, but I still don't see what it has to do with me."

"You're listed as the legal next of kin. All it'd take is a note from you granting them permission to go inside." He added, "If it makes you any more comfortable, I'll go with the detective so nothing's disturbed."

"You sure about this? Seeing Andy, I mean?"

Trish sounded concerned, which made him feel better about her.

"Yes. Positive. So, will you do that for me? And for Andy?"

"Yes, of course I will. But I can't do it until tomorrow."

He wanted to ask her if she could do it now, but heard her sob, so decided to let it go even though it was driving him crazy waiting.

Wendy said, "One more thing."

Lucas replaced the phone and turned to her, thinking, *I need a drink.*

"Sit down. We need to discuss a couple of problems."

Lucas couldn't sit and started to pace.

"What?"

"As trite as this sounds, Lange's doing his job. He's working up a homicide and the first person you look at is the spouse, so don't take it personally. He obviously doesn't know all the things about you I do." She got up and inspected the nearest window. "What I'm saying is, you're still at risk."

"I know that."

"Well, it gets worse." Wendy checked to make sure the window was locked, then checked the next one too. "I keep getting this nagging feeling there's a leak on my end. And if I'm right, it goes straight to Ditto. What I'm saying is, I don't plan on telling anyone about the video until we have a chance to review it and I can secure a search warrant for DFH. Then I'm going to tear that place apart. Even then, I'm going to have to be careful."

Apprehension tingled his arms and legs.

"You suspect there's a leak, or you *know* there's a leak? Which is it?"

"Ninety-five percent in favor."

Lucas waited to see if she'd add anything, but she didn't.

So he said, "You know who it is?"

"Suspicion is all. Nothing concrete."

"Then we just have to be careful."

"You own a handgun?"

That was about the last thing he expected from her.

"No."

He wasn't for or against guns, just didn't have any use for them. Handguns in particular.

"I suspected that. You know how to shoot one?"

Lucas laughed.

"We're not talking quantum physics here. Aim and pull the trigger. Isn't that about it?"

"*After* you make sure it's loaded, the safety's off, a round's chambered, *and* you're aiming it at the right object."

"Got it."

Wendy eyed him.

"Just checking." She lifted her oversized purse from the chair, set it on the table, and pulled out a black pistol. "There was no time to get you a permit, so I got this. Think you can handle it?"

He turned it over in his hand, appreciating the heft. Small and compact, with the smell of gun oil. He rubbed index finger against thumb, feeling the slippery residue left on his fingertips.

He nodded.

"It's a Glock 36 Sublime. Only holds six rounds, which nowadays isn't much. But they're 45 caliber. At close range, that means stopping power even if you only wing your target. Point is, if you need more than six shots, you're aiming wrong. Always go for center of mass, the chest. The serial number's been filed down, by the way."

She handed him the clip and a small box of bullets.

"Where'd you get it?"

"Doesn't matter. What does matter is it's untraceable. Until we have the asshole who wired your car, you're in danger. Keep that close by and familiarize yourself with how to use it."

Chapter 48

LUCAS STOOD AT the picture window in the darkened living room and watched Wendy walk to her car. He wanted to blame her, to hold her responsible for their brief affair, but he knew that wasn't right.

When he called her after storming out of the house that evening, he secretly wanted her to suggest dinner.

He was attracted to her then and was attracted to her now. The difference was when he saw her, his guilt over bedding another woman when he was still legally married ate at him.

That was supposed to be Andy's sin, not his.

He watched Wendy get into the car and shut the door before he turned away from the window. Heavy fatigue settled into his body.

How long had it been since he really slept well?

Probably before Hong Kong. Now alone, restlessness replaced the dense fatigue of moments earlier, and he realized he might not be able to sleep even with an Ambien.

He turned in a slow circle, appreciating every piece of furniture, remembering how he and Laura had shopped for each one. His eyes misted over.

Shit.

He needed a drink.

Scotch rocks in hand, he slowly climbed the stairs to his small study. Turned off the lights and sat in the room staring out the window and listening to the breeze against the eves of the house.

The phone rang.

Lucas jumped, pressed his palm over his galloping heart, and drew a breath before he answered.

"Dr. McRae? Jimmy Wong. I hope this is not too late to return your call. My office said something about an emergency."

"No, no, not too late. Thanks for calling back."

He quickly explained what he wanted.

"I'll copy everything from all cameras immediately and overnight the DVDs."

After hanging up, Lucas thought about calling Wendy with the news but decided not to.

Instead, he decided to try sleeping despite being on the edge with the threat of Ditto.

What was worse, dying in his sleep from a bullet through his head, or going through another night of being awake with worry?

He chewed an Ambien, washed it down with a slug of scotch and went to bed, pretty sure he'd drugged himself enough to at least silence his brain for a few hours.

Lucas awoke three minutes after five the next morning.

Knowing he couldn't fall to sleep, he made a pot of coffee and killed the slowly passing minutes by pacing until seven. He called Josh to make sure he made it back to Walla Walla.

At the agreed upon time of eight, Lucas rang Trish's doorbell.

She answered the door barefoot in jeans and a sweatshirt, looking like she'd not slept well either.

She hugged him, then handed him a folded sheet of paper.

"Here is a notarized affidavit that I am Andy's legalized authorized representative. It should be all you need to have the doorman let you into his apartment." She looked away for a moment, then met his eyes. "I'm so sorry about Laura." She started to cry and said, "Please let me know what you find out about today."

Forty-five minutes later Lucas stood next to Wendy as the doorman stepped aside, allowing them access into Andy's condo.

The doorman said, "I'll leave you here. Be sure and lock the door as you leave."

They entered stale and musty air. The solid hallway door clicked shut behind them, sealing the room with heavy silence. A selling point had been how completely the double-paned glass shielded street noise. Andy had always loved how quiet the apartment was.

For a moment Lucas stood still, taking in the familiar surroundings. The one-bedroom condo had been done in contemporary masculine European design using copious black and stainless steel. And just like Lucas, Andy loved high-end electronics. The apartment had all the newest, high-end equipment.

Wendy sniffed the air, said, "Well, that settles one thing."

"Which is?"

"He's not in here decomposing."

"We already knew that last week. The doorman."

She glanced at him.

"Maybe you did. In a case like this, I always check for myself. The guy might not have even walked in here."

Maybe that's what made her a good cop. Likewise, he always looked at the actual MRI instead of simply accepting a dictated report.

"That's strange. There's no dust on any surfaces." She gestured at the living room area. "He use a cleaning service?"

"I'm sure he did. And probably once a week, knowing him."

"That explains the lack of dust." Wendy made a quick tour, opening bathroom and closet doors. When finished, she said, "You stay right here in the hall and don't touch anything. Or, if you want, you can help me search, but I don't want you off doing anything on your own. Understand?"

"Understand."

When she started for the bedroom, he went with her.

She said, "Look for anything that might help determine what happened to him. No matter how remote it seems."

"Like?"

"You'll know when you see it."

Lucas found it in the top drawer of the desk. For several seconds he held the slip of paper. Unlike the freshly cleaned surfaces around him, this scrap still had Andy's touch on it, and he realized this would be his very last contact with his old friend.

"Hey, found something."

Wendy stepped in.

"What?"

"Here," he said, handing it to her.

She studied it a moment. It was a receipt for a DVD rental at the porn shop where Lupita hung out waiting for customers.

"Yeah, you got it."

Chapter 49

WENDY PARKED THE Caprice between yellow parking stripes and set the hand brake. Before killing the engine, she cracked the windows, a habit developed in Moses Lake from having her dog ride with her almost everywhere.

"I want you to stay in the car while I do this."

Lucas said, "Oh, no. That wasn't the deal."

No way could he accompany her during an interview.

"Hey, there was no deal other than you could tag along to Andy's apartment. We're now in serious territory, and you're not coming."

He wasn't buying it.

"You can't do this to me."

"I'm not doing anything to you. I'm trying to conduct a clean investigation. Say we find something incriminating on DFH and Ditto's defense lawyer gets wind that a civilian was tagging along with me during the investigation. We run the risk of getting screwed on some legal technicality. Be satisfied you're getting this much. I'll let you know everything I find out. Okay?"

"No."

"It's not-negotiable."

Wendy headed for the porn shop's front door.

What a mess.

For starters, it was totally insane to be interested in a guy mourning his wife's death. To make matters worse, he was under active investigation. A murder investigation, for Christ's sake. She knew he wasn't guilty—no way he killed his wife—but still…

And if it turned out Andy Baer *was* somehow linked to Lupita's disappearance, it might become even stickier. As it was, if it hadn't been for that shark Davidson, she would've been forced to alibi Lucas out. Which would've meant Redwing knowing about her jumping in the sack with him. She couldn't afford that risk. In fact, if this lead turned up anything, she was unsure who to take it to. Probably Travis.

Five feet inside the door of the adult video store, Wendy held her badge up for everyone to see, raised her voice to the clerk still another fifteen feet away, "Seattle Police. Sir, I'd like a few words with you."

The little drama had the desired effect of clearing out all the customers.

Wendy leaned on a glass counter, a display case filled with various-sized dildos and cock rings.

She asked the clerk, "How long have you worked here?"

The skeletal man in his early thirties, wearing a black Harley-Davidson T-shirt and baggy shorts, started picking at something behind his right ear.

"I dunno, three years."

She handed a picture of Lupita Ruiz to him.

"Then you must know this woman, right?"

He squinted at it too long. He tried for a poker face but wasn't good enough. She saw a flicker of recognition in his eyes. He handed it back.

"Nope, never seen her."

"Real name's Lupita Ruiz. She probably used the street name Charmane when working this area. She's missing. We're trying to find out where she was before she went missing."

She tried to give the photo back to him.

"Can't help you, lady."

"Can't or won't?" She paused a beat. "I do Missing Persons, not Vice. I'm definitely not here to cause you any problems, but you force me to, I will."

He didn't blink.

Wendy said, "Here's the deal. You and I both know that she was soliciting here. You guys working the register got a cut of the action for not interfering. Hey, no skin off my nose."

The guy shrugged.

"I don't know what to tell you other than I don't know her."

With a sigh, Wendy pushed off the counter and slid the picture back in her purse.

"Well, then, guess you won't be all broken up if we keep a patrol car and a couple motorcycles in the parking lot for the next month or so. In case you haven't noticed, there's been a lot of speeding along this stretch. Chief wants to crack down on them. Thanks for your help."

She turned toward the door.

The guy scanned the empty store.

"Wait."

She stopped and turned to him.

"Yeah?"

"Okay, so I know her."

Wendy's pulse quickened.

"When did you see her last?" she asked.

"Fuck, I don't know. I sell porn and toys. I didn't make her fucking appointments."

"Chill, dude. Already said this isn't about you. Tell me this, she must've used a place close by. Have any idea where it might be?"

"I don't know, but you might want to check out that motel next door."

Wendy held up the head shots of Andy Baer from when he was booked.

"Know this guy?"

The guy stared at the pictures.

"Yeah, shit, seen him around once or twice."

"His name's Andy Baer. You keep a file of rentals, don't you?"

"Yeah. Assuming he used his real name. What I mean is, it shouldn't come as a big shock that a shitload of people use a false name renting videos. I couldn't care less. Unless, of course, they, like, don't return 'em."

"Take a look, see if he's on file."

The clerk shuffled to a counter on his right.

"How's that spelled, his last name?"

She told him; he typed.

"Well, what do you know? He's here, and he's even got a late charge on a DVD."

Wendy's pulse quickened more.

"When was it rented?"

He recited the date.

Christ!

The same date Lupita disappeared, and the day before Andy's car was impounded from the parking lot out front.

Chapter 50

THE MOTEL WAS a two-story L-shaped structure indistinguishable from a thousand others along highways from Seattle to Miami. Hick-brick exterior, flat tar roof, rusting wrought-iron rails, noisy air conditioners hanging out of walls, a cracked asphalt parking lot, a sign boasting cable TV. It'd seen better days.

So had the dishwater blonde who sauntered from the back room thirty seconds after Wendy punched the call bell.

The small, overheated office contained a scarred laminate counter, two vending machines, and an ice maker creating suspicious rumbles. A plasticized sign taped on the wall listed adult film rental rates. Lucas smelled disinfectant, maybe Lysol, and stale nicotine.

Handing the clerk the picture of Lupita, Wendy said, "Ever see her before?"

"Yup. Couple times."

"She rent the room?"

"Nope. The guys do that."

As if it was protocol.

"Same guy?" Wendy asked, unable to mask a note of hope in her voice.

For a moment the woman stared at Wendy with a you-gotta-be-kidding look, then shook her head.

"I want you to check, see if a man by the name Andy Baer ever rented a room."

Wendy told her the specific date and spelled the last name.

The woman opened a small file box and flipped through registration cards.

"I'll look, but even if he used his name, he most likely paid in cash."

She made it sound like Wendy didn't have a clue about how the sex business worked.

Lucas turned to Wendy and offered, "I'll bet he'd charge it if he stayed here. He was a nut about using his credit card to rack up airline mileage."

The woman gave a snort, then stopped, pulled out a card.

"Lookee here. You're right."

Wendy leaned over the counter to see the card.

"Which room?"

The clerk handed it over to her.

Wendy asked, "Is 201 occupied now? I need to look at it."

After checking, the clerk announced it was empty.

Before stepping into the room, Wendy warned Lucas.

"Don't touch a thing."

The room interior was even more depressing than the exterior. A queen-size bed with a queen-size sag in the center. An empty closet with two bare wire hangers dangling from an unpainted dowel. No ironing board, no safe. A small bathroom with rust-stained drains and cracked porcelain. At the foot of the bed, an ancient TV and DVD chained to a cheap laminate stand. The room smelled of mold and dust.

Wendy checked the DVD player, but Andy's delinquent movie wasn't there. She stood, mulling something over.

It'd been more than three weeks since Andy used the room. God knew what traffic had passed through here by now. Of course, Wendy could find out that information if she wanted, but the question wasn't if Andy had been here. She knew he had. He'd rented the DVD at 2:17 and checked into this motel at 2:31. His BMW was impounded from the rental store parking lot the next morning.

Wendy knew how Lupita had worked—scanning the patrons in the porn shop, then approaching them to go next door and watch what they rented, together. Because it was so convenient, most customers left their cars, as Andy must have done. When the car hadn't been moved by morning, the clerk had it towed.

Wendy turned to Lucas.

"Let's get out of here. We have a few more things to do."

Travis was waiting at the fountain by the time Wendy could ditch Lucas, drive over, park, and hike into the center. She sat next to him, glanced around to make sure no one was within listening range, then turned to face him so she could keep her voice down.

"The mortician I was telling you about—Ditto?"

"Yeah."

"I need a wire on his lines. Both cell and land, private and business. Here," she handed him the warrant she'd composed two days ago.

"I assume you're going through Internal Affairs because you don't want anyone on your team knowing about it?"

She smiled.

"Once we have it in place, I'll submit the same paperwork to Redwing."

He nodded.

"Gotcha. Might let us find the snitch, is what you're saying."

She patted his knee as she stood.

"I need it ASAP."

Chapter 51

HEADLIGHTS OFF, LEO Gerhard crept the black Chrysler along the street toward McRae's home. There were no pedestrians or traffic in this quiet residential neighborhood at this time of night. He suspected the occasional car was a lawyer or a doctor heading home after a long day at work.

How else could anyone afford fancy places like these?

Even if he had the money, he wouldn't live like this. Expensive homes cost a fucking fortune. They also meant huge responsibilities, like cutting the lawn, painting the siding, washing the windows—an endless list of jobs that sucked all the pleasure right out of life. Those chumps could have it. His present arrangement of living rent free at the mortuary was just fine for him.

He eased to the curb across from McRae's house and shifted the transmission into neutral, allowing the engine to idle. Only the upstairs master bedroom window remained lit. McRae's Volvo was parked at the curb; a large Dumpster overflowing with debris blocked the driveway. The neighboring homes were dark too, making the area feel almost deserted. A westerly wind whipped leaves on the trees and warned of an approaching rainstorm blowing in from the Pacific.

Gerhard eased off the brake and back onto the accelerator. After a block he curbed the car again, but this time killed the engine. He sat in darkness listening for unusual sounds and watching to make sure a late-night dog walker wasn't heading his way.

Satisfied, he stuffed a ski mask in his windbreaker pocket before slipping on latex exam gloves. He patted his left front pocket to make certain the small Bersa pistol was there. A beautiful weapon. Blue nickel, compact size, manufactured in Argentina. He'd found it in the purse of a strung-out black hooker a couple months ago. Just one more example of the contamination they'd removed from society.

He planned to simply put a round through McRae's mouth and out his head. No note. Just another depressed person electing to end his life without telling the world why. Not leaving a note was more common than people thought. And in McRae's case, who could question the timing? Here was a man either racked with guilt over killing his wife or consumed with sorrow over her death, depending on whether or not you believed he set the car bomb. Either way, suicide would seem logical.

Black jeans, black T-shirt, and black windbreaker concealed Gerhard easily in shadows as he moved soundlessly toward McRae's house. Reaching the Dumpster in the driveway, he found a place to settle in and watch the house yet still be hidden from anyone on the street. Sitting on cement, he nestled his back against cold metal and waited, hoping the rain wouldn't start before it was time to enter the house. This time he wouldn't fail.

Wendy Elliott eased the car to the curb three houses down from McRae's, killed the engine, and sat back in the seat.

Earlier in the day she'd approached Redwing with a request for a forensics team to examine the motel room. In building her case, she explained the details of how Lupita mined the adult video store for johns to take to the neighboring motel. But she also included several misleading pieces to the puzzle, and in a couple instances, purposely gave him false information.

Before talking with Redwing, Wendy phoned Travis and told him the entire story. After a verbal pat on the head and a thanks, he told her to keep at it and that they needed more.

Needed more?

Christ, the connection between Redwing and Ditto was now rock solid. What more did Travis need? Say Bobby Ditto offs a hooker and someone reports her missing. With Redwing in charge of the Missing Persons unit, he could make sure that the report on one of Ditto's victims never surfaced. And if a relative made noise about the case, Redwing could take charge of the investigation himself. There are a hundred ways to make an investigation yield nothing. Besides, a good number of missing persons turn out to be runaways who *want* to be missing.

Where the hell do they go?

A few—usually women—end up as skeletons, murder victims. Another sizeable number just vanish. What if some of those ended up at DFH?

Who would know?

No one. It was a perfect system. Unless they killed the wrong person.

Why couldn't Travis see how logical her deductions were?

She yawned. Stupid to not have picked up some coffee.

She yawned and yawned again—they always seemed to come in threes with her. She adjusted the seat to give her a bit more leg room and a better incline to make sitting more comfortable. Glanced around at the quiet darkened residential street with nice yards and homes. Not particularly affluent, but well maintained. She yawned the final time and let her heavy lids close.

Nothing going on right at the moment, so would it hurt to close her eyes for a few seconds?

Lucas couldn't relax, couldn't stop thinking about this mess his life was in, much less sleep. He clicked on the lamp and picked up a novel. By the end of the page, he realized nothing made sense. He started again at the top of the page but got the same result. He put the book back and started pacing.

Maybe a drink would relax him. Go downstairs and mix a martini? A scotch? Yeah, that sounded good.

Only a small one, just enough to take the edge off his anxiety, then come back up and check the email to see if Wong's shipping information was there.

He stood, eyed the gun on the table next to him.

Until now, the idea of aiming a loaded weapon at someone with the intent of pulling the trigger wasn't in him.

Things change.

Now he believed beyond any doubt that if he came face-to-face with the bastard who killed Laura, he could do it. But there was no need to take the gun for a simple trip downstairs to pour a glass of scotch. Leaving the pistol next to the computer, he walked out the bedroom door.

The kitchen lights flashed on.

Gerhard immediately tensed, afraid of being caught in the light from the window, but then realized McRae would be looking from light to dark, making it impossible to see him. Especially since the Dumpster shielded him from the streetlights.

The charred door between the garage and kitchen had been hastily replaced with one large sheet of plywood, so McRae couldn't come out that way and surprise him.

More relaxed now, he settled in again to wait.

Smiling, Lucas sat at the desk reading Wong's email that came in while he was downstairs.

Wong had shipped the DVDs via DHL to his home address with a scheduled delivery time between eleven and noon the next day. Maybe knowing they would be here in less than sixteen hours would help to reduce the anxiety eating away at him.

He upended the scotch and shut down the laptop, picked up

the gun and moved to the easy chair next to the window.

Gerhard saw the upstairs window go dark and checked his watch.
On average, a person took twenty minutes to fall asleep.

In this case he'd be conservative and allow McRae at least
thirty minutes before entering the house.

Chapter 52

GERHARD SLID THE key into the front door lock and rotated it until it caught and clicked. He paused to listen for any response inside. Every second out here on the porch risked notice by a neighbor, in spite of it being so late. On the other hand, he needed to be cautious and avoid making any noise that might wake McRae. He couldn't afford to leave signs of a struggle.

He heard no sounds from inside.

Then he was through the door, leaving it ajar an inch in case he needed to escape in a hurry. He didn't expect that, but you never knew. Better to be prepared than not.

At the bottom of the stairs to the second floor, he again listened for a any movement but heard only the hum of a fan. He placed his right foot on the first stair and slowly applied weight.

The scotch didn't do much more than round off the edges of Lucas's anxiety. He considered going downstairs for another, but he didn't want his senses blunted, just in case. Again he looked at the gun in his hand. Never before had he kept a firearm in the house. He didn't like it. The sight of it fueled more anxiety in his gut. He feared pistols, having seen too many fatal accidents roll through the ER year after year. He made sure the barrel pointed away from him toward the wall.

Something creaked.

Jesus, what was that?

Sitting up, head cocked, he concentrated on the stillness in the house.

Had he imagined it?

He started to reach for the lamp but thought better of it. Slowly he stood up, not wanting to cause a sound.

Heart hammering his chest, he gripped the gun tighter and listened hard.

Another creak.

Someone was coming up the stairs. It was a sound so familiar it wasn't easily mistaken.

With the gun in his right hand, Lucas reached the door in five strides. He took hold of the doorknob with his left hand, thumbed off the safety, slowly turned the knob.

Wendy awoke, realized she'd nodded off.

How long?

Couldn't say for sure because she hadn't noted the time earlier. She glanced around, but things looked exactly like they had before she nodded off.

Go home and get a good night's sleep?

Hmmm...might be a worthwhile idea.

Or perhaps go search for a coffee shop that was open and come back with a supply of caffeine.

As Gerhard put weight on the second step it creaked.

Fuck! Sounded like a megaton nuclear blast.

One hand on the railing, he stared intently up the darkened stairwell, waiting for any sign of movement.

From somewhere above came a muffled click, like a door latch opening. He aimed the gun at the top of the stairs where someone might stand, his finger on the trigger, ready to fire in case McRae turned on the light and blinded him.

If so, the gun would already be aimed at where he'd be standing.

Lucas peered through the crack between the door and jamb, into the dim outlines in the hall.

There wasn't much detail to be seen in what little streetlight filtered through the windows.

It was more like he *knew* where borders and spaces should be and was scanning for something out of place.

Everything appeared normal. No shadows moved.

More confident now, he widened the opening enough to squeeze his body into the hall while keeping his back against the wall.

He stopped, listening for any faint sound but heard only the hammering of his heart, his mouth bone dry. He squeezed the pistol grip tighter and moved his finger from the guard to the trigger.

Creak.

This time Lucas was certain the sound was the stairs.

One more long step and he was positioned so that if he leaned forward, he could see down the stairs to the front hall. A second later he recognized a shadow that shouldn't be there. Another second, and he knew a person was crouching on the stairs.

Gerhard shifted weight, raised his left foot and planted it on the next stair. The closer he was, the less likely to miss was that really someone up there, or was his mind fucking with him? Aiming at the same spot as a moment ago, he moved up one more step, his finger tightening on the trigger.

Something was really there—it was not just his imagination. Lucas aimed the gun and started to squeeze the trigger.

The form at the bottom of the stairs spun around and started down.

Lucas squeezed off a round, the explosion deafening him. The form vanished.

Suddenly Wendy was wide awake, aware a shot was just fired, and rolled out the door, moving fast, Glock in hand. Up ahead, the McRae house. She saw the door open. A figure ran out.

"Freeze, police!"

The figure—a man?—turned and raised an arm. She saw a muzzle flash, heard the detonation, dropped flat on the parking strip, rolled to her left, went prone, and raised the Glock, the front sight dot glowing in the darkness. No figure now, no sounds other than her rapid breathing. She squinted at the shadows along the hedge forming the south border of McRae's property. Nothing but shadows.

"Wendy?"

She glanced at McRae's house, saw a figure in the doorway. Felt a rush of relief. He hadn't been shot.

She yelled, "Stay inside."

Gerhard flew out the door, partially blinded by the muzzle flash. Fucking bastard, opening fire like that.

He heard, "Freeze, police!" and squeezed off a shot in the general direction of the sound. The voice came from his left, so he cut right, into a tightly spaced row of cypress trees. Stopped, dropped into a crouch facing toward where the voice had come.

No movement. No further shouted orders.

Good, the dancing sun in the center of his eyes was quickly dissolving.

Thankfully, he knew the neighborhood from prior recon.

Silently, gun at the ready, he took one step backward, then turned and bolted for the alley.

Sensing movement along the hedge, Wendy pushed up and started moving, yelling to Lucas, "Go inside, call 911."

She reached the side of the house and stopped to peek around the edge in time to see a large form silhouetted in the alley streetlight vault a low fence, running left.

She went full out toward the fence, used a recycle bin to propel herself over, and dropped into a crouch, both hands aiming the Glock at the empty and silent asphalt with two puddles reflecting the weak fluorescent light of the streetlamps.

She heard only silence.

Staying in the shadows as much as possible, she moved from one garbage can to the other, leapfrogging, afraid of walking into an ambush. Up ahead, at the end of an alley, she spotted an open garage, totally black inside.

No way she could get past it without setting herself up to be blown away.

If she were Gerhard, that's where she'd make a stand.

Gerhard cleared the fence, hit the alley, flamed the afterburners, running flat out, not bothering to glance back on account of what had slowed him. Besides, anyone firing on the run would have to be fucking lucky to hit him. Best thing was to put as much fucking distance between them as possible. Reached the end, cut right, continued flat out for a block, then cut left, circling back to where he'd parked the car. Lucky to not have parked on McRae's street.

Four blocks later he reached the unlocked car, jumped in, and was turning out into the sleepy residential street when he made out the first faint siren in the distance. Slowly, he drove back toward the city.

By the time Travis walked out McRae's front door, it was after 4 AM. Travis hadn't asked where Lucas got the gun or even if he had a permit. Instead, he just gave Wendy a funny look like he *knew*.

With the house cleared of everyone but Wendy, Lucas wanted to try to sleep, if only for a few hours. After double-checking to make sure the front dead bolt was securely engaged—for all the good that did—he told Wendy he was heading back upstairs. She said she'd spend the rest of the night on the couch. She doubted whoever that was would be back but didn't want to take the risk.

Lucas told her about Wong's email and said, "I checked the confirmation number a couple hours ago. Delivery is scheduled sometime between ten and noon. That's less than eight hours away at the max."

She nodded.

"Well, that'll settle one thing. It's either Andy or not. Either way, it'll be a relief to finally sort that out."

Chapter 53

THE VIDEO OF Lucas's and the three groups of four surgeon dissections—from all three cameras over each of the tables—filled six DVDs. Wong intended to edit them to about one hour of key segments but hadn't started yet. Wong sent copies of the initial hour from each camera with each DVD clearly labeled by a black Sharpie: overhead camera 1, right side 1, etc. The number indicated which of the tables the cameras were covering.

Lucas chose the disc from the overhead camera.

"This would be the closest approximation of my view when I first uncovered the head."

A fresh wave of anxiety swept through his chest.

"Well?" Wendy asked.

Shit, he'd been just sitting there holding the disc like an idiot.

He decided to watch it in the family room instead of on his computer. The TV screen was larger, and the high definition should give good detail.

He motioned toward the other room.

"Let's go in here."

He placed the DVD in the tray and watched the machine swallow it. For several seconds the player spun, figuring out the proper format, before the screen lit up. Instead of the image he expected, a menu appeared below the title: Transoral Approach to the Clivus. They waited, watching the DVD counter increment. Finally, the actual video started, showing the surgical towel exactly as he remembered.

From the TV speakers he heard his voice say, "The first demonstration will be the anterior approach to the Clivus."

The knot in his stomach tightened.

His voice on the disc continued with, "We start the incision here."

He looked down, unwilling to watch the towel slide away from masking the head beneath it, realized what he was doing and forced his gaze to the screen.

His hand entered the picture and took hold of the towel and pulled it away.

And there was the head, on his left side, hair clipped to the scalp, the skin color distorted from the lack of oxygenated blood.

He gasped.

Then froze the image.

For a moment he and Wendy sat side by side staring at the image on the screen, neither one speaking.

Finally, Wendy asked, "What are you thinking?"

The moments in Hong Kong came flooding back: the initial shock, the stunned moment of recognition, the turning away to vomit uncontrollably.

"Lucas?"

He realized he was looking away, his mind racing back through the good times he and Andy shared. He turned to her.

"It's him."

"You sure?"

He didn't want to look again at the head, but between this initial glance and the one in Hong Kong, he was sure.

Well, pretty sure.

The color was...

"Yes."

"How can you be sure? The other day you said that no blood

distorted it when you saw it in Hong Kong."

"It does, but it's him." He thought about what he just said and added, "We can have Trish look at this too and give her opinion."

Looking at the picture of the detached, lifeless head, Wendy said, "I'd rather not have to resort to that." Wendy seemed to mull things over a moment. "You said something about a scar?"

Of course!

I should've thought of it before.

"Yeah, there is. Andy had chronic middle ear infections as a kid that resulted in mastoiditis. He had to have his mastoid sinus cleaned out. There's a scar behind his right ear. The first thing I had them do was disarticulate the jaw, so we should be able to see it." He glanced at the pile of DVDs and picked one at random.

"Wong exchanged Andy with another table. The one I ended up was a female. We need to find the one disc with a female, and that will be the one that ended up with Andy."

He slid the new disc into the player and set the old one by itself to keep them straight. They watched the beginning, saw another, unfamiliar male and popped out the disc. He inserted the next one, hit play.

Suddenly, Wendy gripped his arm painfully tight.

"Hey, ease up," Lucas said.

He reached over to move her hand, but Wendy was staring at the TV with all color drained from her face. He looked from Wendy to the screen and realized the view was panned in on the female head.

"What's wrong?"

"That's Lupita."

Chapter 54

"NOW YOU HAVE it," Lucas said to Wendy. "Proof Andy's head was in Hong Kong. Along with Lupita's. It also proves Ditto's organization supplied both heads. Doesn't that give you enough to bring Ditto down?"

"Not yet, it doesn't."

Lucas's chest tightened as both firsts clenched.

His suspicions were right. He'd been right all along, but what good had it done?

"Why not?"

Wendy said, "Can you prove the DVDs haven't been altered? Or where they've been and who's had them since they were recorded?"

Lucas didn't answer even though it was ridiculous to think Wong had altered them in some way. But he saw the problem she pointed out. Any defense attorney would be all over that argument.

He muttered, "Shit."

Wendy said, "We need something better."

She sounded like she had the answer to that.

"Like?"

Wendy stood, started putting on her coat.

"Ditto's records. I'll work on getting a warrant."

Lucas gave a sarcastic snort.

"You really think that if he's dealing in supplying murder victims, that he's really going to have accurate records?"

She gave him a weird smile.

"Something like that."

Then she was gone.

Wendy was waiting at the Seattle Center Fountain when Travis ambled over and sat down beside her.

He asked, "What you got?"

She explained that the DVDs from Hong Kong provided visual identification of Andy Baer and Lupita Ruiz's head.

"Those DVDs should give me probable cause for a search warrant specifically for Ditto's records—the death certificates and where they were obtained—for the specimens used in the Hong Kong demonstration."

Travis nodded.

"That may help you in the missing persons cases—although that remains to be seen—but how does it help in your primary case?"

"I'm thinking we can make this become a two-for. That's the whole point of this discussion. I want Internal Affairs involved but totally suppressed until we have enough to bring Ditto *and* Redwing down. That means only you, I, and the judge know what's really going on."

Travis thought about it for a moment.

"We need to be damned careful how we go about it. How soon do you need the warrant?"

"Soon as possible."

"Give me a moment to call Judge Walker, see if she's available to see us. She's the one who signed the warrant on Ditto's wire. You have the affidavit written out?"

"I do."

Travis pulled out his cell phone and dialed.

Later that afternoon Wendy sat down across the desk from Redwing, said, "Got a break in the Ruiz case."

A hint of surprise flashed across his face but only momentarily.

"What? I thought you were supposed to be working some other cases."

She told him about the DVDs and the identification of Lupita Ruiz and Andy Baer as probably cause for a search warrant, specifically for Ditto's records for the specimens used in Hong Kong and also for a wire on Ditto's phones. What surprised Wendy was that after the initial surprise, Redwing didn't hesitate.

Redwing asked, "You have the papers prepared?"

"Yes."

"Then I'll approve it, but I don't think we can get a judge to sign off on this for another three days or so."

Wendy shook her head.

"I already have one available and ready to sign off. Judge Walker."

Redwing didn't seem happy to hear that but agreed to move ahead with obtaining the warrant.

Chapter 55

"WHAT IS IT this time, Detective?"

Ditto stood next to the reception desk, the matronly receptionist busy at a computer monitor, as if this little drama weren't happening.

Wendy handed him the warrant.

"I want copies of the death certificates and all related paperwork for the four heads that were used in Hong Kong during the date in question."

He smirked.

"It would be my pleasure. Follow me."

He led her to his office, sat down at the computer.

Before he could even type a command, Wendy said, "Not electronically. I want to see the actual paper."

Ditto smiled.

"No problem."

Wendy didn't return the smile, just waited and watched, her mind sorting through the various scenarios that might be playing out. Ditto didn't seem rattled at all, which could mean one of two things: he'd been tipped that the warrant was coming and switched papers. The second option was that she was completely wrong about his involvement in the missing women. She watched him at the filing cabinet, going through a drawer of hanging folders. He withdrew one and handed it to her.

"It's all here. Should I have copies made for you, or do you wish to inspect them here?"

Wendy sat down and flipped through the file. Four death certificates. Four TSA and customs forms. The dates were correct. The seals looked valid. But the names on the death certificates did not include Lupita Ruiz or Andy Baer. Interestingly, the donors' names were not required on the TSA or customs forms.

Now what?

For several seconds she was frozen in place, her mind spinning.

Well, shit, anything can be faked. She'd validate the death certificates with the Department of Records.

Wendy stood, said, "Copies of all four death certificates would be very helpful."

Ditto held out his hand.

"It will only take a minute. You may wait here."

She didn't hand the folder over.

"I'll go with you."

"Not a problem."

Wendy followed him into another room with a large copier.

"Here you go." Ditto gave Wendy copies of the four death certificates. "I hope this satisfies you. But I must advise you that any future conversations will be handled by my attorney. In addition, should you persist in these personal attacks against my integrity, you can expect to be sued for slander."

The smug son of a bitch.

Wendy felt her face burn with anger.

Ditto added, "I don't understand why you don't like me, but obviously this crusade of yours has become personal. What exactly have I done to provoke this?"

Without answering, she turned and walked out.

Wendy opened the car door, threw the copies at Lucas before sliding into the driver's seat, and slammed the door. She jabbed a finger at him.

"Not a goddamn word. Let me cool off first."

Then she fired the ignition.

Lucas asked, "You okay to drive?"

Glaring, she spun around.

"What'd I just say? Not a goddamned word."

Lucas picked up the scattered sheets of paper and shuffled through them. Death certificates. He looked for Andy's name but didn't see it. Nor did he see Lupita's name. There were, however, two males and two females. The females' ages were listed as forty-five and forty-nine. But there was no way the woman he saw in Hong Kong was over thirty-five.

"There must be some mistake," was all he could say.

"Only mistake I made was not shooting that smug, arrogant son of a bitch."

Wendy flipped a toggle to trigger blue flashers hidden behind the car grille. A siren screamed as she accelerated.

Lucas saw cars ahead pull to the side of the road.

"Where are we going?"

"To check the death certificates. All four are listed as King County deaths. I plan to cross-check every goddamned one."

"The Department of Records?"

"Damned straight. If we can get there before the office closes."

Chapter 56—King County Department of Records

WENDY AND LUCAS sat side by side on hard oak chairs in front of a heavily smudged computer screen as Wendy typed in the password that would give them access to the electronic copies of the four death certificates.

The search field opened.

"Okay, give me the first name," she said.

She entered it as he recited it. The she asked for the date of death. Once these fields were filled in, she hit enter.

A moment later a copy of the death certificate popped up. Field by field, they cross-checked the information.

Everything matched.

All four certificates exactly matched those on file with King County.

Wendy sat back and shook her head. "They're all valid death certificates."

Lucas said, "But they're just not the right ones for at least two people; Andy and Lupita."

"Right. There's just no way to prove that."

Downtown Seattle

Luis Ruiz pointed at Wendy.

"You said yourself he saw them in Hong Kong. No fucking way it's not them." He pointed at Lucas. "Fuck, you saw them on the video, right? His friend. Lupita. Saw them both."

Ruiz wore a glitter print hoodie over a red Chicago Bulls T-shirt, black Pelle Pelle jeans with legs bunched up over multicolor Adidas sneakers, and a gold chain fat enough to rig an 18-wheeler.

Wendy, Lucas, and Ruiz stood in an asphalt parking lot next to the alley that ran the length of the block, one of the few remaining downtown lots not yet converted into high-rise condominiums. Small, just a half block in depth. The Alaskan Way Viaduct sliced under First Avenue to the north, cars shooting past into the Battery Street Tunnel. Rhythmic thumps vibrated through the wall of a hip-hop nightclub to the south. The alley door opened, casting a rectangle of yellow light into the alley as the music suddenly grew louder. Ruiz turned to look. The door closed again.

Ruiz's two homies stood guard ten feet to either side of him, one watching the alley, the other with his eye on the street. The stink of urine and rotting garbage from the Dumpsters grew stronger, then eased each time the breeze picked up.

Wendy said, "I'm sorry I had to tell you she's dead."

"Fuck!"

She could hear the emotion in his voice. The two homies shifted weight uneasily and looked around as if embarrassed by it.

Ruiz said, "Tell me again what Ditto looked like when you asked him for the death certificates."

On the drive here she debated how much to disclose.

"He wasn't surprised. He knew I was going to ask for it."

"You mean, like, he has a source in the police department?"

"Obviously."

Ruiz seemed to think that over, his rage barely contained.

"Tell me again how we know those death certificates are

real?"

"We checked."

"Checked what? What's to say the motherfucker's not filling out counterfeit certificates? Man can put any name he wants on them. Yours, mine, his."

He pointed again at Lucas.

Wendy motioned for him to cool down.

"Let me finish. See, that's the thing. They *are* legit. All four of them. Each death was recorded here in the county. We checked the Department of Records. We put the certificates side by side and compared every damned detail. They're exactly the same. What I'm telling you is, Ditto gave us copies of legitimate records."

"You're not listening, bitch. What I'm asking is, okay, sure those records may be copies, but how do you know for a fact those names are for people who died?"

Wendy lowered her voice, hoping maybe Ruiz would take the hint and pipe down too.

"That's what I'm trying to tell you. We checked. We looked up relatives for each one of those deaths and called them and verified the name of the person on the death certificate. And we got the same answer every time. They're dead. Every damned one of them is dead. What's more, all four died within the past couple months from legitimate causes. There is no way we can say those records aren't legitimate. They are."

Ruiz walked a tight circle, pounding his palm with a fist. He stopped, glared at her.

"If that's true, how do you explain my sister showing up in Hong Kong?"

Wendy shrugged.

"Same thing you're thinking. The records lie. The records he showed us are legitimate, but they aren't the records for the people in Hong Kong. That's the only way it works. And it's exactly what you're thinking."

"Well, then fucking do something about it. Don't come tell

me the investigation's dead. Do your fucking job."

"Believe me, I'm on it."

"The fuck you are!"

It occurred to Lucas that maybe Wendy was trying to provoke Ruiz into doing something. Like maybe putting a .38 hollow point between Ditto's eyes.

Shit, he and Wendy both knew Ditto was involved in covering up Andy and Lupita's deaths. They just couldn't prove it.

So maybe Wendy was trying for her own brand of justice. And it probably wasn't the first time a cop assumed the role of judge and jury. The way Lucas felt about Ditto, it was justified.

"I'm open to suggestions," Wendy replied.

Ruiz fumed, shuffling his garish Adidas and kicking a discarded 40-ounce Coors can, spinning it under a tricked-out Hondo Civic.

"Fuck, man, you got the video. That's worth something."

"Yeah? Like what?"

"It shows the motherfucker's lying."

Wendy shook her head.

"Tell me something I don't know. Every one of us standing here knows that. That's not the problem. The problem is proving it. Sure, we can all look at the video and sign affidavits that two of the four specimens are from Lupita and Andy, but Ditto has the death certificates and paperwork for specimens that his man took through customs both here and in Hong Kong. Meaning, if it comes down to his word against ours, who will they believe? Him."

"But——" Ruiz started.

She cut him off.

"Then there's the issue of chain of evidence. More precisely, there is *no* chain of evidence. Any defense lawyer would blow that piece of evidence right out of the water. And before you ask, I already spoke with the prosecuting DA about it. When I described the situation, she laughed and shook her head, said, 'This is the digital age. You ought to know that. Anything can be morphed. Even a video. You can make anyone look like anyone you want.' She wouldn't even consider it sufficient evidence to have Andy declared legally dead."

Ruiz kicked at the ground.

Wendy said, "Then there's the whole other issue. To go after Ditto, I need to have a crime. What are we claiming Ditto's guilty of? Lying? We have no evidence of murder."

Ruiz fisted his palm again.

"Fuck!"

Wendy glanced at Lucas, like she wanted him to say something supportive.

But what was there to say? Besides, he was trying to control his own rage at Ditto. For all the good that would do. Christ, talk about being impotent and useless.

Lucas said to Ruiz, "I feel your pain. I feel the same way. This isn't over yet."

But in his heart, he knew there was nothing left to do.

It was over.

Chapter 57

LUCAS COULDN'T SLEEP.

An hour earlier, he'd given up trying and resigned himself to a night of tossing and turning until it was obvious there weren't enough hours left to make sleep worthwhile even if it did come. At which point, he rolled out of bed and brewed a pot of coffee.

Insomnia happened occasionally the nights before an extremely difficult case. He'd lie in bed mentally working through the surgery, trying to anticipate each move, along with problems that could arise. The approach, the dissection plane, the three-dimensional configuration of the tumor, the location of vital structures in relation to where his instruments were. If his patients even had an inkling of how sleep-deprived he sometimes was by the start of their surgery, they'd be horrified.

All night he ruminated on Ditto and how he had gotten away with murder. Maybe Ditto didn't actually kill Andy and Lupita, but he certainly had disposed of their bodies in spite of what the records showed.

How did Ditto do that?

After pouring a cup of black coffee, he trudged to his study, and dropped heavily into the desk chair. On a pad of yellow legal paper, he jotted down every fact he could dredge from memory about DFH and Ditto. Every word Gerhard had said, as well as other bits of information from Wendy and her visit with the anatomy professor at the med school.

As he worked, an idea niggled at him. It didn't come from anything one person had said, rather, it formed from an amalgamation of facts that coalesced into one thought.

Holy shit!

For a stunned moment he sat and wondered how he'd missed it. Excited, he reached for the phone.

"Wendy. Lucas."

He paced the second-floor hall, phone right against his ear, thinking through how Ditto might have worked it.

Even coming right out of sleep, she sounded concerned.

"What's wrong?"

"I've been thinking." He realized it was past two in the morning. "Sorry to wake you," he said, returning to the desk with the pad of legal paper in front of him. "But remember the conversation you had with the professor at the UW?"

"Boynton. Yeah. What about him?"

"Didn't he say something about wondering how Ditto could get enough material to meet demand?"

"He did. That's one of the first things that got me interested in him. Ditto, I mean."

"Did he say they have so much trouble meeting their own needs, they sometimes are forced to buy bodies from Ditto?"

"He did."

"How does Ditto do it?"

"You woke me up to ask that? The only way he can do it is to produce his own bodies. As in kill people. For Christ's sake, that's what we're trying to prove. Where are you going with this?"

"The thing that keeps sticking in my mind is that. Ditto's too successful. Doesn't Boynton claim he's shipping more cadavers and body parts than this region can reasonably support?"

"Yes, but if you believe Ditto, he's getting material from as far away as Portland, Spokane, and Vancouver. Who's to say that isn't enough population? Maybe, maybe not. Besides, when you ask others about Boynton's claims, they argue that Boynton isn't as aggressive as Ditto. Also, Ditto is running his funeral business. There can be several explanations why he could be doing better than Boynton."

"Maybe it's all in the accounting."

"What are you talking about?"

"We know he substitutes bodies. Has to be. How else can he have legitimate death certificates for people who don't match the actual corpse? Andy and Lupita couldn't be the only ones. I think we can prove it."

She was silent a moment.

"How?"

"A formal audit. Look at the numbers. I bet if you total up everything, you'll find more bodies going out than coming in."

Wendy didn't say a word.

Lucas waited.

Finally, she said, "*We know* that. Or maybe I should say we *suspect* that. The problem is there's no way to force an audit without probably cause. Give it up."

"Bear with me. How many unclaimed bodies you think turn up every year?"

"Lucas, that's one of the first things I checked. Unclaimed bodies go straight to the ME's office. They're cremated, and then they're disposed of in a common grave every quarter. And the ME's office is so totally inflexible about that policy, they redefine the term tight ass. Besides, by the time an unclaimed stiff's ready to be disposed of, it's way past being of any use to Ditto's body part business. So you can forget about the ME as his source."

"Right, so he's not getting bodies from them, but what if he's getting their paperwork? Get it? If a body's unclaimed, what's to keep the name on the death certificate from appearing on Ditto's records? It could be an extra valid death certificate and one would know the difference. In addition, since some of these people don't have an identified next of kin, he could use the name and death certificate numerous times without anyone knowing."

To make sure she got it, he said, "It's an old accounting trick. Double entries. And it would work. Think about it. He kills four people and has four more who die of normal means but are sent to his funeral home for cremation or burial. He's got eight bodies and four legitimate death certificates. He gives one death certificate to one of the ones he killed. If we check it, we'll find it's legit. The only way anyone would find out that he's making double entries is if someone cross-checked the names on the ME's records against those at DFH to see if any are the same. Or if they did an audit to show he's supplying more bodies and parts than actual come in. If he weren't in the body parts business, there'd be no way to tell. No one has ever had cause to audit him, so it's just about perfect."

Several seconds of silence ticked by.

"Goddamn it, you're right. That could work. But only if someone in the coroner's office is giving Ditto copies of death certificates. Holy shit."

Chapter 58

WENDY SAID TO Travis Hunt, "Lupita worked the same area around the porn shop, the same place Andy rented the video. He rented a room at the motel next door the same day Lupita went missing and the same evening Ditto's Suburban is seen in an alley on the next block. The day after, Andy's car is impounded from the porn shop parking lot. Then both heads show up in Hong Kong supplied by Ditto's company. Even though that video can't be used as evidence, it can be used to verify my story."

Wendy glanced over at Lucas to see if he wanted to add something at this point. When he didn't, she went on and continued to explain Lucas's theory of fixing the DFH records.

"See how it works? Say Ditto needs four bodies for a demonstration, and he doesn't have them. He goes out, finds people who won't be missed, and kills them. Now he has the bodies, but he still needs the death certificates. He contacts his accomplice at the ME's office, and that person supplies him with enough death certificates. He can't reuse old ones because the approximate dates would be wrong if anyone ever checked."

"Why are you telling me this?" Travis asked in a hushed voice.

She, Lucas, and Travis sat at a window table purposely

remote from other early morning customers in a funky twenty-four-hour café smelling of steam and fryer grease. Wendy sat next to Lucas with Travis facing them on the other side, Travis's body language saying he was frustrated with the request. She knew why, but had to go through with it to make sure Lucas knew she was pushing the case.

Lucas picked up the menu wedged between a red Heinz bottle and a stainless-steel napkin holder and appeared to read it, leaving Wendy to answer.

She said, "C'mon, Travis, it should be obvious. I can't go to Redwing with this. I want a warrant to run a list of the names of unclaimed bodies the ME has disposed of in the last six months against the names of bodies Ditto claims were donated. I want to look for matches and for duplicates. Simple enough. What's the problem?"

"The problem? You got several. For one thing, we don't have probable cause. For another, assuming we were granted the warrant, the moment we ask Ditto for his records, he and his lawyer will know you're behind this and file another complaint against the department for harassment. By the time we sort things out, who knows what might happen to those records."

Silence.

Wendy remembered she forgot to emphasize what keyed her to Ditto and DFH in the first place.

"How about this for probable cause? Ditto's Suburban was in the alley behind the motel where Lupita was last seen."

"Got proof of that?" Travis challenged.

Wendy said, "Haven't you heard me? The vehicle was called in. It's on record. What more do you want?"

"No, not that part," Travis said. "The part about where Lupita was last seen. Unless you're withholding something, all we know is she disappeared *sometime* that evening. *Maybe.* No one has an exact time or an exact place. Sure, she worked the area, but can you prove she was there at the same time Ditto's vehicle was spotted?" He paused briefly, and said, "Every damned bit of your evidence is circumstantial. You say it was Baer's head in Hong Kong. You say—"

"But it was," Lucas jumped in, apparently unable to tolerate the legal jostling any longer. "The scar proves it. Hell, ask Trish, his boss, or any number of people who knew him to look at the video. They'll verify it."

Travis waved that away.

"We've been over that. The video is worthless as evidence."

Wendy glanced at Lucas, saw him doing a slow burn but said nothing.

What could she say?

She couldn't explain the other ongoing investigation.

Travis said to Lucas, "Let's get something straight. For what it's worth, I believe you. The problem is getting a judge to buy your story now that Ditto claims harassment." Travis looked from Lucas to Wendy. "Understand what I'm telling you?"

Wendy nodded, but Lucas remained stony still. Travis pushed his chair back from the table and stood. For a moment he stared at Wendy, communicating a silent message that only a partner would understand.

Finally, he said, "Here's what I'll do, I'll make a few inquiries and try to massage this through a back channel. But if it comes back no deal, you'll be okay with it?"

"As long as I know you gave it a try."

Travis pulled a key ring from his pocket, started sorting through the keys.

"Keeping Redwing out of the loop makes it tricky." Travis picked out what looked like a car key. "Metz is the only judge I feel safe going to. But last I heard he's out of town until the end of next week. You all right with waiting that long?"

Wendy understood he was stalling.

"I have a choice?"

He grinned.

"No, but I thought I'd ask."

Wendy nodded again.

"I owe you one. Thanks."

Travis' grin widened.

"Actually, this makes us even."

Frustrated, Lucas watched Hunt leave.

Wait a week, ten days? Way too long.

By then Ditto would know about the warrant and would either alter the records or destroy them in an office fire or maybe an explosion like the one that killed Laura.

Wendy was studying him.

"What?"

"Even if Travis gets a warrant, we can't wait that long. You know damned well Ditto will do something to cover his ass."

"I'm not thrilled about it, either, but you must admit it's better than nothing. You just need to hang in there and trust me on this."

"Bullshit. You guys have a leak in the department, and you don't even have a clue who it is. Ditto's going to find out."

Lucas started for the door, thinking of ways to get what they needed before Ditto could react. He had to do something other than stand by and watch the man who'd murdered Laura and Andy go free.

"Lucas," Wendy called as he walked out the door. "Lucas!"

Seething, he stopped, turned to face her.

"What?"

Her face was etched in worry.

"Just what the fuck you think you're doing?"

What was there to say? Nothing.

She was a cop and her priority was to work within the system. But the situation was way beyond that now. Bobby Ditto had to be destroyed, no matter what it took.

"I'm leaving."

"You think I'm blind? You're planning something that has a good chance of landing you in deep shit. I don't want to see that happen."

"Are we done here?"

"No. That gun I loaned you. Where is it?"

"At the house."

"I want it back."

"This minute?"

"Damned right. The way you're acting, you're on the verge of a classic fuckup. I don't want to deal with the paperwork if you do. We're driving over to your house now."

Chapter 59

LUCAS PULLED THE letter from the printer, sat back to read it one last time. It would serve as a last will and testament if things went south tonight. It also explained the reasons for the actions he was about to commit. And if things worked out the way he hoped, then no harm, no foul. Destroying the letter would be the first thing he did upon returning home.

If he made it.

He resisted the strong urge to call Josh. Just to hear his son's voice one last time and tell him he loved him. But Josh would become suspicious and start probing, so it was best to just put the note on the kitchen table where Josh could easily find it.

Reading his words filled him with regrets. For not being a better husband. For not telling Laura more often that he loved her. For not being a more attentive father. For not trying harder to convince Andy to stick with therapy. For a thousand little things in his life that he could have done differently.

Lucas positioned the letter on the kitchen table and weighed it in place with a saltshaker. After one final look around the house, he walked out the front door to his car.

He sat behind his steering wheel mentally reviewing the plan. This morning, as soon as Wendy drove off with the gun, he'd phoned a pathologist friend who had connections with the coroner's office. The friend had been able to obtain a list of all unclaimed bodies processed through the ME's office during the past six months. People who died without family or spouse to dispose of them properly. The list was now folded and in his pocket.

Obtaining the list was the easy part. Getting access to Ditto's files required a hell of a lot more thought. He needed help. No doubt about it. And he couldn't just call on anybody. It had to be someone comfortable working outside the law and with, well, to be blunt, criminal skills. If that someone had motivation to nail Ditto's ass, all the better.

Someone like Luis Ruiz. Earlier that evening…

…they meet a few minutes after two on the shore of Gas Works Park. As they stood looking out over the water, Lucas sketched out his plan to lure Ditto out of the building so he can break into his office. Ruiz listened carefully and then refined it, seeing problems McRae never would've thought of. To Lucas, this is a good validation for choosing Ruiz.

Afterwards, they climb into Ruiz's Honda Civic and scout Ditto's building on the east side of Queen Anne Hill between Dexter and Eighth Avenue. A four-story office building roughly divided into thirds, with DFH occupying the southeast third. Apparently DFH had its own basement garage access.

Now Lucas checked to make sure his cell battery was fully charged. Finished going through his mental checklist, he drew a deep breath, fired up the Volvo, and headed toward Lake Union.

Chapter 60

STREETLIGHT. JESUS. HE hadn't even considered that. His attention had been on figuring out the most likely place to monitor the garage and front entrance without being seen.

Lucas glanced around for a less conspicuous place to stand, someplace he wouldn't be bathed in mercury vapor light. Or was it sodium vapor?

Whatever.

Standing on the corner like this made him obvious as hell to anyone who bothered to look out a window. Didn't matter that he'd worn all black tonight; jeans, sweatshirt, and watch cap. He shivered despite lingering warmth in the night air.

On the corner across the street from DFH was one of the few remaining old utility poles, its wood splintered from climbing spikes. It smelled of creosote. He hid behind it in case anyone from Ditto's office looked out at the street.

Lucas watched the building for ten minutes, looking for activity. Only three lights on, making the place seem empty. In spite of the relatively warm night, his fingers grew so cold they tingled. He shook his hands, but it didn't help. His breathing picked up and his gut knotted. He felt exposed and vulnerable.

Shit, why couldn't Wendy have left him the gun?

A better question was: why had he given it to her?

What would she have done if he simply refused to give it back Yeah, he could imagine what she would've done.

He checked his watch and then rocked his head left and right, trying to release his tight neck muscles. By now Ruiz should be over in the Georgetown area waiting for the call.

A car approached and slowed.

Checking him out?

Was it the same one as a few minutes ago? He couldn't remember. It pulled to the curb across the street from the front of DFH, and the driver cut the lights. Lucas faded into the shadows as best he could and watched. Nothing happened, and it was too dark to see into the car.

He waited.

Nothing.

A few moments later the interior light of the car came on as a woman stepped out of the passenger door. She leaned in then stood, turned, and walked briskly into a small parking lot to the side of the building. He heard an ignition fire up, then saw headlights come on. A moment later a car pulled out of the parking lot, turned right, and accelerated. The car at the curb started, the driver pulled a U-turn and headed off in the other direction.

The sound of an ignition...he thought about Laura, what it must have been like to turn the key and have your world turn into a fiery explosion. Hopefully her death was instantaneous. One moment here, then oblivion.

That son of a bitch.

If he couldn't kill the bastard, he'd destroy him the best way he knew how: by devastating the business that seemed to be Ditto's life. Then he'd make sure the rest of his life was doled out day by day, year after year, with nothing but a postage stamp-sized cement floor, concrete and steel walls, a stainless-steel crapper and a bunk.

The second-floor light of the DFH building went off, leaving only two top floor lights on.

Jesus, there was no point waiting any longer.

He dialed Ruiz's cell who answered immediately.

Lucas said, "Go ahead. Call."

Ditto was leaning back on the couch with legs straight out and heels on carpet, stroking himself when the phone rang.

The DFH line, rather than his private one, which meant he had to take it and couldn't let it roll over to voicemail. The good news was that calls at this time of night usually meant business. Business was always good news.

He picked up the TV remote and froze the image of a woman in fishnet stockings giving head to a butt-ugly, muscle-bound guy with tattooed arms. Had to admit, Baer had good taste in porn. He answered with a simple, "DFH."

Ninety seconds later, call finished, Ditto disconnected and dialed Gerhard's extension.

"Hey, got a pickup for you. Some beaner's mother died, and he doesn't know what to do with her."

Ditto felt pride at how well his advertising campaign obviously penetrated the regional market. This guy, for example. With an accent like that he was probably a migrant worker, maybe even illegal, which would mean cash.

Ditto continued, "Got something to write with?"

"Shoot."

Ditto recited the address, then added, "Oh, I forgot to ask if he wants the ashes. But unless he mentions it, just skip it and get the contract signed. Got that?"

"Affirmative."

"Good. Call when you get back. I'll be sure to be up. We can see what kind of condition it's in. If it's fresh, we take care of it tonight."

After disconnecting, he picked up the remote and looked at the girl again before hitting play.

Damn, she's cute.

Lucas crouched behind a green Browning-Ferris Dumpster, waiting for the metal garage door to start rolling up. When it did, it made a racket he couldn't believe. Then a black Suburban climbed the short sloping driveway to the street. Lucas was poised on the right side of the vehicle because it'd be harder for the driver to notice him there. The downside, he now realized, was not being able to see who was driving. Could be Ditto. Could be the person on call.

Then again, did it matter?

The Suburban's brake lights flashed as it stopped at the top of the drive.

Shit.

The driver was making sure the door was completely shut.

The metal door reached its apex, remained still for five seconds before starting down with a fresh symphony of metallic screeches.

The door was half closed, leaving Lucas no other option but to risk being seen. Hunched down, he scurried down the short driveway and rolled, clearing the door a second before it clanked shut. But he must have broken a safety beam because the door immediately began to rise again.

Lucas frantically glanced around, saw a black Chrysler and scurried to it as he heard the Suburban's door open. He crouched between the Chrysler's trunk and concrete wall and held his breath. He heard the slap of shoes enter the garage and then stop. For several long moments he waited, then heard the footsteps move away from the garage entrance, followed by the slam of the Suburban's door.

A moment later the garage door began to lower, probably triggered by a remote inside the vehicle. The door clanged shut. Lucas stole a glance around the rear fender and saw the glow of red taillights through the other side slats of the garage door. For another long moment both the vehicle and Lucas remained frozen. Then the vehicle accelerated and the taillights vanished.

Only then did Lucas glance at the ceiling for a security camera. Sure enough, one was aimed at the door and probably had covered him as he rolled under. Well, there was nothing he could do about it now. Either he'd been noticed or not.

He took a few moments to study his surroundings but didn't see other obvious security measures. This part of the basement was brightly lit from overhead fluorescents. By its size, he assumed it accounted for maybe a third of the building's garage space and was obviously used exclusively by DFH. A wall of bare cinder blocks separated this section from the remaining garage. A black Mercedes-Benz was also parked here.

Beside the garage door, the only other exits were a metal fire door immediately to his left and an elevator across from him, probably for transporting bodies. His cell still showed good signal strength, so he speed-dialed Ruiz.

"I'm in and he's on his way," Lucas whispered, then powered off the phone.

Last thing he wanted was for it to ring. Even if he set it to vibrate, it could give away his location.

He checked once more for hidden cameras, thinking he'd put up an obvious one as a decoy but hide the others. Assuming, of course, Ditto was all that security conscious.

The only way to find out was to get moving. Lucas debated whether to use the stairs or elevator and decided on stairs. He looked for something to prop the door open with and noticed a rubber wedge on the floor next to it. After pulling on latex exam gloves, he slipped into the stairwell and used the wedge to hold the door open before he started up a flight of bare concrete steps.

Chapter 61

LUCAS STOPPED ON the first-floor landing to listen for sounds from the other side of the door. He realized the door was metal. A mariachi band could be playing on the other side, and he probably couldn't hear it. He slowly pushed the horizontal door release to see if the door was locked. It opened with no more than a soft click. Leaning in, head cocked, he listened for the sound of approaching footsteps but heard only an eerie silence.

Now in the darkened lobby of DFH, he allowed the door to reseat itself. Rubbing a bit of warmth back into his arms, he waited for his eyes to adapt to the weak light that came in through the windows from the streetlamps. He mentally reconstructed what he'd seen during his brief visit here.

Jesus, his fingers were freezing, his heart racing.

It dawned on him that although he hadn't used force to enter, the criminal charge of breaking and entering might still apply. Officially he was committing a felony. Worse yet, he could imagine himself lying on the floor in congealed blood, Ditto calmly explaining to the police, "It looked like he had a gun, so I fired."

On second thought, if Ditto caught him, he'd probably just shoot him and send his head in the next shipment to Hong Kong or Berlin or wherever.

Turn around and leave? It'd be easy enough to do.

But he couldn't go back, not after what he owed Laura and Andy.

By now his eyes were adapted to the weak light, so he headed down the hall to Ditto's office.

Once inside, he closed and locked the door, angled the blinds shut before turning on the overheads, and settled in at the desk. He wasn't certain how he knew—maybe from his previous visit, or maybe Wendy had mentioned it—that Ditto used the computer to check the records of the Hong Kong specimens, so that seemed the most logical place to start searching.

The tiny LED at the bottom of the blackened display glowed amber, meaning the system was probably in hibernate mode instead of off. He swiped the mouse, heard a faint screen crackle followed by the hum of the power supply fan. The screen brightened into a standard Windows log-in box.

Shit!

Stunned, he sat in silence. Had he really expected to gain access to Ditto's records by simply sitting down at the computer?

Ditto checked his watch. Gerhard should be at the beaner's place by now. He should've asked him to call in a report. Not that it really made any difference. Business was business. But an unusable body would make for a short night. They'd simply throw it in the oven and flip the switch and clean out the ashes in the morning for the bank.

On the other hand, a primo body always required a good deal of effort. So, factoring in the time Gerhard needed to load a body and drive back, they should have things wrapped up by three at the latest. Which might give him four hours sleep before he needed to be up and dressed for the first appointment of the morning.

Either way, something would need to be cremated, so he might as well save a couple minutes by going downstairs to set out the instruments and start warming Old Smokey.

Shit, shit, shit!

How could he have not thought of this? Lucas stared at the screen and felt like an idiot. The username wasn't the issue. That was already filled in. The password was the problem.

Yeah, sure, he'd heard stories of people cracking machines by guessing passwords, but that meant knowing personal things about the user. Anniversary, dog's name, birthdays, that type of bullshit. He didn't know squat about Ditto. Plus, that kind of guesswork took time.

He glanced at two Detroit Tigers posters. Another of some hockey player and some other crap.

But saw nothing that reached out to him and said, "Here you go. A password clue."

He could try typing in *tigers*, but any security-conscious systems allowed only a limited number of incorrect log-in attempts before shutting down and Tigers seemed too easy.

Lucas moved to a large filing cabinet and pulled on the top drawer. Locked. He pulled harder, but the damned thing wouldn't budge. The lower drawers opened without a problem, so this told him the most important papers were in the top drawer.

Back at the desk, he found a letter opener and used it to try to pry the drawer open, but all it did was bend the opener. Next, he tried to push the entire cabinet over, but it didn't move. Probably bolted to the wall. This only increased his suspicions it held Ditto's sensitive records. But short of an acetylene torch or dynamite, he wasn't getting in there tonight.

Royally pissed, Lucas returned to the desk and stared at the screen. Stupid damned oversight.

Damn it!

He'd come this far, only to be turned away. Every second he stood here was one less he would have to search. He sat down in the desk chair and looked around him. The computer monitor was a sleek flat screen without Post-Its or any other notes attached. Which was, he remembered, a place people often leave a password.

He scanned the few things on the desk. A phone, an old-fashioned address book, a pen holder. He picked up the pen holder and turned it over. Nothing taped to the bottom surface.

Shit.

He opened the address book. Nothing on the first page. He opened the P-tab. On the first line was an eight-letter alphanumeric string with two letters capitalized. If anything was a password, this was it. Carefully, making certain of no mistakes, he entered the string. Satisfied it was entered correctly he took a deep breath and hit enter.

Ditto hummed contentedly while arranging two scalpels and an air-driven hacksaw. The call out tonight removed some of the pressure of meeting the monthly quota. In fact, it put them ahead for the month, leaving him in a jubilant mood. He toyed with the idea of asking Cathy to fly up to one of the San Juan Island resorts tomorrow. Just call ahead for a bed-and-breakfast at a place she liked. Gerhard could handle the business until they returned Sunday.

Life was good.

Then again, he philosophized, we don't realize how well off we are until something comes along to threaten the foundations of our life. Only after surviving a threat, do we look back and take stock of the things we take for granted. This gave him pause, causing him to step back to admire the equipment he owned and the business he'd painstakingly grown from nothing. The sight swelled his chest with pride.

It was a damned shame Dad wasn't here to see how well he'd done.

But the incident with McRae had taught him another very important lesson. He needed to take time out for a complete reassessment of DFH. A risk analysis to consider better methods to protect his assets. He and Gerhard should analyze ways to improve procurement that minimized risk and maximized gain. This McRae incident should instigate a lessons-learned discussion.

One thing was for sure—it'd been a huge mistake to take the hooker and her john at the same time. Worse yet, the john turned out to be someone who was missed, thereby breaking one of his cardinal rules: minimize risk. Risk management was precisely the reason for having set up the rules. Looking back on the incident, that one mistake ultimately caused the problem.

The hooker?

Fuck, no one had a clue.

Well, except the detective. Taking Baer caused it all.

Yeah, life was passing him by. Ditto needed to spend more time with Cathy enjoying himself.

Feeling restless, he went to the window and looked out onto Dexter Avenue. Not much traffic. Typical. Yet something didn't feel right.

What was it?

Chapter 62

"FUCK!" GERHARD SLAMMED the steering wheel with his palm.

He checked the GPS again and then looked out the driver's side window at an industrial park. On the passenger side was razor wire, a few clapboard buildings, and what looked like warehouses.

The fucking address didn't exist.

Or if it did, it sure as shit wasn't in this ratty part of town. Barely able to steady his fingers from the anger, he punched Ditto's number on speed dial.

Returning from the crematorium, Ditto opened the apartment door in time to hear the phone ring. He moved to the kitchen to check the display and saw Gerhard was calling on the private line instead of the DFH number.

"Yes?"

Gerhard sounded irritated. Which was unusual for him. Of all the people Ditto knew, Gerhard was the most even tempered.

"That address you gave me. Give it to me again."

"Sure. What's up?"

He walked to the living room where the note was on the

coffee table.

"I'm not seeing what I should be seeing."

Ditto read the address to him.

Gerhard said, "In that case, we got us a big mother problem. All I see is fucking warehouses. This is an industrial area."

Ditto's anxiety ratcheted up a notch.

"You sure?"

"Fuck, yes, I'm sure. Only thing in front of me is razor wire."

Ditto didn't believe he'd copied down the wrong address. He'd had the guy recite it twice, just to be sure.

"Hold on a moment. Let me call to verify."

Setting the phone on the table, he used his cell to dial the number the caller, Robert Gonzales, had given him. It rang once before switching over to a recording.

The number you called is out of service.

He disconnected and traded phones again, his suspicions crystallizing.

"Get your ass back here ASAP. I'm going to check something. Anything changes, I'll call."

If nothing else, Ditto liked to think of himself as conscientious when it came to business. Like routinely copying down incoming telephone numbers when answering a call. Any call. It might gain importance two minutes after hanging up. Like right now, there it was, the number that had appeared on caller ID, which was different than the one Gonzales had given him.

He dialed this number. It rang until eventually clicking over to voice mail.

"Yo, sucka. You reached me. Leave a message."

It was Gonzales's voice but without the heavy fucking Cheech and Chong accent.

Why call a funeral service and dish out a bogus story?

He could think of only one reason, and it wasn't good. Like maybe someone wanted him out of the building. But that didn't make sense.

Something was definitely wrong. Time to batten down the hatches.

He pulled his Beretta 92 from the nightstand. After making sure it held a full clip and a round in the chamber, he set out to search the building, figuring he'd end up in the basement about the time Gerhard pulled in.

Assuming, of course, no one else was here.

Lucas entered "Ralph Thompson" in the database and hit enter. Thompson's record popped up immediately, making it the third unclaimed body on the books of both the King County coroner and DFH. The coroner recorded it as an identified but unclaimed body with no known next of kin. In contrast, the DFH records claimed the body had been donated by Thompson's wife. Both records were tied to the same valid death certificate.

He had to hand it to Ditto, coming up with such an intricate scheme. It flew totally under the radar, unless someone intentionally cross-checked the names like he was now doing.

And why would anyone ever do that?

As he started to push back the chair, a voice said, "Step away from the computer, McRae."

Lucas jumped, adrenaline jolting him. He turned toward the voice, saw Bobby Ditto in the doorway aiming a gun at him. Lucas zeroed in on the barrel and became paralyzed.

"I said step away from the computer."

Lucas looked from the barrel to Ditto's face, then back again, unable to move.

"Move," Ditto ordered.

Lucas slowly raised his hands and walked away from the desk.

"Move right." Ditto flicked the gun in that direction. "Completely away from the desk so I can see all of you."

Lucas did as instructed.

"You just had to keep at it, didn't you? Couldn't give it up. Wouldn't believe what we told you." Ditto entered the room, motioned the barrel toward the door.

"You first."

Lucas moved in that direction.

"Take it easy."

Ditto stepped back, keeping about ten feet of distance between them.

"Out the door to your right."

Lucas tried to calm the panic in his chest.

He had to do something before Ditto killed him. But what?

For now, the best thing to do was keep Ditto talking and burn as much time as possible.

"People know I'm here," Lucas said.

"So fucking what? What are they going to do about it?"

Lucas realized how lame his statement sounded and tried again.

"Just so you don't do something stupid."

"Stupid?" Ditto laughed. "I don't do stupid things. Careless? Maybe a few times. But never stupid." He waved the barrel again. "Through the door, asshole."

Lucas entered a room of yellow tiles and well-sealed cement floor with a drain under a stainless-steel table. In one corner was a crematorium. His bowels turned to ice. Ditto planned to kill and dismember him. He had to keep him talking. He turned to Ditto.

"How do you justify killing people for parts? That's what you're doing, isn't it?"

Ditto flicked the barrel left to move Lucas toward the center of the room.

"I'm shocked you even ask when the answer's so self-evident."

Lucas didn't budge.

Fuck him. He can drag me over there.

"Not self-evident to me. Explain it."

Ditto eyed him a moment, as if torn between shooting and answering.

"Sutton's law, man. 'Because that's where the money is.'"

Ditto added, "If you don't buy that one, maybe this one will appeal to your left-wing liberalism. Let's say you're the minister of health for some godforsaken third world country and you find a windfall of three million bucks. Suddenly, this gives you the choice between providing free dental care to hundreds of thousands of your people or building a state-of-the-art heart transplant center that might treat a few people a year. Which would you choose?"

Lucas stayed frozen in place, searching for something to fight with.

"I don't get it. What's your point?"

"The answer's obvious. Or at least it should be. The right choice is the one that provides the greatest good. In this case, dental care for the masses. You can't argue with that, can you?"

"No, but that's irrelevant. What's that got to do with murdering people for body parts?"

Ditto shook his head.

"You make it sound so arbitrary, so capricious. It's not like that at all."

He raised the gun and aimed at Lucas's heart.

Lucas shuffled a step to his right.

"Then explain it to me because I don't get it."

The gun lowered a fraction of an inch.

"You of all people should appreciate just how much good a well-preserved body can do. How did you learn anatomy? On a cadaver, I bet. What were you doing in Hong Kong? You were showing other brain cutters how to do a very specialized surgery, if my memory is good. In other words, you used one head to benefit how many, thirteen surgeons?"

"Ah, the old ends-justify-the-means argument."

Ditto shrugged.

"You must admit the logic fits. Especially if we're removing only the losers from society."

So far Lucas saw nothing he could use as a weapon. Making

it look more and more like his only option was to simply rush Ditto and fight for the gun.

"Not a good point. You forget that was my friend you killed. He was far from a loser."

"Gerhard didn't know that at the time. It was a mistake. And for the record, I'm sorry about it. Sincerely. We were after the whore, not him." Ditto pressed his lips into a tight *O* as if thinking about what he'd just said. The gun lowered slightly.

"I bet that if you thought about it a moment, you'd agree there are people out there who just suck the blood from the rest of us. We would be better off without them. By taking them off the streets, I can use their bodies to do more good for society than they'll ever be worth in their miserable damn lifetimes."

Jesus, Ditto sounded as if he really believed it.

Lucas tensed, readying for a lunge.

Before he could move, Ditto aimed the gun at his chest and started to squeeze the trigger.

Chapter 63

THE GUNSHOT ECHOED off the concrete walls. Lucas threw himself to the right—too late—and waited for the impact, which never came. He looked around wildly and saw Ditto laying on the floor, motionless.

Stunned, ears ringing from the blast, Lucas stared down at the blood pooling under Ditto's lifeless head.

What the hell happened?

Then he heard something cut through the ringing and realized it was a voice. He spun around. Luis Ruiz was standing in the doorway, aiming a gun at Ditto. Lucas caught the whiff of cordite.

He heard Ruiz yell, "Motherfucker."

Or at least, that's what it sounded like.

"What?"

"Said, that sucka's dead. Now give me a hand." Stepping over to the body, Ruiz shoved the gun into the pocket of his cargo pants. He grabbed Ditto's legs and started dragging him toward the cremation oven. He stopped to look at Lucas. "Shit, bro, can't you see I need help with this motherfucker? Sucka weighs a ton."

Lucas didn't move.

"But—"

"I don't need no attitude from you. He was gonna cap yo ass. What'd you expect me to do, watch? Now get over here and help me."

Ruiz opened the over door, slipped on an asbestos mitt, pulled out the shelf.

Lucas thought about what Ruiz was going to do. Thought about what would've happened if Ruiz hadn't killed Ditto. Thought of Laura and Andy. Thought about witnessing Ruiz murder Ditto. Probably not to save Lucas's life, as much as to avenge Lupita's murder.

It certainly wasn't self-defense. Still, Ruiz could always claim he was defending Lucas and deny they'd both broken into the place. Then it dawned on Lucas.

"Where's Gerhard?"

"Downstairs in the garage. Why? That make any difference? You gonna help me or stand there acting like a fool?"

Lucas moved to Ditto's other side.

"Gerhard let you in?"

"Fuck, no. Dude's dead too."

"What happened?"

"You wasting time we don't have. Need to get our asses out of here."

"I need to know."

Ruiz threw up his arms.

"Fuck! I made the call like you wanted but never drove there. Thought you were so fucking nervous I better hang around, cover your back. When Ditto's man drove back into the basement I followed him in."

"That wasn't the plan."

"Fuck the plan. So far, looks like my plan's better. You be one dead crispy motherfuck if I hadn't bailed you out. That what you want?"

He had to admit, Luis had a definite point.

"Now, give me a hand."

Together they lifted Ditto onto the oven tray, slid him

inside, cranked the head up to max.

Luis grabbed a stretcher, started for the hall, motioned for Lucas to follow.

By 4:15 AM, the ashes from both bodies were cool enough to sweep from the oven into a black Hefty garbage bag. They made no attempt to keep Ditto's separate from Gerhard's. By then all the blood on the floor was washed down the drain and the drain rinsed with Clorox. Lucas figured a crime scene technician might still be able to find residual blood in the drain, but considering the room was used to embalm people there was enough reason for it to be there, so why even bother looking?

Half an hour later Lucas and Ruiz stood at the end of a dock at Lake Union. Ruiz untied the garbage bag and upended it, pouring Dittos and Gerhard's remains into the dark cold water. After shaking out the dust, he balled up the bag. They spent no moment of tribute, silence, or prayer, the entire process of disposing the two men taking less than thirty seconds.

After one final glance around them, Ruiz said, "Best we get the fuck out of here before someone sees us."

Ruiz tossed the wadded-up black Hefty bag into a green, foul-smelling Dumpster three blocks away.

Chapter 64—Three Days Later

LUCAS SAT AT his desk paging slowly through a photo album chronicling his life with Laura and Josh. Her clothes were still hanging in the closet. One of these days he should force himself to collect all of them and…what?

Donate them to Goodwill, he supposed.

It was the healthy thing to do. To move on with his life. But for the moment, he wasn't in any hurry.

He paused to peer out the window and wonder what Ruiz was doing and how he was dealing with what they'd done. After dumping Ditto's and Gerhard's ashes in the lake and throwing the garbage bag in a Dumpster, they walked away from Lake Union to Ruiz's car. Ruiz drove him back to where Lucas's car was parked, the entire time never saying a word. It was as if an understanding had formed that needn't be verbalized. It reminded Lucas of years ago when he slipped over the side of the sinking boat, leaving Andy to deal with the police.

Lucas got out of the car and looked at Ruiz.

Ruiz nodded at him, said, "Stay loose."

Then he drove off.

Stay loose. Jesus! How could he?

They'd just murdered and cremated two human beings.

With good reason, maybe, but still…

Lucas resigned himself to living with those moments in DFH until the day his mind shut down forever.

Stay loose.

Two words. They could mean man things. Remain cool and never admit a word. Forget about what we just did. Or maybe Ruiz intended it to mean we'll get away with it or we won't. Either way, they'd settled their personal scores with Bobby Ditto and Leo Gerhard.

Lucas remembered the numb feeling as he drove home. He'd showered and briefly considered lying down but knew sleep would be impossible. Instead, he'd made a pot of coffee and drank cup after cup until his stomach turned sour, his hands shook, and the caffeine high kept him bouncing from thought to thought.

The whole time he roamed the house picking up various things—a vase, a framed picture, one of several ballpoint pens Laura endlessly accumulated next to the kitchen phone—and looking at them as if seeing each one for the first time.

For hours he did this, wondering how he would ever piece his life back together and worrying about when the doorbell would ring and a cop would be there.

The cop would say, "You're under arrest for the murder of Robert Ditto."

And read him his rights, maybe handcuff him, drive him to the West Precinct where he would call Davidson again, figuring if O.J. Simpson could go free, there was still hope for him.

Okay, so say he was picked up and questioned about Ditto's death. What could they prove?

If he and Ruiz held the line and didn't admit to anything, there was no telling what might happen. He might just get away with it. But he and Ruiz would be in constant fear the other guy would talk, so they had to trust each other to say nothing.

For the past two days he had flashbacks of Ditto aiming the gun at him, and each time he felt the same panic despite knowing Ditto was dead. Both nights he drank too much yet still needed

Ambien to shut his brain down. Then he crashed for three or four hours only to have the day start all over with more flashbacks.

He couldn't handle the thought of going to work, but knew he would have to go back soon.

The phone rang. His first reaction was to let it ring. He knew of no one he wanted to talk to. But then a voice in his brain told him it would be better to at least try to enter the real world again.

He picked up.

"It's Wendy. Okay if I drop by?"

He checked his watch. It was almost six. He'd vowed not to drink tonight, but anything after six seemed fair game.

"Why?"

Would she be the one to tell him he was under arrest?

That would be fitting in a karma sort of way.

"I have news you might like to hear."

"Yeah, come on over."

"Good, 'cause I'm outside your place."

They stood at the door staring at each other awkwardly, Lucas not sure what to expect but certain that he must look guilty as hell. He figured Ruiz would at least have a shot at bullshitting his way through an interrogation, but doubted he could. He'd try but was certain he'd tangle himself in a lie. Maybe he and Ruiz should've discussed it to coordinate their stories.

Wendy asked, "May I come in?"

She wore the same pantsuit as the first time he saw her.

"Sure." He closed the door and asked, "How about the living room?"

Somehow the kitchen still seemed to be Laura's space.

She sat down in a chair and crossed her legs.

"Hey, relax. I'm not here to jump your bones." She cleared her throat. "In fact, I have good news. Lange finally cleared you of complicity in Laura's death."

So, she wasn't here because of Ditto. What a relief.

Stifling a smile, he asked, "What changed his mind?"

He still felt bitter for being the prime suspect in the case.

"Turns out Travis was finally able to obtain a warrant to look at Ditto's records. Guess what he found?"

The alarm from a moment ago was back. Any hint of a smile faded.

"You were right about the accounting. They checked his records against the medical examiner's. Same death certificates but different people. The only problem is, other than Andy or Lupita, we can't identify any of his victims. The good news for you is that we're looking into having both declared legally dead. With what we have now, there's no reason to believe you or Wong fabricated those videos. And the Hong Kong cops got a statement from Wong attesting to that. At least, for you, that part will come to a close."

Head cocked to one side, Wendy studied him.

"But the really strange thing is Ditto's missing. So is Gerhard."

She let it hang.

Lucas looked away but said nothing.

"You wouldn't know anything about that, would you?"

"Me?" he said, feigning surprise. "No. Why should I?"

"No reason you should. Just thought I'd ask. Funny, Ruiz answered the same way, by turning it into a question."

More silence.

"So," she said, "you have no questions about it?"

He wasn't sure how to answer without saying something incriminating, so simply said, "No."

"Okay." She stood and smoothed her pants before starting toward the door.

"You were also right about Ditto having help."

He stood, ready to walk her to the door. He wanted her to stay and talk about other things, but wanted this conversation to end before he slipped up and made a mistake.

"Yeah?"

"Yeah. Redwing, the head of the Missing Persons Unit. He

was the one feeding Ditto information. The way it worked is Ditto would pass him the names of people he took off the street. Redwing would keep an eye out, and if the names showed up in a missing person report, he saw to it the case was never assigned to anyone. And because these people were easily missed, no one ever asked another question. And if someone did, he made sure the case never went anywhere."

She was at the door now, hand on the knob.

"One of the things I couldn't tell you was we put a wire on Ditto's phones. We caught Redwing passing him information."

Lucas asked, "What'll happen to him?"

"Probably not much. He'll have a hearing, but in all likelihood the best case is the department will fire him without a pension. Worst case, I dunno. He's already been suspended pending the hearing. Oh yeah, one other thing."

Lucas's heart skipped a beat.

Here it comes.

"The video Andy rented the day he disappeared was in Ditto's DVD player."

They looked at each other for a moment. He thought it best to say nothing.

Wendy started out the door, hesitated, and turned to him.

"Take care of yourself, Lucas. I'm sorry for what you've been through."

"Wait."

She stopped and looked at him.

"I'd like to see you again, after…I get my head straight. It's been a lot, these past few weeks."

She smiled.

"I'd like that. Let me know when the time's right," and then she was out the door, heading to her car.

Chapter 65—Two Weeks Later

LUCAS CUT THE small outboard motor and let the rented fishing boat drift far enough away from the buoys to be out of the traffic through the Ballard Locks. Fall was coming early this year, the sky filled with low pewter clouds but no chop on the chilly water. Enough bite in the air to make you button up. He and Josh sat in silence, the boat rocking gently. A seagull cried and a jet passed overhead.

Lucas picked up a tin that looked like one you'd receive during Christmas filled with either fruitcake or cookies. It was heavier than expected, and he hugged it to his chest a few beats.

"Time?"

Josh nodded.

"It's what she asked for if anything happened to her. We talked about it a couple times."

Josh nodded again, eyes misting up.

With a giant lump in his throat Lucas's eyes misted too.

"Anything you want to say?"

Josh shook his head.

"I'm so sorry, Laura."

Lucas hesitated before upending the tin and pouring the ashes into the green-gray water.

Acknowledgments

In no particular order, my thanks and gratitude to the following people who helped me prepare this story:

Judy Stoudt, U.S. Customs
Daniel O. Graney, PhD
Daryl Gardner
Mary Osterbrock
Marjorie Braman
Robert Astle